T0061602

# BREAKING
## the
# FRIENDZONE

# BREAKING
## the
# FRIENDZONE

## MAY LYNN

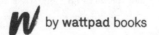

by wattpad books

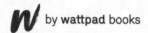

An imprint of Wattpad WEBTOON Book Group

Copyright© 2022 May Lynn.
All rights reserved.

Published in Canada by Wattpad WEBTOON Book Group,
a division of Wattpad Corp.

No portion of this publication may be reproduced or transmitted, in any form
or by any means, without the express written permission of the copyright
holders.

36 Wellington Street E., Suite 200, Toronto, ON M5E 1C7 Canada

*www.wattpad.com*

First W by Wattpad Books edition: October 2022
ISBN 978-1-99025-911-1 (Trade Paper original)
ISBN 978-1-99025-912-8 (eBook edition)

Names, characters, places, and incidents featured in this publication are either
the product of the author's imagination or are used fictitiously. Any resem-
blance to actual persons (living or dead), events, institutions, or locales, without
satiric intent, is coincidental.

Wattpad, W by Wattpad Books, Wattpad WEBTOON Book Group, and
associated logos are trademarks and/or registered trademarks of Wattpad Corp.
and/or WEBTOON Entertainment Inc.

Library and Archives Canada Cataloguing in Publication information is
available upon request.

Printed and bound in Canada

1 3 5 7 9 10 8 6 4 2

Cover design by Cassie Gonzales
Illustration by Jay Flores-Holz

To my husband . . . I ship you.

# prologue

## LACEY JO MASON

"Lacey! Dinner!"

The boy beside me was the first to look over my shoulder in the direction of my mother's voice. His blond curls blew wildly with a rogue gust of wind that caused our feet to disappear beneath white sand—the same grit that clung to my bare legs, arms, and my favorite yellow dress. We'd been playing in this spot for hours, and this was the first time today he wasn't smiling.

"We didn't finish our castle," he said, looking bummed.

The disappointment was mutual.

Just shy of six, I thought I would make no friends here. Compared to New York City, the communities forming the Hamptons were their own world. The beach was bare, nothing more than a stunning view for the windows of the extravagant homes that lined it. The people who lived inside these places were just as boring, in my initial opinion. Living here was a way to brag about financial status, but money was something new for my parents. My mom insisted on the move, but was rarely home to enjoy this purchase due to work. And even though my dad was now a stay-at-home parent, he had no interest in keeping me entertained, or even staying home. For a week I had played on the beach alone. After following the sound of music, this was the first kid my age I had met. He had danced his way to the beach from the house beside mine—with an iPod, shovel, and pail in hand.

"Lacey Jo!"

This time I turned, spotting my mom waiting on our porch. With one hand shielding her eyes from the sun, the opposite hand was raised in the air to summon me home with a single finger. Looking from me to the boy, she smiled, making me do the same. She was beautiful, and I loved everything about her. We already shared the same long brown hair and blue eyes, but it was intentional that our dresses were the same color, and I envied the large sun hat atop her head, wanting one just like it. She was stunning, and I strived to be like her in every single way I could.

"Can you play later?" I asked, turning back.

"Maybe. If my mom comes home, no."

I assumed this meant no. My mom always came home after work. On the weekends, her work was done from home. But as I watched his frown sink farther, I knew this wasn't the case.

"She never comes home," he muttered.

I hesitated to let him out of my sight, afraid I wouldn't see him again because of a single meal. He *had* spent the day determined to make me a castle, after all.

"Are you here all summer?" I asked, remaining hopeful he

wasn't just vacationing like many others in the area. "I live here now."

His frown disappeared, and his smile returned with an excitement that I knew meant we were neighbors. "We live here all the time! What's your name, pretty girl?"

I blushed. "Lacey Mason. What's yours?"

"Maybe I'll tell you tomorrow," he said playfully, scooping up his belongings. "Bye, Lacey!"

Scrawny, tan legs kicked up sand as he rushed back to his house. After he disappeared behind a pool house, I took time to envy the castle at my feet. It was perfect with a moat and courtyard. He hadn't mastered the towers, but he was determined. However, his hard work would be washed into the Atlantic Ocean by morning.

"Lacey!"

"I'm coming!"

I gave my dress a final shake before running to the stairs. My mother stood at the top, holding out her hand for me to take. As I did, another breeze mixed the air with fresh saltwater and her lavender perfume. The combination was heavenly.

"Who was that boy?" she asked, peering over my shoulder.

I shrugged. "My boyfriend."

"Your . . . your *what*?" Mom giggled as she bent to swipe more sand from my legs.

"He's a boy . . ." I said, feeling embarrassed, "and he's my friend . . . I think. So, he's my boyfriend. Right? He wouldn't tell me his name. He's weird, but I like him. He said I was a princess, and he made me a castle!"

"Lacey,"—Mom continued to laugh—"all boys are weird. Don't call him your boyfriend, though. Daddy won't like it. You're not even six. He doesn't want you to have one of those for at least another fifteen years. More like twenty."

"What do I call him, then?"

With a smile, she removed the sun hat from her head and placed it on mine. "He's just a friendly boy, Lace."

# chapter one
## LACEY

"I'm surprised you agreed to come with."

We had just left the 95 and branched onto Montauk Highway. It was official—I was back in the Hamptons for the first time in seven years. The plan was to never come back—too many memories, both good and bad, and all that hurt. My dad's surprise was nothing compared to my own. It was a last-minute decision. I literally halted his car as he tried to leave and threw my bags into the backseat.

"It's just for a few weeks . . . for Rachel. She came to Michigan after Knox and I split. It's only fair."

"They were together a long time. Right?"

The small talk was awkward. Unfortunately, we still had another hour before we arrived, and he was being chattier than usual. Any sort of discussion about ourselves would make this even more uncomfortable; so why not just discuss my friend's breakup instead?

"Three years."

"Wow. Were they engaged?"

I finally turned to look at him to see if he was serious. When his gray eyebrows lifted, waiting for an answer, I cringed. If Rachel had been here to hear that, she would have ginger-snapped.

"What?" Dad asked, shifting his attention between me and the outstretched road.

"She's twenty-two!"

"So?"

"That's way too young, and three years is not that long."

"I married your mother at twenty-one after knowing her barely a year."

"That's different."

"How so?"

"Because *yours* was love at first sight."

Silence fell, Dad pinched his lower lip as he agreed, albeit unspoken. It was one of Mom's favorite stories—her chem lab romance. It was their first day of class. She was the first one in the room; he was the last. The only seat left open was beside her, and she looked up at my dashing dad, whose grin instantly "melted" her. They had been midway through a failed lab that shot a pink, sweet-smelling foam from their desk to the ceiling, sending my mom into a serious fit of giggles. The professor asked how my dad had turned a green liquid pink, and my dad answered he had successfully made a love potion and could prove it. He then turned to Mom to share their first, earth-shattering kiss. He only broke it to announce to the room he'd fallen in love. A year later, they married.

"Anyway,"—I attempted to change the subject away from

Mom—"you can drop me off at Rachel's. We're going out tonight. Where will I be riding out my hangover tomorrow? Where are we staying?"

"With William Drake."

I choked on the hot Cheetos I had just shoved into my mouth. It took a few smacks to my chest before I could breathe normally, but I still couldn't speak. My esophagus was burning, and my mind was too busy rushing in a million different directions. The one place I wanted to avoid was our old house, and this would put us way too close. Then there was the panic at the thought of seeing Luke . . .

"It's just for the weekend. He wants to talk business, but I haven't agreed to return to run the lab yet. I'm in no rush to work for him again." Dad peered to his right to gauge my expression, surely finding just what he was expecting. "Lucas lives in Chapel Hill. He won't be there."

With my relief came an eye roll. "Of course *he* does."

North Carolina was only the home of the number one pharmacy program in the country. Ann Arbor was no small feat, either, but it wasn't the same. Chapel Hill was the dream—my mother's alma mater. The place where my parents met. Even with my savings, grants, and letters of recommendation, it wasn't enough to land me a spot in the program. Apparently, if Daddy makes hefty donations, a spot is obtainable.

"You're going to own a company together someday," my dad reminded me. "Eventually, speaking to each other will be a requirement."

I sank farther into my seat, wishing this car ride and discussion were over. "*If* there's still a company to run by then."

The way I saw it, I wouldn't have to speak to Lucas Drake again for at least three years.

My buzz didn't stand a chance against Rachel's. We sat on the floor of her childhood bedroom, where she was now living again, and ate burgers from a local restaurant we'd loved as kids. We washed them down with wine from her parent's wine cellar—too much of it. Unlike my breakup with Knox last year, she seemed to take this well for a girl who had no say in the end of her relationship.

"You really don't know what happened?" I asked, sensing that she had been holding back from me all night.

Rachel shrugged as she twisted the corkscrew. "We made it too complicated."

"He broke up with you, but you say *we*. And you don't seem to be upset with Chris."

Her cheeks turned the color of her hair. The cork popped free just as she hiccuped and giggled. How was this the same girl who had called me sobbing a mere twenty-four hours ago, saying she'd *messed up*? What exactly had she messed up?

With a wineglass the size of my head in hand, she stood and opened the doors to a walk-in closet bigger than my college dorm. I had forgotten just how extravagant everything needed to be here. Just in my seven years away, the Meyer home had been renovated to keep up with today's trends—if you could call having every wall, floor, and piece of furniture white a trend. Even the bedroom looked different from when we had played here as kids. Out of all the friends I had made during our four years living here, Rachel was now the only one I still spoke to. Odd, with our lives being so different. I was on the college path, while she had opted for the partying route and skipped college all together—much to her parents' dismay. If I had asked my ten-year-old self which friend I thought I would have for life, the answer would have been much different. In fact, Rachel and I didn't become close again until after my mother's accident. We'd had a long-distance BFF relationship ever since.

"This one." She pulled a silver dress free from the wide array of clothing. It hung by a string no thicker than a shoelace. It was sexy—a cowl neckline with just enough bunched polyester fabric to cover a bustline. Its shiny material looked like it was made of glitter. Rachel swung it around to show the open back. "Your legs and ass will look amazing in this."

"Mine?" I asked, now convinced she was drunk. No way could I pull it off. "That will barely cover my ass."

"That's the point. Duh." She shook the hanger to make the dress shimmer.

"Where exactly are we going tonight? I thought we were hitting the bars? I don't need to be practically naked for those."

"We have to go to Blue. You'll need to be practically naked there. It's more fun that way."

Blue. Only a club would have a name like that. The Hamptons wasn't exactly a beacon for nightlife; unless you counted cocktail and dinner parties to show off your umpteenth home renovation—I'm sure one was held for the Meyer home. This meant we were leaving the Hamptons tonight.

While I'm used to the partying scene associated with being a college student, partying with Rachel wouldn't be the same. This wouldn't be a college scene. It would be somewhere expensive. Not only would there be a charge to get in but the cost of drinks would likely be triple what I was used to. The entire reason for my dad being back here was a dwindling bank account. The money my mother had saved was nearly gone, and my college fees weren't helping.

"Stop counting dollar signs." The dress was thrown into my

lap. "If you wear that dress, you won't be buying your own drinks. The rest is on me. We'll use Dad's driver. We are both getting laid tonight."

I dropped my back to the floor and groaned. She was frustrating. "Rach . . ."

"Don't start with me." She cackled, returning to the closet to find her own ensemble for the night. "You need this just as much as I do."

Guys were so much work. Getting laid was that much *extra* work. And for what? Not one of them had ever gotten me off during intercourse; not even my ex. So, I was supposed to show myself off like a prized pony, hoping to be picked and taken back to his place just to go home and finish the job myself? My hand and I had a glorious thing going. It hadn't let me down yet; unlike every penis I had met.

Two fingers snapped in front of my face, bringing me back to reality, and I found my best friend bent over me with a new pack of Venus razors. "We are going to drink away the thought of every man who did us wrong until we are carried out of that club like the queens we know we are. Now, get your ass into that shower and shave *everything*."

I knew better than to argue with her. I took the razors, got to my feet, and took the dress with me.

By the time we were both ready and climbing into the car, it was nearly eleven. What little wine buzz I had had was long gone. The same could not be said for Rachel. I was certain the entire bottle had gone into the shower with her, which no one could fault her for. The girl was hiding just how broken up she was over Chris and was doing a shit job of it. We just didn't handle our breakups the same way. After Knox, I needed Rachel, a binge-worthy TV show with over four seasons, a tub of Ben & Jerry's, and a lot of tissues. Rachel needed dick, and I needed to support that.

She rattled off the address of our destination to her father's driver, confirming that we'd be leaving the Hamptons tonight. And while Rachel rehashed tonight's plan to the woman who would take us to Blue, I was busy watching the New York scenery change back from beach house mansions to the few rare skyscrapers of Long Beach, New York. The buildings only grew in height and width the closer we got. It had been so long since I'd been anywhere near here that it took a mass of traffic behind a stoplight for me to realize just where I was. After we inched our way up a few car lengths, we sat adjacent to a high-rise office building with nothing but windows for walls on its exterior. Its red-and-purple logo beamed so brightly from its top floors that it reflected in the sheen of my dress. Keeping my legs crossed and my dress as far down as I could get it, I scooted myself closer to the window so I could see my name reflected in the red letters.

DRAKE-MASON PHARMACEUTICALS.

It was my mother's legacy; it was my future. And beside it, I felt ridiculously small.

"How bad is it?" Rachel asked, just as the car moved again.

The LED lights left my view, along with the building I hadn't seen in years. "Bad enough they want my dad to reopen the lab."

"Would he seriously do that?"

I shrugged. I never thought so, but my dad was here and willing to discuss it. He had held a grudge against William Drake for years after the closing of the department he managed. The entire business had grown from the lab. Dad didn't speak about it much, but when he did, it came with a serious dose of pent-up hostility. Drake-Mason had begun with three people and ended with two. William Drake purchased Mason Labs, my father's research combined with my mom's pharmacy and business knowledge, and thus, Drake-Mason Pharmaceuticals came to be. In three years, I was due to inherit the shares my mother had set aside for me, along with her own, which were currently held by a trust. My dad's shares were long gone—sold to cover our bills throughout the years. As of right now, Drake-Mason was a sinking ship. I was close to losing another piece of my mother, and the thought of it made my stomach churn.

"You know what, Rach? Maybe drinks and someone to take my mind off things might be good after all."

Our car came to a stop. The change in Rachel's posture accompanying her excitement agreed. "Oh, you're going to thank me tomorrow after you get some."

*We'll see.* I wouldn't be holding my breath. If I got laid, great. If not, fine. Either way, I wouldn't go out of my way to impress any guy tonight. Rachel was right—they could come to me. And the way Rachel had dressed us, I was sure the only time I'd need my wrist wallet was for my ID.

We both exited from my door, stepping onto the curb outside a club labeled Blue but intentionally lit in neon pink. I was questioning their choice of signage while being dragged to the front of a line that currently wrapped around the side of the building.

"Meyer," Rachel said confidently as she strode past the bouncer, her hand still gripped tightly around my wrist and leaving me no choice but to follow. She didn't even give the guy a chance to look at the clipboard he was holding, but he also didn't argue with her. One look at Rachel and her last name were all it took to get us to the doors. "You're in for a treat, Lacey Jo!" she shouted.

I could already feel the pulsing beat of the music beneath my feet, and we weren't even inside yet. A second bouncer pulled one side of a double door open for us. My wrist was tugged again, and this time, Rachel turned to wiggle her brows just before entering a club of people swinging their bodies in a sea of blue lights. Now I understood the choice of my silver and her white dress. We were sure to stick out in the crowd.

"No Hamptons boys!" I yelled above the music while weaving through the dancing bodies that packed the place.

Rachel smiled wickedly ahead of me. "I didn't know their tongues felt any different!"

I was sure she was right, and they wouldn't feel any different. But I also didn't need those tongues using talk of their trust funds as a way into my bubble tonight. My mind needed a rest from the topic of money, and I knew a few drinks would give me that break. The offers began before we even reached the bar.

# chapter two

## LUKE

I debated having a beer as I watched each light in the main house switch from on to off. A handful remained lit, telling me my father was still awake. Not surprising. He rarely fell asleep before midnight, and it was nearing eleven. He'd be sitting in his den reading *The New York Times*, as he did most nights when I still lived with him.

Everything in me was screaming not to go inside—not to put myself into a situation where the temper I got from him would get the best of me. I also knew not going inside would make it that much worse in the morning. It was my first time home since leaving for school last December, and there was nothing about the Hamptons I missed. Especially this house. I really didn't miss North Carolina, either, but at least there I was somewhat free of William Drake.

It was exceptionally warm for late May, and opening the

sliding door from the porch that led to the four seasons room came with a blast of cool air. Billie Holiday on vinyl accompanied my journey through the darkened house and grew louder until I was standing in the den's doorway. My father sat in his favorite wingback chair with *The New York Times* in hand, as assumed, and a cigar smoking in the ashtray beside him. Without looking up from his current read, he picked it up, flicked the ash free, and placed it in the corner of his mouth.

"I wondered how long you'd wait to come in here," he said, still refusing to look away from the paper. "Collin said you arrived nearly two hours ago."

Collin was correct. I hadn't realized the full-time driver was now a part-time tattletale. He was more security than anything. My dad loved to believe he was more important than he actually was. The beach was littered with everyone, from movie stars to actual royalty, so even though he had more money than most of them, the paparazzi weren't exactly lined up to see the son of an oil tycoon and Big Pharma CEO's day-to-day life. A basic security system would have sufficed. Sometimes I believed my dad kept Collin around simply for company. He was the only one willing to put up with William Drake this long.

I leaned my shoulder against the doorjamb, indicating that I wasn't willing to hang around long. "I was unpacking."

He dropped the paper into his lap and pulled the cigar out of his mouth. "Only you?"

I knew where this was going. "Just me," I confirmed.

His disappointment in me was nothing new. In twenty-three years, I hadn't done a damn thing right in his eyes, and tonight wouldn't be any different. He may have had a say in many parts of my adult life, but this was not up for discussion.

"You're fucking up."

"I beg to differ," I said, still feeling his words hit me in my gut. It wasn't the first time he'd said it and wouldn't be the last. "I don't love her. It was inevitable."

"You put a ring on her finger, Lucas! You cannot turn this into me forcing you to love her. You loved her enough to ask her to marry you."

My head shook. I was purposely clenching my jaw to prevent myself from arguing with him further. I never said I didn't fuck up by putting the ring on her finger. I should have known better when the ring wasn't *big enough*. Her agreeing with my father on my career path, and then telling him about my doubts was the last straw. I was convinced Tiffany only saw my name, and the money that came with it. Me deciding I wanted out of the Drake-Mason shadow should have stayed between the two of us, but it was a threat to the life she was expecting. It wasn't the first time we'd broken up. It would definitely be the last.

Now I was home for the summer without the girl who was the reason for coming home. Tiffany had taken a summer job with my father as his personal secretary while he was waiting to replace his current one, who would retire next week. She was likely staying somewhere nearby with friends since I left without her, but I hadn't bothered to ask where. She was not my problem anymore, and I attempted to leave the room before he could make it mine.

"Lucas!"

I had managed to make it two feet before his voice stopped me. "Yes?"

"You can hide away in that pool house all summer, but I'm still expecting you to be at brunch in the morning. We have a guest."

I turned. "A guest?"

"I invited Jack Mason for the weekend. He's in the guest wing."

"Jack Mason?" I repeated, convinced I had misunderstood

him. "Jack Mason is here? In this house?"

"We need him to reopen the lab. His research is pivotal to keeping us afloat. He took that with him."

"Why the hell would he say yes to *you*?"

"Because," he began smugly, "if I'm correct, he's hurting for money. He hasn't held a steady job since we closed his division, his shares are gone, and he's also putting his kid through pharmacy school. Ann Arbor isn't cheap. And as much as he hates this company and me, he won't let it fail out of spite. It would only hurt Lacey."

*Lacey.*

Those were two names rarely brought up in this house. Jack came and went for meetings for a while, right after Mary's accident. Lacey, however, I hadn't seen since the day my mom left us seven years ago. It was a hard day to forget. I lost my mom and my best friend that day—and both events were my fault. Even though we didn't speak about it, the plan had never changed: Lacey and I were set to inherit and run the company together, just as our parents had. I hadn't known she was living in Michigan until now. Jack had been living in Pennsylvania for the last few years.

"It's important you be there, and that you show interest. Kiss his ass."

I rolled my eyes, this time actually walking away. In our language, it was a yes. I'd be there. I'd pretend to show interest in the company and act as though my plan aligned with my father's. The joke was on all of them. There was no way in hell I was going to sit in my father's place. My days were spent ensuring that I had enough work for the next few months to keep out of my dad's line of sight and keep my savings growing.

The pool house wasn't the worst place to spend the summer. It had everything I needed from a bedroom to a kitchenette and bath.

And waking up to the sound of waves and a view of the Atlantic was something some people would kill for. This property was one of the biggest in the areas.

Before sliding the glass door open, I noticed that my phone, which I'd left on my suitcase, was lit up. Seeing Justin's name instead of Tiffany's was a relief. I'd only been off the plane for ten minutes before my phone had been blasted with texts and voice mails from her. They were instant deletes. This summer I was putting myself first.

"Hey," I answered, falling onto the couch.

"You in New York yet?"

Justin's school year was spent in Massachusetts. Unlike me, he enjoyed coming home to spend time with his family during break. Of course, his employment was probably going to land him a residency on this very beach. Harvard Medical School would allow him to keep the lifestyle to which he'd become accustomed. He was going to keep me sane this summer.

"I got in this afternoon." I took note that wherever my best friend currently was, it was loud. "You?"

"I'm at Blue. Meet me here."

"Man, I don't have it in me tonight." I kicked off my shoes, feeling the exhaustion of the day. "I still smell like the airport, and my dad is already on my case over this Tiffany bullshit."

"That's exactly why you need a night out. Trust me—you need to make a showing."

I laughed, knowing what he was insinuating. "Oh yeah? You've located tonight's prospects already?"

"Leave now," he said before ending the call.

I threw the phone onto a couch cushion with a sigh. Even if I left now, I wouldn't get there for a while, but maybe a night out wouldn't hurt. If I wasn't on my *A* game for brunch in the morning,

I could blame Justin for my hangover and attitude. I got to my feet to shower.

The line into Blue was nuts, wrapped all the way around the block. I gave my keys to the valet and thanked him. Eric was the bouncer tonight and stood as soon as he saw me approaching. His enthusiasm already had the rest of the line pissing and moaning. Yeah, I was going to be that schmuck tonight and skip the line. Perks of frequenting here the last few years.

The back of our hands hit and then the fronts before I was pulled into a hug that had my feet leaving the cement. His hand patting my back a few times nearly knocked the wind out of me. I wasn't a twig, but Eric made me look like one.

"Justin said you'd be making an appearance." He placed me back on the ground.

"Yeah. He didn't give me much of a choice."

"Crowded night," Eric said, pointing out the obvious and returning to his work. "Good luck finding him in there."

I had texted Justin and was still waiting for his reply. When in doubt, head toward the bar. If Justin was out, it meant he was already many beers in. Guinness, if I were guessing. I checked my phone once more before entering a jam-packed space with dizzying blue strobe lights. It was a world I was accustomed to. I loved everything about the noise, the ambiance of everyone being flooded in the same color while swaying their bodies together. Blue was known as an upscale—and sexy—place to spend your evenings. No doubt why Justin had chosen it tonight.

The bar area was called the pit. While the club itself was filled with every type of blue light imaginable, the pit was black with motionless blue accent lighting. You could go there, sit, and not fear a light-induced seizure. It was in the shape of a giant ring, and it was in the very center of the club. I sent off another message, letting Justin know that was where he could find me.

Even though there was a black leather stool open, I didn't take it. There was plenty of room between two groups of girls with their backs to each other for me to lean my elbows onto the bar while standing. It took about five minutes to be greeted by the bartender—not surprising, since they always took care of the women first. And tonight, there was no shortage of those.

I ordered a rum and Coke. Anything harder and I was risking having to leave my Jeep in Long Beach. Usually, on nights such as these, I'd crash at some hotel and put it on my father's tab. Risking not getting home in time for tomorrow's brunch was not a chance I was going to take. I'd never hear the end of it. When the first one went down a little too fast, I ordered a second. And when that one went down even faster, I started a tab. This seemed to catch the attention of a girl beside me, who swung her body around to avoid her friends and flashed a smile at me.

"Hi," she said, leaning in closer. "I'm April."

Her drink of choice was tequila. It didn't even take looking at her shot glass to know. I could smell it the closer she came. She was a beautiful girl, but she was *way* too drunk already.

"Luke," I said with little enthusiasm. I looked over my shoulder, hoping Justin was somewhere in sight. No luck.

"Luke, I think my next shot should be on your tab."

Money really was annoying. I knew her interest was piqued when she heard the bartender ask me by name if I wanted a tab for the night. Typically, that option was only given to those using bottle service. It was only offered to me because usually I would be here with a group of friends, and that's exactly how we would play it. Tonight, however, I wouldn't be living it up on the second floor with a table.

"I think I'll pass, April."

The blond's Botox-filled lips pouted. "Why's that?"

Why couldn't my answer be enough? She turned around because she realized I had money. What a catch. I ignored her question when I heard an infectious laugh that made my head turn in another direction completely. Across the bar, on the other side of a circular island holding all the club's liquor, sat a beautiful brunette who had caught the attention of a bunch of guys already. She was leaning one elbow on the bar, and circling her straw in an almost empty drink, and some guy had said something to make her laugh and fuck if it wasn't the most beautiful sound I had ever heard.

"Because I'm buying her a drink," I answered April, motioning with my head to the stranger across the bar. I ignored whatever April said in response, but she disappeared. I flagged down the bartender.

"Hey!" Justin's hand hit my upper back. "About fucking time!"

"Did you forget where we live?" I asked. "It's not a quick drive to Blue."

Justin took the newly vacated seat beside me. I remained standing, knowing I'd shortly be moving to the opposite side of the bar to meet the girl I'd be dancing with tonight. My eyes were still on the pale, bare skin of her shoulders, waiting for her to turn around. I asked the bartender to give her a refill and put it on my tab. She leaned over to the girl beside her to tell her something, and that's when I noticed she was sitting next to someone I knew. When Rachel finally looked my way, I tried to flag her down. Her eyes doubled in size. She smacked the other girl's arm and said something to her. Finally, the girl turned around. Big, piercing blue eyes now had my undivided attention. My goddamn stomach fluttered, caught in some sort of moment with the most beautiful girl I've ever seen in my life. My smile grew but was met with disdain before the girl turned back around.

*Well . . . shit. What the fuck just happened?*

I elbowed Justin. "Who's sitting beside Rachel Meyer?"

"Are you serious?"

*Why would I not be serious?*

The bartender placed a fresh drink beside her and then pointed my way. Again, she turned. Again, we connected. And again, I was shot down when she ignored the drink and continued what now looked to be a heated conversation with Rachel. I elbowed Justin harder this time, hitting his ribs.

"Ouch! What the fuck was that for?"

"Go over there with me." I motioned to the area occupied by the mystery girl and Rachel.

Laughing, he stole my drink and took a swig. "She turned you right back into a twelve-year-old. Honestly. You can't man up and go talk to her?"

I couldn't. She turned down my drink. I needed a wingman. Justin grew up directly across the street from Rachel, and he was my in. If I could get him to distract Rachel, I might stand a chance of catching the attention of her friend. The window to accomplish this was closing fast. They were without a doubt the hottest girls in this place tonight, and the guys they'd been talking to earlier were now in my way.

Grabbing Justin by the arm, I pulled him out of his seat, dragging him only until he caught his balance, at which point I nudged him to walk ahead of me. This needed to look like it was all his idea. The only way for this to go wrong would be for this girl to find him more charming than me. He could be a dick like that.

"This isn't a good idea." His head pivoted to mock me. "Send her a drink. Don't drag me into this shit."

"I did. She ignored it."

"Honestly, do you blame her?"

*What the hell is that supposed to mean?* I didn't get the chance to ask before I was shoved forward, landing directly in front of Rachel and her friend. Both halted their conversation and threw some seriously judgmental shade. I glared at Justin. *Thanks, asshole.*

"Told you," Rachel said before picking up the disregarded drink and wrapping her lips around its straw.

"What do you want?" The brunette asked. Her annoyance was blunt and like acid churning in my stomach. She made a point to look anywhere but in my direction.

Not a good start.

Needing a change in attitude, I shifted my attention elsewhere. "Who's your new friend, Rach?" I asked.

"Huh?" Multiple glances were exchanged between Rachel and the girl I was determined to win over. "Is he serious?" she asked Justin. "He has to be joking."

"I'm not? And that didn't answer my question. What's your name, pretty girl?"

"What did you call me?" she asked, bewildered, as her head snapped upward. Finally. I had caught her attention.

"Pretty girl," I repeated and offered my hand. "I promise I meant it as a compliment. I'm Luke."

She stared at my hand like I was going to bite her if she took it. Justin and Rachel were laughing behind me, and this girl's smile twitched like she might join them. The smile was a good sign. I was getting somewhere. She was a ten. With that smile, an eleven.

I grinned to play along. "So, about that name . . ."

Her infectious laugh returned. Her head shook *no*. If she was friends with Rachel, I would get her name, eventually. Rachel didn't live that far from my father's place.

"Fine." I kept my hand extended. "I don't need a name to dance with you."

She turned to Rachel, bursting with more laughter. "This is actually happening. *This* has made the entire night worth it. This *is* really happening, right?"

Rachel, equally enthused to the point of tears, nodded yes. Well, I had made their night. I wasn't claiming victory yet, but it was a step in the right direction. She was amused, at the very least.

"Does that mean I get your name?"

"No. It doesn't." She looked up at me, finally giving me more than well-deserved eye contact.

The connection made my chest expand, followed by a feeling of déjà vu. She swallowed hard—she was feeling it too. Not only did she seem familiar but the entire conversation did.

"Dance with me. I have to know you."

"I feel as though I already do, *FB*." She glanced back to a giggling Rachel before me.

*FB? Like . . . a fuck boy?*

Was she a friend of my ex? Was that why she was laughing . . . because I was barely out of a serious relationship and hitting on someone new? I couldn't have her thinking that, or I wouldn't get anywhere with her tonight.

"I'm not a fuck boy."

"Never claimed you were."

"Rachel, get your *friend* here to dance with him so I can return to my night. He won't let this go. Just look at the poor guy." Justin attempted to help by wrapping an arm around my shoulders. "He's pathetic right now. Have you ever seen Luke like this?"

I stuck my lower lip out to pout. I was literally pouting for this girl. She could have told me to beg at her feet like a dog, and I would have kneeled on this dirty bar floor.

Rachel pursed her lips, glanced at her friend, opened her mouth, and snapped it shut again. "She has a rule tonight. No Hamptons boys."

*Well, that's a shit rule.*

"You know what, Rach? I think I'll drop that rule for FB."

"But I thought we were going to drink, dance, and get lai—" Rachel was cut off by her friend's hand covering her mouth.

I needed to hear the rest of the sentence. It sounded like she was about to say *laid*. My inner monologue was begging to assist.

"Not tonight," she disagreed, while I lost all hope. "This is too hilarious. Okay, FB. Dance with me."

I extended my hand again. A moment earlier, I thought I'd be the one dragging her between the swarm of dancing bodies, but it was the other way around. She was sure of herself as she led me into the crowd. But I would be the one leading tonight. I spun her until her back was against my chest, where I felt the vibration of her giggles mixed with music pumping around us.

With one arm up to wrap around the back of my neck, she began swaying her hips to the beat of a popular remix. I placed my outstretched hand on the slick fabric of her dress, across her stomach, keeping her right where she was. She didn't even flinch. Her confidence was sexy and intoxicating as she ground her ass into my pelvis.

New songs came and went, and with every single one we became more comfortable touching each other. My hands were all over her, and hers were on me. The room was sweaty and hot—as every club is—but the sweet with a hint of spicy perfume she was wearing drowned it out. It was an aphrodisiac, fogging my mind and drowning out everyone else around us. I was getting hard, and she knew it. She also didn't seem to mind, as she pressed herself against me as much as she could.

"You're killing me," I whispered against her ear.

Her head leaned into my shoulder. "Good."

I knew she was grinning. She was being playful, enjoying that I was hard for her in front of hundreds of people. Two could play that game. My lips pressed against her jawline, just below her ear. I removed one hand from her swaying hips to squeeze one of her breasts. With my lips now on her throat, I felt the moan she released. The buildup of sexual tension was becoming too much not to see it firsthand. I swung her around, brought her toned body back into mine, and took her lips.

There was a moment of hesitation as her body tensed in my hold. In that second, I felt I had made a mistake, ruining all the progress of the night. But it quickly faded; she released the tension, and our tongues met in a heated kiss.

"Luke." I felt her breath on my lips as she whispered my name.

Her long eyelashes fluttered before lifting. Ocean-blue eyes. The moment they met mine, I was lost in them. They were literally stunning, and so familiar. They were searching for mine just as hard as mine were hers. I couldn't take it. My hand wrapped around her waist, pulling her back into me, pressing my forehead against hers. I closed the small space between our lips again, without hesitation. The club went on moving without us as we remained still and wrapped up in each other until we both needed air and broke the connection of our mouths. I was dizzy from the sound, and the heat, and this girl. I wanted to be alone with her—somewhere I could learn her name and get greedier without interruption.

"Want to get out of here?" My voice came out breathy, still panting from the circles we'd spun tonight.

She nuzzled her face into my palm, nodding yes. "I have to tell Rachel I'm leaving."

I pecked my lips against hers. "I'll be at the door."

# chapter three

## LACEY

"Shit," I muttered, watching Lucas William Drake weave his way through the crowd.

My fingertips were pressed to my lips. They still tingled from where he'd kissed me less than a minute ago. It wasn't just my lips still tingling. None of this was supposed to happen. My intention had been to allow him to continue making a fool of himself by not remembering me—the girl he once claimed was his best friend. At first, I thought he was joking, or lying, to get me to speak to him again. However, it turned out he honestly didn't remember me, and I wasn't sure if I should be relieved or feel worse for allowing him to turn that Lucas Drake–shaped knife in my gut even more.

He wasn't supposed to kiss me. And it sure as hell wasn't supposed to feel like *that*. Blood on fire, knees quaking, skin tingling, mind-blowing fireworks . . . all in that one kiss. My knees were still wobbling as I returned to the bar to find Rachel. She was right where I left her, sitting beside Justin and just as shocked as I was. The two remained intentionally and playfully silent when I approached.

*Shit.*

"So, I'm going to go with Luke." I used my thumb to point to the main entrance.

"Did you tell him yet?" Justin asked. "Lace, I've never seen him so scared to talk to a girl before. You need to tell him."

Justin Carmichael had recognized me immediately. After my dad's promise that Luke was in North Carolina, I never imagined he'd show up here. There was no doubt in my mind now Justin was the reason for the surprise showing. Clearly, he neglected to mention I was here. I should have been pissed, but whatever, I got a good laugh from it. After all these years, Luke looking like an idiot for a few *hours* was the least he could do.

"I'll tell him on the way home. I'm staying at the Drakes' house this weekend. At least now he has a reason to hate me. Nothing new."

Justin's smile fell. "He doesn't hate you. He's not the same person you remember."

A falling out for no reason, and seven years of silence, begged to differ.

"Lacey, you kissed him!" Rachel's giggles were loud—and Jack Daniel's induced. "You *kissed* Luke!"

"He kissed me." A single finger was held up to clarify.

Luke instigated the kiss. I played a game with him, and may have ground my ass into his erection, but I never intended to kiss him. As for kissing back, I definitely didn't intend that. But then, it wasn't supposed to be panty-dropping. *Damn him.*

"So, we didn't witness you kissing him back?" Rachel shared a look with Justin. "Okay, then. If that's the story you're going to go with."

Annoyed, I waved them off with a promise to call Rachel in the morning.

I found Luke exactly where he'd promised to be—standing beside the entrance, now void of the blue glow I'd seen him in all night. He was different, but oddly still the same boy I remembered. The rogue blond curls he had as a child were short now and tamed by a haircut that forced them to stay in place. He'd grown at least a foot since our last encounter and had to be pushing a few inches over six feet. And he was all muscle—a fact I had confirmed when my body was pressed against his all night, and reinforced by his fitted black shirt, which was hugging every inch of him in the best way.

He was the spitting image of his father.

"Do you know Justin?" he asked, peering back to the bar where his friend was still sitting.

It was hard not to laugh. I bit my lip to stop myself. "I don't know. Do I?"

This was still too fun. Watching his confusion only made me want to draw this out longer. He shook it off. It was nearly two in the morning, and we had quite the drive ahead of us. Not to mention a walk to wherever his vehicle was currently parked. Hopefully, it wasn't far, because my feet were killing me, and there was no way I was walking barefoot. We had barely made it to the curb when a Jeep Wrangler stopped ahead of us, and the valet tossed Luke the keys.

"This is yours?" I eyed the vehicle warily. It lacked doors.

"I hope so. Otherwise, the owner is going to be pissed that the valet just gave us the keys."

Flashy, cherry red, and brand-frickin' new—it didn't quite meet the Hamptons aesthetic, but at least my feet were done being murdered for the night. Luke offered his hand. I took it, using it as the boost needed to get up and into the vehicle without showing everyone what was under my dress.

"So, how about that name?" he asked, pulling at the seat belt and offering it to me. I shook my head *no* as he cutely protested with a groan. "Okay. Well, then, your place or mine?"

*Would now be a good time to tell him that my place is currently his place? Nah.*

I didn't necessarily know if he was staying with his father. I was assuming. Either way, he was taking me there. The Wrangler entered traffic, which had died down considerably since Rachel and I had arrived at Blue. My hair began blowing wildly in my face.

"Yours."

"You got it, pretty girl."

I dropped my head back against the seat, gazing up at a star-filled sky. It was the second time tonight he'd used it as a term of endearment—a fond memory that he was cheapening.

"Bet you call all the girls that."

His hand gripped the wheel tighter, and he shook his head. "Not as many as you'd think. One comes to mind."

Yeah. One came to mind for me too—the girl he didn't remember. Puberty was rough for me. The last time he saw me, I was fifteen, chunky, flat chested, with braces, and acne across my nose that I failed to hide with foundation. I wasn't wretched by any means. I also didn't stand out. Luke made me feel like I did. Now he didn't even know me. Must have been nice to repress the memory of our last encounter, because I couldn't forget it if I tried.

The last time I'd seen Luke was the day his mom left. My mom and I made a special trip to the Hamptons to make sure Luke and his dad were okay. The door was slammed in my face as he told me to *fuck off and go home*. While most people might have been able to shrug off this interaction, I was a fifteen-year-old girl hopelessly in love with Lucas Drake. Those were harsh words coming from the boy who was my world. When I say he broke my heart, it actually shattered that day, because he was also my best friend. My mom stayed up with me the whole night after a hellish car ride home while I sobbed my eyes out. She comforted me, explained that Luke was a Drake male—and with that name came expectations and a reputation. He wasn't worth crying over and I should let him go. Luke made that decision an easy one. He never spoke to me again, and that was fine. Because a few months later, my mom was gone, and I was busy trying to figure out a world without her in it.

I waited years to share a first kiss with Luke. Tonight, I had it. My mother was probably spinning in her grave.

"So, what do I need to do to get your name?"

My shoulders shook with laughter. This little game really was amusing.

"Okay, fine. Tell me something about yourself. Are you from here?"

"Was I born here? No. Do I currently live here? Also, no."

"So, you have a summer home here? You know Rachel, and she doesn't leave the comfort of the Hamptons often."

He was right about Rachel, but . . . "Nope."

"Then how do you know Rachel?"

I couldn't answer that yet. I couldn't say I'm an old friend, or how we met, because Luke was the one who introduced us. Same with Justin. I decided to direct the questions back to him, starting with the one that had been on my mind since we hit the dance floor of Blue. Luke had moves.

"Where did you learn to dance like that?"

His smile widened. "I taught myself. I'm saving to open a dance studio."

*A studio? What about pharmacy school? What about Drake-Mason?*

The more I thought about it, the more genius the lie became. Get girls home by flashing your money, sleep with them, then tell them you want to own a studio so they see those dollar signs go up in smoke and they won't hang around. *Impressive.*

"What about you? What do you do?"

My head shook *no* again. Pharmacy school would be a dead giveaway. We still had a good hour left on this journey, and I was going to milk this as long as possible.

*Tell him, Lacey.*

"You're a hard girl to crack—you know that? You're stubborn."

"I've been told that."

Our drive remained playful and filled with unanswered questions. We pulled into William Drake's drive in the early hours of the morning. We drove past my father's car, and Luke still didn't piece together that I was home for the weekend with my dad. He parked and told me to wait for his help to get out. I appreciated it. Falling on my face before telling him would have been embarrassing.

I took his offered hand and slid my way from the seat until my heels hit the ground, reminding me how sore my feet were. I giggled and groaned with the pain while Luke's hand rested on my hip. When I looked up to thank him, I was greeted by his warm, soft lips against mine.

This was why I should have told him earlier. Now I was dizzy and caught up in one of his amazing kisses all over again. I definitely shouldn't have been the one to deepen it, but I did. I leaned into him until his muscular arms were wrapped around me. He lifted me up, giving relief to my feet but adding to the grief of my starved lady parts that now pressed against his pants. I was too invested in what was happening with our tongues to even realize where I was being carried. I was a bag of mixed emotions—telling myself to tell him the truth, craving more of his taste, and not wanting the fireworks from this kiss to end. It didn't until my back was pressed up against an exterior wall, where Luke needed the extra leverage to keep me off the ground while searching for his keys. My eyes opened to discover that I was now against the pool house—a place we used to play in all the time as children.

"Luke . . . I . . ." I was struggling to find words. He was keeping me against the wall with his knee between my legs, and I was becoming a hot mess each time he lifted it to keep me up. His unforgiving mouth was all over my neck and chest, kissing and nibbling on any exposed skin his mouth could access. "I have to . . . to tell you something."

There was a jingle of keys and the sound of the door swinging open. My back left the wall, and I was once again only supported by his arms. My legs tightened around him, and with the move came the realization of just how hard he was. I was running out of time to tell him, and at the same time, I had never been so hungry for sex in my life. I impulsively rocked my hips against his, dropped my head back, and cried out with a moan I didn't know I was capable of.

He moved us through the house until we were in a bedroom. It was dark, but there was some light coming in through the window facing the pool outside. He tossed me onto the bed, where I bounced before becoming a breathy mess sprawled out across the duvet. I leaned up on my elbows to see him unbuckle his belt and pull it free. It was tossed to the floor before he started unbuttoning his pants. My pussy was throbbing with anticipation, partially muting out the voice in my head, which was screaming how bad an idea this was.

*I need to tell him.*

"Luke..."

He shed his pants and shirt, leaving me to admire the changes in his physique since he hit puberty. He was all muscles that bulged and flexed with the smallest of moves, like when he ran his fingers through his hair and smiled. Christ, he was fucking gorgeous. Guys actually could look like they stepped right out of the Calvin Klein ad? Because then there was his underwear and it left nothing to my imagination. Luke was huge—his whole body was a theme park, and his cock was a promise for a good time. My lady parts were now eagerly waiting in line for a ride.

The bed dipped as he crawled his way between my legs until he returned to my lips. My upper thigh was firmly gripped and squeezed while his hardened cock teased against my lace barrier. We both felt the heat escaping me. I couldn't lie about not wanting him if I tried.

"What do you need to tell me?" he asked.

This was it. I needed to tell him, and it had to be now. Yet, my shaking head was disobeying me, and so were my eager hips, which were trying to keep against him for any sort of pressure against my aching clit.

"Nothing," I whispered.

I was being so stupid. This had gone from making Luke look like a fool for a few hours to making me into one. I set out tonight to get laid. Not to fuck my future business partner. But God, he felt so good everywhere. His firm body, the soft lips, and his hands that were now all over me—this was too good to stop. I hadn't been touched like this since... well... ever? It had been a year since I'd had sex, but I couldn't recall the foreplay ever getting me this worked up. And we had barely started.

His hands continued wandering, squeezing my breasts before nibbling at them through the fabric covering them. I whimpered, wanting more. While his mouth was busy there, he'd finally made his way to the hem of my dress, and we both agreed it was in the way of tonight's intentions. I sat up just enough for him to pull it off. It fell to the floor, and his lips were back around my exposed nipple, causing me to cry out and writhe beneath him.

"I'm dying to taste you," he said, just as two fingers slid beneath the only fabric left on my body. He parted me and slowly traced my slit with one finger before circling my clit with the other. "Mm, soaked."

And him talking dirty was only going to make it worse. He teased my entrance until I was practically begging for more. Yeah, the lace underwear needed to go. And now. Luke tugged them off in a flash and tossed them. I wasn't even sure where they landed when they were off, and, at the moment, I didn't care. Apparently, I wasn't the only one eager to get them out of the way. Luke knelt between my legs abruptly, grabbing my knees, parting them, and pushing them to my chest.

"Hold these," he demanded.

Done.

I did as I was told, hooking my arms around each thigh and pulling them closer to me. Luke cradled the cheeks of my ass in his palms, using them to lift me to his awaiting mouth. The connection caused me to cry out. My folds were lapped excruciatingly slowly by his warm tongue. Then again. On the third round, he stopped at my clit, paying very special attention to it. Keeping his tongue pressed firmly against it, he began endless circles that had my knees shaking in my grasp. In the lightless room, there was nowhere to look but at him, and he watched me watching him. The focus was so intense, I could have sworn I could feel the start of an orgasm in the distance.

That was impossible—but then it wasn't.

"Fuck!" I cried out.

My knees dropped and my feet hit the mattress. The orgasm tore through me like a raging fire through a forest, with no part of me left untouched by its blaze. This heat was unlike anything I had ever experienced—leaving me seeing stars as I rode Luke's face. He squeezed my ass, keeping me attached to his tongue as I writhed against him. He was relentless, and I was grasping for anything to steady me—the sheets, his hair, my own breasts. My soul was fighting to escape my body. As the heat faded, I was left feeling practically melted.

"Jesus," Luke panted for air, "you have the most beautiful orgasms."

*How did that just happen?*

I sat up again, wrapping my hand around his neck and forcing his mouth to mine. His arousal-soaked tongue swirled with mine as I took his cock out from his briefs. It was so ready for me—rock hard and pulsing against my palm. He hissed into my mouth as I stroked him. Using my thumb, I circled his crown as a tease, loving the way he eagerly twitched from it.

"What do you want to do with it?" he asked, cupping my jaw. "Show me."

My pussy clenched with need. But it was going to have to wait. I sat up farther, and Luke backed up until he was standing. After a few more strokes of my hand, I wrapped my lips around him, swirling my tongue around his tip. Luke inhaled a sharp breath. And when I began moving him in and out of my mouth, he raised his gaze to the ceiling and moaned from deep within his chest. The sight was working me up all over again.

"I need your name," he said. "Christ, give me something here."

I smiled around him. I was taught never to speak with my mouth full. Luke hissed and released small curses until he couldn't take the sucking anymore and popped himself free from my mouth. I would have sucked him until he came, but I knew the eagerness for more was mutual. He pecked my lips and whispered he would be right back before disappearing. The room was now aglow in a pink light that told me it was sunrise. There was panic in my gut, knowing I was supposed to be at breakfast with my dad in a few hours. But the way Luke eyed me upon his return made my stomach twirl and my lungs leap. There were condoms in his hand. One stayed, and the rest were tossed onto the mattress beside me.

I didn't know where to look as he rolled it on. I could have stopped it right now before we truly passed the point of no return, but then he was above me again with his tongue in my mouth and, *God!* Why did he have to be so good at this? We were a mess, trying to maintain the kiss and get closer at the same time. With my fingertips digging into his back, Luke wrapped one of my legs around him and entered me with one swing of his hips.

I gasped. I moaned. I clung to him for dear life as he drove himself into me repeatedly. His thrusts were powerful, timed to perfection and maintaining a rhythm that had me on the verge of a second orgasm.

"Come for me." He practically growled it into my ear.

My anxiety wanted to fight him on it, but he upped his speed and drove me right over the edge. The second one was even better than the first, and with it I screamed his name. The intensity had me struggling to keep my eyes open. Him being inside me made it so much better.

When my eyes did open, Luke was now cast in a golden glow from the window. He noticed it too—the sunrise threatening our time. "I have a meeting to be at soon," he said, blissfully unaware I'd be attending the same one. "But I'm not stopping until I watch you come again. Then, I'm getting that name."

"You can try," I giggled. "I think I'm out of orgasms. The name isn't happening."

His dirty smirk and thrust made my head fall back with a closed-eyed moan. "We'll see."

I wasn't sure which one he thought he was going to get from me, but he would not give me time to figure it out. He was going again and not holding back. And I was now so loud I was sure I could be heard from outside the pool house.

"Put your arms around my neck and do not let go."

He didn't have to tell me twice. I wrapped myself around him, and he lifted me from the bed. Locked in another of his fireworks-inducing kisses, he used his forearms to lift and drop me onto his cock repeatedly. I couldn't get enough of it—it was the muscle for me. He came through on the promise of the third orgasm, cracking me in minutes.

"I'm going to come," he said with a groan into my neck.

"On me," I said. The thought was driving me wild.

"Yes. Fuck," he hissed.

I was tossed back onto the mattress. The condom was torn off and thrown to a nearby dresser. His arm bulged as he gripped his cock and pumped himself, once, twice, and on the third time, released. His hot cum shot up my open thighs and belly, coating me deliciously.

I fought to catch my breath. The air had suddenly left the room. I just allowed Lucas Drake to practically split me in two. *Shit*.

After using his sheets to clean as much of myself as I could, I sat up and reached over the side of the bed to get my dress. My underwear was nowhere in sight, and I was willing to lose them forever to escape this room. My phone lit up as I grabbed it, showing me that it was just after six. I had two hours to get into the house and be ready for this breakfast. I definitely needed a shower.

"You don't have to run off, you know?" he said, still standing completely naked beside the bed. "I'm dreading this meeting. I could skip it."

I tried to avoid his stare. "I, uh,"—my head shook *no*—"am supposed to meet up with someone this morning."

"Boyfriend?"

That was laughable. And I did. "No. Not in the slightest."

I stood, locating my shoes and finding them remarkably more comfortable than they were a few hours ago. My wallet was still beside them. I gave up on the underwear and headed out of the room and toward the door leading out to the pool.

"Wait!" Luke called out. Out of the corner of my eye, I saw him fumbling as he tried to hurry after me and put on his boxer briefs at the same time. His knee collided with a small table beside the couch. He cussed and clutched the spot he hit. "Wait! Wait! Jesus! Hold up a minute!"

I kept moving until his hand was around my wrist. He twirled me just as he'd done the night before, to get me to face him. My head fell to his chest, where I inhaled his spicy cologne. I took a deep breath, knowing I should tell him right now. I reminded myself just how bad it felt the last time I walked away from him— when he told me to fuck off, get out, and then never spoke to me again.

"Please tell me your name. How am I supposed to find you? I need to see you again."

I laughed playfully. "I'm sure you will."

I attempted to pull away, but it was no use. He pulled me in for another drawn-out kiss. I eased into him, hating myself for it. "Please," he whispered against my lips. "Don't make me play the fate game. I will turn over every part of this town to find you. Starting with Rachel Meyer."

He wouldn't have to go that far. In a couple of hours, he would be reminded of the girl whose heart he broke seven years ago. Tonight had been fun, but it changed nothing. We weren't friends.

"I don't believe in fate," I said, wiggling my wrist until he released it.

"What do you believe in?"

"Karma." The word rolled off the tongue before I could stop it. This wasn't revenge on Luke. We had both enjoyed the night, but part of me wanted the word to sting a little. He just looked more confused. I swung the door open, the space between my legs still throbbing, and walked out to a chilly spring morning.

"Please tell me your name?" he called out.

Without looking back, I swung my wallet over my shoulder with a smile. "Maybe I'll tell you tomorrow, FB!"

# chapter four

## LUKE

I could smell the bacon from outside. To avoid spending any extra time with my father, I entered via the sliding doors as I had done the night before. Kitchen staff were working tirelessly, setting the dining table with the family crystal, preparing food, and a mimosa and Bloody Mary bar. I stole a piece of bacon from a piled platter. My next stop was going to be the Bloody Marys.

This breakfast was bound to be a shit show. I couldn't fathom my dad asking anyone for help. If he was serious about reopening the lab with Jack, Drake-Mason was hurting worse financially than I imagined. I enjoyed that thought more than I should have. The place itself wasn't terrible, but the thought of filling my dad's shoes was nauseating. Pharma, science, stocks, lawyers constantly battling lawsuits—I wanted no part of that life. It didn't matter, though. I had no say in my future. It had been drilled into my head since I was a kid—I would run the company just like my father did. Because if I didn't, who would? One other person came to mind, but I had no idea what her stance was on filling her mother's position. I hadn't talked to Lacey Mason in years and knew she wouldn't come anywhere near me to tell me herself. The thought of running the company with someone who hated me was equally exciting.

I only had anxiety about anything Drake-Mason related, and today was no different. I took another piece of bacon and bit into it before exiting the room to check my phone for the millionth time in the last hour. Rachel still hadn't texted me back, even though the message now showed it had been viewed. I tried calling Justin multiple times, even though the chances of him still sleeping were high. *Someone* knew my mystery girl's name, and I was determined to find her. I hadn't lied when I swore to turn over this town. I hadn't slept a wink last night, and I wasn't even tired. My mind was throwing images of beautiful tan legs wrapped around my face, big blue eyes that begged for more, and a laugh that had me smiling even now. I needed to know everything about her.

Rachel and I weren't exactly the closest of friends anymore; a fact that was confirmed by us not being friends on any social media apps. Her shit was locked down tight too. Other than a profile picture of her on the beach, I couldn't see any of the people who were friends with her. However, I could see Justin's friends, and Justin was friends with Rachel. He needed to wake the fuck up so I could use his phone. I was about to call him again when I heard an overdramatic sigh from behind me.

"You're late."

"I'm not," I said, tucking the phone back into my pocket where it would need to remain. "I'm just not at your preferred level of early."

My dad wasn't amused. He passed me and entered the kitchen. The staff falling completely silent showed just how beloved his presence was. He barked something about the frittatas while I mentally prepared myself for the disaster that was about to play out. Reentering the room, I went for the alcohol. I poured myself a large Bloody Mary and stole a few extra olives to tide me over. It was likely most of this food was for show. No one really sat down to eat while discussing business.

Even though he was pissed I was already eating, my father took an olive from my palm for himself. "Remember to tell him how much you're enjoying school, and how you're eager to start at Drake-Mason in a few years."

"So . . . lie?"

"Yes," he said without thinking. "Wait. What? No! *Lucas* . . ."

"I'm joking."

I wasn't joking.

"Save your humor for another day."

Mindless business robot. Got it.

The glare he shot me was short-lived. His game face was back in no time, hand outstretched, grinning with a charm that could make your teeth ache. "Jack, I hope you slept all right. Did you have everything you needed? I could have Collin make a run into town for anything you need."

He wasn't lying when he said kiss Jack's ass. Christ. Now Collin was security, driver, *and* his personal errand bitch?

"I had everything I needed," Jack said, accepting the handshake. "Slept like a rock."

It had been years since I'd seen Jack. The silver hair was new, and for someone who had slept like a rock, his eyes had lines around them now, making him look more tired than he apparently was. Except for the aging to his skin and hair, he was just as I remembered him. I had little to go off of, though.

"Lucas," Jack said, turning his attention to me, "look at you.

You must have grown a few feet since I last saw you out on that beach. Spitting image of your old man."

My least favorite thing to hear. *Thanks, Jack.*

"It's good to see you." We shook hands.

"I didn't know you'd be home for the summer," he continued. "Pharmacy school has kept you busy, I'm sure. God knows, Lacey can't even escape it in the summer. This was the first year she's come home for the break."

"Yeah," I agreed, sliding my hands awkwardly into my pockets. Time to kiss his ass. "It's been a wild few years. How is she liking it?"

"I'll let her tell you all about it. I apologize, she got in late, but she should be down soon."

*. . . what?*

My mind could barely make sense of what he had just said when I heard a familiar voice apologizing behind me. I could feel the blood leaving my face.

"Lacey." My dad's outstretched arms were ready for a hug.

I watched, horror-struck, as she filled them—dark brown hair still wet from the shower, toned legs peeking from beneath her sundress, and blue eyes that I now knew she got from her mother.

*Pretty girl.*

"Look at you! All grown up! I can't believe it."

"Mr. Drake, I'm so sorry that I'm late. I ran into an old friend last night," she said, shifting those ocean blues to me, causing a lump to rise in my throat. "A few times."

*Christ.*

My heart was trying to beat its way out of my chest. Lacey Mason. My mystery girl was Lacey Jo Mason, and I didn't know how to process this. I had to do something, because standing here staring with my jaw on the floor definitely wasn't on the list of approved actions for this meeting.

After leaving my father's arms, Lacey took a few steps in my direction. She tucked her hair behind her ear while her cheeks turned a bashful shade of pink. "Good to see you, Luke."

"Lacey." I nodded and awkwardly hugged her, wanting to be anywhere other than standing in front of our fathers at this moment. "It's been a long time."

"Feels like minutes," she said coyly, just loud enough for the two of us to hear. "You look good, Luke. It's nice to see you again."

"You could have told me," I whispered, knowing I was holding her for longer than I should have.

Her head shook as her mouth parted to respond, but she was cut off by the announcement that breakfast was ready. She pulled away, and all I wanted to do was grab her hand and run off to be alone for five goddamn minutes. I was seriously supposed to take a seat across the table from her and act like last night didn't happen? I was barely in my chair and she was doing just that—striking up a conversation with my father about pharmacy school and life in Ann Arbor. Every single time she laughed, I felt the oxygen leave my lungs.

*How could I have not recognized her?*

I tried not to stare, but damn, she was making it hard. I kept my elbows on the table, against house rules, with my hands joined in a fist I kept in front of my mouth to hide my facial expressions. She had been my best friend for years, and I didn't even recognize her. It was a shit move on her part. But how could I even justify being mad when I deserved it? I couldn't. I wasn't even sure I *was* mad about it. Part of me was relieved last night was with her. Because I now knew exactly where to find her, how to talk to her, and hopefully how to unfuck what I had royally fucked up all those years ago. Lacey Mason was my biggest regret, and maybe I had this weekend with her to fix as much of it as I could.

The louder my dad's laugh became as they talked about his latest golf game—telling Jack he hadn't played courses I knew he had to make Jack feel like he had one up on him—made it clear that the sucking up had begun. I couldn't focus. Between waiting for Lacey's little side glance in my direction and being mesmerized by the way she traced her collarbone with her fingers as she listened to their discussion, I could barely enter their conversation.

"Well,"—my dad swung one leg over the other and crossed his arms, leaning back into the king's chair at the head of the table—"let's talk some business. Shall we?"

The food remained untouched. I wasn't even hungry anymore. Lacey picked up a piece of crisp bacon at least three times without being given the chance to eat it. Instead, she twirled it and placed it back on the plate. Aside from William Drake, there were three people at this table, but Lacey seemed to be the only one interested in *talking business*. She sat up straighter and zeroed in on my father.

"As I'm sure you know, our stock hasn't been what it used to be."

"So I've seen," Jack agreed.

"Times have changed. Big Pharma is bigger than ever. They're buying out the little guys, and although we've done well to stand on our own, we're a one-trick pony. We have one drug, our drug, and it used to be the number one prescribed beta-blocker. Now, we're fifth with nowhere to go but down."

Silently, Lacey glanced at her dad, who was holding a napkin so tight his knuckles were white. There were quite a few elephants in the room this morning. One couldn't be avoided—and that was the closing of the lab.

"Why am I here, Drake?" Jack's voice no longer held the

enthusiasm it had had a moment ago when talking about his golf swing.

"Well," my dad said, remaining confident, "as I briefly mentioned over the phone, there have been discussions about research and development. And those talks have obviously drifted to the lab."

"*My* research." Jack clarified for him. "*My* lab."

My father's lip twitched. "Yes. Your research and lab. We would like to reopen it and have you pick up where you left off."

"Jesus." Jack's mouth tightened. His frustration was evident and warranted.

"Dad . . ." Lacey was cut off by his raised hand.

"You said there was no money to keep it open. Now you really have no money and want to piss away what's left?"

"Jack, we didn't have the means at that time. It wasn't just me who made that decision. Mary . . ."

My head snapped just as fast as Jack's. First to my dad, then to Lacey to watch her chin fall to her chest. Could he make this damn meeting any worse? Mary didn't need to be brought into this.

My dad straightened again, unable to look Jack in the eyes. "She understood the money would be better suited for marketing. We needed to recoup what we'd spent on research to start again. We waited too long—my fault. But if we are going to keep this company afloat, we need to act now. I'm willing to throw my own money in as an investment to get you started. We need fewer side effects, minimized action time, and to release a few different strengths, *possibly*. Generics are killing this business, Jack. We made this. I know you don't want to see *our* brand leave the market."

There was little hope for my dad's plan as Jack shook his head *no* with his eyes tightly shut. But it was Lacey who looked completely defeated by it. She blinked rapidly, staring down at her lap.

As much as I hated the thought of taking over the company, she was now answering my earlier question: she wanted it.

"You shut me out of it. It's not *ours* anymore," Jack said. "My research was nowhere near complete. Not even close to human trials. You don't have the years needed to get it to market."

"I can get us ten. Five from my investment and five from redirecting workflow. We've begun making changes within, including offering early retirement to the original crew—what's left of them. We've also taken on more interns who are working for free, or close to it. And our finance team is eyeing our books and accounts carefully, making sure no penny is left unfound when it could be put toward keeping our work alive. I assure you; I've thought of everything."

Now he had Jack's undivided attention. "You're paying someone to review accounts to find five years' worth of missing pennies? That hardly seems beneficial."

"I just said I'm *not* paying interns to find five years of missing pennies." My father grinned. "Stop acting like you don't want to play in a brand-new lab. It pays better than it used to. Come in this week, and I'll show you the numbers firsthand."

Even though Jack was acting hesitant, I knew he was taking the offer. His knee was nervously bobbing. My dad wasn't the only one playing here. The longer Jack drew this out, the more of a benefit he'd get out of it. My dad needed him, and now Jack knew it. He could ask for anything, and my dad would serve it to him on a platter.

"I have nowhere to stay," Jack confessed. It practically confirmed my father's assumption about him struggling with money. "I'll need time to get a place near Long Beach."

"Nonsense." That obstacle was waved away by Dad, who was now standing and beaming that he'd gotten the job done. "I have another place just down the beach. I was set to renovate and sell, but I can hold off on construction until you're situated. You won't even have to worry about the commute. I'm happy to share the drive. It'll be great for Lacey too."

Hesitating once more at the outstretched hand, Jack finally took it. My focus was only on Lacey. She returned my look with equal surprise.

*Did we just become neighbors again?*

The day had resulted in a drastic change of plans. Lacey and Jack moved to the other property. I could see it from the pool house. It was way down the beach, but it was there. And she was there with it.

I collapsed into my bed, tired from yesterday's traveling, no sleep, and an early morning filled with sex. I could faintly smell it on the sheets, along with her perfume. The playbacks of it repeated in my head as I closed my eyes. But the word *karma* was unforgiving. I exhaled, giving up on the sleep, and watched the ceiling fan spin above me.

Even if Lacey hadn't said it outright, she was holding a grudge. I was torn between believing our night had been out of spite versus being something . . . more. I had ruined our friendship—I owned that. I didn't recognize Lacy—didn't want to own that. But again, I'd fucked up. I just couldn't believe that first kiss was nothing more than a play to get back at me for being stupid. I felt something, and I felt her reaction to that something. I covered my face with my hands and growled, beyond frustrated with my ability to make a mess of everything.

I'd just about decided to live from the bed for the day when my phone buzzed on the nightstand. It was lit up, inching its way closer to the edge with every ignored ring. I couldn't see who was calling, but my guess was my ex. I didn't know when she was arriving at JFK airport, but I would not be suckered into picking her up. I rolled to my side and lifted my head to see Justin's name flashing. I swiped the screen, selected speaker, and dropped back to the pillow.

"How stupid are we feeling this morning?"

"You can be a real dick sometimes, you know that?"

Justin's hearty laugh confirmed. "How did you take it? Bet that was a fun ride home. It was good for you both. There's a lot of history you two need to resolve."

I should have had more to drink with breakfast. I left the bed to see if the minifridge was stocked. "The ride home was fine. Learning who she was during breakfast . . . not fine."

"Breakfast?" Justin asked. "Luke, you didn't . . ."

"Our history remains unresolved and now more complicated."

My search of the fridge came up with nothing. Meanwhile, my friend continued giving me an earful about how both Lacey and I had both been stupid last night. That might be true, but I didn't want to take back what we'd done. I mindlessly pressed the phone to my ear as I left the pool house for fresh air. There was a wooden ramp leading from the elevated lot down to the beach below. I leaned my hip into it and watched the water, feeling my heart knock in my chest when I saw Lacey walking on the beach alone.

"Justin, I have to go."

"Don't you dare. I'm not kidding. You need to . . ."

I hung up before he could continue the lecture. Shoving my phone into my pocket, I ran back to the main house to raid a fridge I knew was full. Lacey and I needed to talk, and beers were going to assist. With my hands full, I headed back outside.

By the time I returned, Lacey was sitting in the sand with her knees drawn to her chest. Her sandals were off and lying beside her. She watched the waves roll in while her brown hair blew in the midday wind. I slowed my approach, but something told me she knew I was here. For a few seconds, I stood and watched her in silence.

"I think I met you right about there." I pointed a few feet away from where she sat. "You were in a yellow dress with a dragonfly on it."

"And yet you couldn't remember my face," she said with little enthusiasm, refusing to look at me. "It's a big beach. I didn't select this spot because of you. Don't flatter yourself."

Her family's old beach house was directly behind us. Many families had owned it over the years since the Masons sold it. It wasn't even the same color as it had been when Lacey and I were kids. Back then, it was painted stark white, like most of the homes around here. The newest owners had chosen a navy blue with accented pine-shingle siding. My father hated it.

"I know you have more memories on this beach than just me," I agreed.

I tossed what I was holding to the sand and took a spot beside Lacey, not caring if my slacks got dirty. She briefly shifted her gaze to me then looked away when she saw I'd noticed. Even with the salty water in the air, I could smell her sweet shampoo each time the wind blew.

"You don't have to do this," she said. "We don't know each other anymore, Luke. We haven't in a long time."

"I want to change that."

"Change it?" she repeated with an annoyed laugh. "You completely shut me out of your life. You chose it. Not me. Why do you get the say in changing it?"

"My mom had just left me—alone with my dad, even though she knew how much I hated him. I didn't handle it well." It was a partial truth regarding what had happened that day. It wasn't why I shut her out, but it was the reason I reacted the way I did. I took all of my frustrations out on her, and it wasn't fair.

"You lost your mom and shut out your best friend." Lacey's fingers drew in the sand. "But when I lost my mom not long after, you were the only person I wanted to talk to, and I couldn't."

*And I wish I could take it back.*

"I can never apologize to you enough for that. I'm sorry, Lacey. I'm sorry for what I did that day—what I said and how I acted. I'm sorry I closed you out. I'm *so* sorry you lost your mom, and I wish I could go back and smack myself for not reaching out to you when it happened. I was a horrible friend."

She nodded as she continued to draw in the sand. I wasn't sure if it was a good nod or bad. I watched until I could make out a cursive *FB* drawn with the tip of her finger.

I smiled at it. "Friendly boy."

At that, she really laughed. "You thought I was calling you a fuck boy. Dork. I still can't believe you didn't recognize me."

"In my defense, the last time I saw you, you looked more like your dad."

"Ouch." She cringed. "Thanks?"

It didn't matter who she looked like. Lacey was beautiful. She always had been. But the crush I'd had through my adolescent and teen years was nothing compared to the attraction I felt now. Just sitting next to her had my bones achingly aware of her proximity.

I offered her a beer. Then I tossed a Ziploc bag of leftover bacon in front of us. Her giggles filled the beach as she opened it, took a piece for herself, and then offered me one. This was a start. Twenty-four hours ago, or even three hours ago, I would have never thought this was in the realm of possibility. Now, I didn't just have a weekend with Lacey Jo Mason. We had the entire summer together on this beach, and I was going to fix what I broke.

# chapter five

## LACEY

As we walked through Macy's, Rachel struggled to hold the multiple purchases she had acquired during our day of shopping. I was holding a single bag with a pair of clearance heels, while Rachel had a minimum of seven pairs from different stores. We hadn't left one yet without visiting the checkout. Part of me knew she was used to Chris carrying everything for her. She'd been pissing and moaning since the first place.

We were supposed to be shopping for me. With one weekend now turning into an entire summer at the beach, I had not packed enough swimwear. The plan had been to stay with my dad this summer, not help him move his life back here to the beach. I still couldn't believe he had agreed to reopening the lab.

After a lunch at a local Thai bistro, we decided on manicures and pedicures. Again, the beach was the last place I thought I'd be this summer. I had seriously underestimated how much of my body would be on display. A pedicure was the least I could do.

From the time we had entered and taken our seats, Rachel had been on her phone, her thumbs rapidly texting.

"Where are we going next?" she asked without looking away from the screen.

"Lingerie. I want to go to that place next door. I'm hoping they sell some cute swimsuits."

She grinned and quickly responded to another text. "Perfect. I need new lingerie. I read in *Cosmo* that you should buy lingerie in the same color as your man's car."

"Who are you messaging?" I ignored the random fact that was probably made up.

"Mostly Chris." She finally put the phone down on her lap. "That time was Justin."

"Rachel . . ." I groaned. "You are not back together with Chris, right? Tell me you're not."

"We've just been texting."

I could tell by her tone it was about to become more than just texting. I was stuck here for the next few months, and she was going to be hung up on her ex the whole time. Was this not the same guy who had her in tears the other night? Hadn't we gone out to celebrate the end of her relationship?

"What happened with him, anyway?" I asked. "I know you said you messed up. But what did you mess up?"

Her smile fell, and she forced her phone screen to go black. She waited until the manicurist left to process our payments before she turned to me. "I wasn't doing enough to keep him motivated."

"Motivated?"

She shifted uncomfortably. "Motivated in the bedroom. Lacey, I've tried everything. He doesn't stay hard."

"Uh," I practically scoffed, "how is that *your* problem? He dumped you for that?"

She didn't have to say another word. She got dumped because Chris couldn't keep it up. Why is it that if a woman doesn't finish, she's shit out of luck, but if a guy can't stay hard, it's the woman's problem? Chris was making Rachel feel as though it were something she was doing wrong. Did he honestly believe breaking up with her was going to fix that? Rachel was a red-haired knockout. Guys lined up to have her attention.

"Can we change the subject?" she asked, wiggling her blue-painted toes. "What's going on with you and Luke? That kiss was seriously steamy."

I cringed. "About that . . ."

It took from the time we left the salon, and our arms were filled with multiple sets of undergarments in various shades before the entire story of my night with Lucas Drake had been told. Rachel's jaw remained on the floor for most of it, and I couldn't blame her. I still couldn't believe it myself. The best sex of my life was with the person I never wanted to speak to ever again. Whenever I'd think of Luke before, there would be this sickening guilt in my stomach, but also this rage because of how angry I was at him. Now, every time Rachel said his name, my frickin' lady bits twirled.

"So, are you going to do it again?"

My brows furrowed. "Do what again?"

"Luke?"

I slid the hangers harshly across the rack, really not bothering to look at what was on them. "No."

"You just said the sex was amazing!"

"Rach!" I hushed her. The store was not empty. There were quite a few other women around, and they didn't need to know about my night of amazing sex with my ex-best friend. A night that would not be repeated. Not ever.

"Luke got hot. Admit it."

I looked up from the price tag of a cute mesh bra to find Rachel waiting for my answer. My cheeks heated. Luke wasn't just hot; he was gorgeous, however, that didn't change the fact that it wasn't happening again. He was still a Drake. He was still the boy who cut me out without a second thought, and my mother was more than right when she said not to pursue him for those reasons. That conversation with my mom was one of the last I had with her, and I kept her words close to me for that reason.

"My mom never liked the idea of Luke and me. Plus, I don't need him breaking my heart again. Best to just keep a distance from him this summer."

Rachel's head was nodding, telling me she'd heard what I said, but she went quiet. Not to respond was unlike her. She glanced at her phone and then at the entrance of the store. Something wasn't right.

"No comment?"

"Hmm?" She began searching the rack again, pulling off a hanger containing a vibrant blue bra and panty set.

"I said I'll be staying away from him this summer."

"Sure." She offered a toothy smile and shoved the hanger against my chest. "Go try this on. Right now."

It was a little flashy for me. Contrary to the other night's events, I wasn't in the habit of showing people my undergarments. After a year of no sex at all, the chances of getting laid a second time were slim to none. I needed swimwear. However, my friend was not giving me the option to disagree as she pushed me and the selection toward the fitting rooms at the back of the store. She didn't stop until she was shutting the door behind me.

"Don't come out until it's on. And don't you dare try on that beige T-shirt bra. Gross."

I tore my tee off, frustrated with her need to control my

spending today. I was sure I was going to like it on, and that would make me want to buy it. I kicked my jeans to a spot under the bench of the room. I nearly jumped out of my skin when Rachel's hand appeared above the door.

"May I see your phone, please?"

"My phone?"

"Yes," she said. "My map isn't working from here, and there's another store I'd like to hit up after this one."

Whatever. If it stopped her from finding more things for me to try on, that was fine. I retrieved the phone from my discarded jeans and shoved it into the awaiting hand.

"Thank you," she chirped.

I returned my focus to the undergarments. After discarding everything but my thong, I donned the blue lingerie and definitely didn't hate it once it was on. In fact, now I was certain I had to have it. The all-lace bra pushed my breasts up and in, with no cleavage toppling over. The bottoms were more like a cheeky lace short that made my ass look way rounder than it was. And the navy blue against my pale skin was perfect—a color I didn't know I needed until now.

"Okay." I swung the door open. "You were right. I like it."

I stopped abruptly. It wasn't Rachel sitting in the waiting area. Luke's eyes left my phone. I froze, unable to comprehend how and why he was here right now. He only broke our gaze to scan my body slowly from head to toe before grinning. My skin heated everywhere.

Luke leaned back in the seat. "Wow."

The word quickly snapped me back to reality. I folded my arms over my breasts as if that would help me hide what he'd already seen.

"What are you doing here?" I asked. "And why do you have my phone? Rachel!"

"Yeah?" she called from a closed dressing room.

"I'm going to kill you."

"Yeah," she agreed.

Luke stood, holding out my phone. I snatched it from him and returned to the dressing room. He took a few steps to follow without actually coming into the room. Instead, he placed both palms on the wall outside of the door and leaned in.

"Why did you need my phone?"

"I made modifications to it."

"What modifications?" I scrolled through my apps, but nothing had changed. "What did you do to it?"

"Well . . ." We locked stares in the mirror. His smile widened. "For starters, I added my number to it."

I bit my cheek to stop myself from smiling back as I tossed the phone back on the pile of clothes on the floor. God, he was frustrating. Why did he have to be so cute and so damn charming? Just like when he came out to the beach yesterday afternoon. I tried to stay mad, but he made it hard.

"Let me take you to dinner tonight."

That wasn't happening. My head was shaking *no* as I picked up all my crap and began flipping it from inside out. He was about to have a door closed in *his* face, but he stopped it with a single hand along its top.

"Luke . . ." I sighed.

"Don't act like the other night didn't happen."

"*We* should act like it didn't."

He took another step into the room and allowed the door to swing shut behind him. I took a step back until my knees hit the built-in stool. He towered over me. I sucked in a breath as his fingertip brushed against my bare stomach.

"There's proof of it right here."

I swatted his hand away playfully, covering the hickey with my hand. "You don't know that's from you."

"No?"

"Nope."

He hmphed. "I could have sworn I left one there. If you spread your legs, I'll show you another one I can claim on your right thigh."

"You're ridiculous."

He couldn't disagree, so instead he laughed, retreating one step. "Please come out with me tonight?" Luke lifted both hands. "I promise to be on my best behavior. Let me get to know you again."

"I can't. I'm helping my dad get settled."

It was a lie. As riveting as time spent with my father was, I preferred spending my time with Rachel. Plus, Luke's dad had promised me a tour of Drake-Mason sometime next week, and I was dying to see it. Luke was disappointed, but it was for the best. He opened the door and let himself out.

Justin was sitting in the chair now, looking bored as hell while waiting for his friend. He stood and glanced my way before Luke grabbed his chin to shift his attention away from me. Just then, Rachel's door opened, revealing her in a sexy black corset with a matching garter, and Justin practically dove in front of her.

"What the hell are you wearing?" he asked, hiding her front with his back.

"Lingerie, moron! This is a lingerie store!"

"Go put clothes on!"

"Uh, the point of this is to lose clothes. Not put them on."

Luke and I shared a look. These two bickered like an old married couple. They had been doing the same at the bar the other night. The more guys that surrounded Rachel, the closer Justin got. The two had been close when we were kids, and I hadn't been sure if they still remained that way. Clearly, yes, because between the three of them, no one seemed to act like this was something new. He was like a protective older brother. It was kind of cute, in an annoying way. It took Luke literally grabbing Justin by the arm and directing him away to stop them from arguing.

"You have my number if you change your mind," Luke reminded me. "You can't hide the entire summer."

And I was guessing he now had mine. As for hiding this summer, he could bet on it. It may have been his first olive branch, but even I knew it wouldn't be the last.

I returned to the dressing room, listening to Rachel mutter about Justin's stupidity from hers. I redressed quickly and left the room to toss all the bras and swimwear back onto the return rack. My phone buzzed in my pocket, and I had little doubt who it was.

*Buy the lingerie, Lace. It was hot.*

I bit my lip, staring at the text, then back to the blue bra and panty set. For its price, I could have bought two swimwear sets from a clearance rack. But how the hell could I turn down that request when it came with such a compliment? I picked up the set, tucked it beneath my arm, and waited for Rachel to finish trying on hers. After about a half hour and many versions of similar corsets, she finally picked three she loved. I had a feeling these were going to be used in an attempt to *lift* someone's spirits in the bedroom.

"You know I heard all of that, right?" She winked as she tossed her items to the counter. "Exactly how many hickeys are we talking about?"

A lot.

"What's the deal with Justin?" I asked, wanting to turn the discussion around.

She giggled, handing her card over to the cashier. "Lacey, your mom never met Luke as an adult, and neither have you. Dinner wouldn't kill you. It wasn't really fair of her to tell you who to like."

So much for changing the subject. "Yeah, well, she was dealing with a crying teen at the time. Can you blame her? It still doesn't change the fact that it would be good to keep my distance this summer. I have to run a company with him eventually."

Rachel rolled her eyes, knowing she was getting nowhere by being on Team Luke. After collecting her bag, I placed the lingerie set on the counter, where the security tag was removed and it was placed in a bag and pushed back my way. But I was still holding my debit card.

"I haven't paid . . ." I stated the obvious.

"It was already paid for," the cashier replied. "The man from the dressing room seemed to like it."

Good God, the embarrassment. Nothing went on in there, but her expression made it obvious that she thought something had. It was a few minutes at the most. If that's all it took, it would have been unfortunate for everyone.

Rachel's elbow collided with my ribs. "He bought you lingerie! You have to let him buy you dinner!"

Dinner was not happening. But now I had money still in my account and his compliment fresh in my mind. What was it Rachel said she had read in *Cosmo*?

"Do you have it in *red*?"

# chapter six

## LACEY

With storm clouds came unease. The last time I had seen the beach this dark, I was eight. I remembered how fast it went from bright, to cloudy, to so dark you would have thought it was night—not nearly noon. The waves had been rough all day, but by the time Luke and I decided we should each go home, they were choppy, loud, and at times, rogue in just how far they'd come up the beach. We waited too long. The wind was ruthless. It knocked me forward, backward, and threatened to take me right along with it. I clung to the stairs that led to our porch and had never experienced the relief I felt when I made it to the door. It dissipated the moment I attempted sliding it open, only to discover it was locked.

I was terrified. I banged my fists on the glass to be let in, watching pillows from our lounges fly away to be lost forever. I couldn't wait. I ran back down the stairs, falling once and skinning my hands and knees. The only place I could go was to Luke—who

I knew was home and safe. I sobbed as I hit the front door begging to be let in. The door swung open, and I was immediately pulled inside and wrapped in a hug as I cried.

I wondered if Luke remembered that day the way I did.

"Lace?"

Rachel stood at the closet holding two hangers—one with a classic black pantsuit with a white-and-black patterned blouse and one with a tasteful black dress. We'd picked out both while shopping the day prior, and we were trying to choose which one I'd wear for my tour of Drake-Mason tomorrow. I couldn't focus; the tour was the last thing on my mind.

"Pantsuit." I placed my head against the window. The sky rumbled, and I shivered.

"Are you still afraid of storms?"

"She is," my dad answered for me as he entered the bedroom.

"Whoa, Mr. Mason, looking snazzy."

Rachel was right. I was used to seeing my dad in jeans with polo shirts most days. Black slacks, a deep gray dress shirt, and a tie that marbled both colors were not pieces in his wardrobe yesterday. Obviously, Rachel and I weren't the only ones who did some shopping. The tie was draped around his neck, and he looped it as he thanked Rachel for the compliment.

"That storm is supposed to miss us. I'll be at Drake-Mason all day. You good here on your own?"

My stomachache said no. I hated being alone during a storm, but I learned a long time ago to suck it up. The storm I had been caught in as a child was later given a category one hurricane rating. While fine for most adults, as a child on the beach, there was nothing scarier. I'd had nightmares about it for years after that.

"I'll be fine."

Rachel was here for the time being, but she had a date later. I didn't have to ask; I knew it was with Chris. She deserved better. But I wouldn't be the one telling her not to spend time with him. In her eyes, something about him was worth it. Since I would be on my own, I'd binge-watch a TV show and try getting other things out of my system. I needed to have a talk with Rachel before she left, and it wasn't something we could discuss in front of my dad. Once he had nodded and left the room, my entire body shifted in her direction.

"We need to talk."

"About how fine your dad is? Yes. Damn."

"Gross!" I chucked the pillow I'd been using to lean on toward her head. "No!"

"Accept it. The man is a DILF."

Ugh. "Can we not talk about how hot my dad is? I have a problem."

"A problem?" she repeated. "What sort of problem?"

"I can't, er, I can't . . ." I was talking more with my hands than my mouth.

"You can't . . . ? Can't what?"

"I haven't gotten off in three days."

Her reaction said everything. She instantly bit her thumbnail to stop herself from smiling like a fool but failed. Her cackle was so loud I was thankful we had heard my dad shut the door upon leaving.

"Since . . ."

"Luke." I finished the sentence.

"Oh, this is good."

"I beg to differ!" I stood up and paced the obnoxiously large bedroom I would be occupying this summer. "No guy has ever gotten me off until Luke. Now, I can't get myself off because it was that frickin' good, and I'm so in my head about it. This is a problem!"

"Easy fix! Let's call him!" Rachel reached for the cell phone on my comforter.

I practically threw my entire body onto the bed to prevent her from getting anywhere near it. We were absolutely *not* calling Luke to come over here and get me off. Not an option. She could not leave this house until she promised to never speak of this conversation with him.

"This is hilarious," she stated. "It's only been three days."

*Three sexually frustrating days.*

"What have you tried? Fingers? Toys? Shower?"

"Fingers and the shower. I don't have any toys."

"Okay." Rachel joined me on the bed. "What about thinking about Luke as you do it?"

I was purposely trying not to think about him or our night together. Part of me thought—knew—it was the reason for the problem. Luke gave me something I wasn't sure I'd ever have again, and it was better than what I could do myself. Our sex was hot. Orgasming with him repeatedly was not something I could forget. Now, my lady parts didn't want it if it wasn't like *that*.

"Give into the Drake D, girlfriend." She slapped my thigh before she stood up and held out her hand. "I promise not to tell Luke about this if you promise me that you'll try fantasizing about him. I bet it works. And that's a sign for you to let him do the work next time."

I pouted and gave her phone back. That wasn't happening.

---

The bathroom was set up to be the epitome of relaxation. The exterior window let in only a little light with the darkened clouds, but I closed the plantation shutters and lit the room with a jasmine and sandalwood candle. Since normally I would have had my music playing while bathing, I opted for silence. Warm water, light on the bubbles, dark and quiet . . . it was perfect.

So why was I not crying out from a well-deserved, mind-blowing orgasm?

I was trying everything in my arsenal all over again. The showerhead, fantasizing about movie stars, and kink. My middle finger had now circled my clit so many times that I was becoming sore. I had never concentrated on anything so hard in my life. Everything brought me back to Luke.

I sleepily let my mind go there—back to our night together. I recalled the smell of his cologne as he sucked on my skin and breasts. With my bottom lip tucked between my teeth, I pinched my nipple before I dragged my fingertips over the skin he kissed. I started from the space between my breasts and traveled to my navel, teasing my skin and imagining his lips there.

"*Luke*." I stupidly allowed his name to fall from my lips. I'd sworn to myself I wouldn't let this happen. It was too easy to remember the way he touched me, kissed me, licked me, *fucked* me . . .

The tub water sloshed in choppy waves when I worked my pussy the way he did—rough and determined. My fingers were soaked, and it wasn't from the bath. My toes curled. My stomach tightened. My lips parted—ready to cry out his name this time. It was happening.

And then it all came to an abrupt stop.

With the sound of my phone making the most obnoxious chirping noise I had ever heard, came overwhelming frustration that had me taking it out on my bathwater. I hit it so hard that the floor around the claw-foot tub was now a massive puddle. Someone was going to pay for the interruption; I was already plotting their death as I reached for my phone.

It was some sort of alarm attached to a calendar app—one I couldn't find an icon for, and yet it was refusing to stop until I entered a password. I was trying every combination I could think of and becoming angrier with each failed attempt. The phone was about two seconds away from being submerged in water with me when a text tone accompanied the alarm.

*My middle name shortened.* The text now associated with Lucas Drake's name briefly showed up in an alert and faded again.

Lucas William Drake. *Will?*

After entering it into the text box, the app sprang to life. Him being the reason I wasn't screaming with an orgasm wasn't lost on me as I finally discovered how to silence it. My hijacked phone was now displaying today's date with a red block of time. After tapping my thumb on the box, it opened to my scheduled commitment: *We're having dinner. Your place. I have a key. I'll meet you in the kitchen. See you soon.*

More water sloshed to the floor as I sat up straight. *Dinner. He has a key. He's showing up here, and he has a frickin' key?*

I swung a leg over the side of the tub, meeting the wet floor. I slipped my way to my feet, wrapped myself in a towel, and ran back into the bedroom. Faint sounds of rustling bags and cabinets opening and closing told me he was already here. There wasn't even time to think, let alone prepare for company. I pulled black leggings and a cropped sweatshirt out of my suitcase and was thankful they weren't inside out when I glanced in the mirror. My hair was still dripping as I tied it up.

"You coming?" Luke called from the kitchen.

"No. I haven't been, thanks to you," I muttered as I pulled open the door.

My nose told me Italian before I even reached the kitchen. It was confirmed when I found Luke leaning against the cabinets with a take-out bowl of pasta in his hand. He looked damn proud of himself as he shoved a forkful into his mouth and used his elbow to nudge a bowl of spaghetti in my direction. As much as I wanted the food and the man shoving it my way, I wasn't going to let his charm sway me into making any mistakes. Moaning his name from my bath was already one, and now he was standing here in the flesh, looking even hotter than he had during our last few encounters. Gray sweats, a white tee, and a black track jacket that hugged his muscles perfectly.

I ignored the pasta and went to the fridge to retrieve a pitcher of water. My ass needed to cool down about ten degrees.

"Thought I turned down your dinner invitation?"

"Incorrect. You said you were busy."

I selected two glasses and placed them on the counter. "What if I was busy tonight?"

"Well, I thought of that, too, but your dad is at work. And I don't believe for a second anyone would leave the house in this storm."

I'd honestly forgotten all about the storm while I tended to my . . . *needs*. Now my senses were hyperactively aware of the whirling wind and the pattering of the rain on the roof and patio. So much for it missing us. I played off the fear and poured us water.

"I don't need you to entertain me, Luke. I'm a big girl. I have plenty to do while I'm here."

"Oh yeah? What were you doing before I got here?"

I bit my cheek. If he hadn't shown up, I would have orgasmed and napped. The perfect combo and not something sharable.

"Just doing some unpacking."

His grin made my body ache. "Right."

Luke took another bite of his food while I gave in to the temptation of the bowl he'd reserved for me. There was a smaller bowl beside it with a salad and some sort of vinaigrette, along with another container of garlic bread and packets of parmesan. I hadn't eaten all day, and the garlic alone was enough to make my stomach growl. I went for the bread first.

"You can't just hijack my phone and break in every time you want to hang out."

"Seemed to work just fine. I got you to eat with me. You'll come to enjoy these little hangout sessions of ours. As you can see, they're rewarding."

His charm had me fighting a giggle. He was damn pleased with himself, and it worked this time. I wasn't sure there would be a next time. My second order of business was going to be taking back my calendar app. The first was the key.

I held my hand out. "Give me the key to this place."

"Hell, no." He scoffed. "I had to make conversation with my dad this morning to get it. You do not know how much I hate that."

I had a pretty good idea of how much he hated it, because in all the time I knew him, he never got along with his dad. I knew nothing had changed there; especially after having breakfast with the two of them. It didn't matter, though. I was getting the key back. Since gray sweats left nothing to any woman's imagination, I took advantage of it. The keys were clearly in his right pocket. Beside another bulge I didn't need to question. I wiped my hands with a dishrag and placed myself in front of him. I grabbed his jacket with one fist and batted my lashes a few times.

"May I help you?" he asked with a chuckle, not falling for it.

I cupped the keys from outside the pocket. "Mm-hmm."

"Don't you dare, Lace."

I sank my free hand into his pocket until I had a fistful of cold metal keys in my grasp. There were two sets, but one was definitely a single key on a key chain. It was in my grasp for barely a second before I was laughing too hard to focus. He tickled my sides until the key fell somewhere near our feet. I'm not sure whose giggles were louder—his or mine, but eventually I cried *Mercy!*

His hands remained where they were as the room became still around us. I braced my hands on his biceps, trying to catch my breath. The distance between his lips and mine was barely measurable. I stared at them, craving his mouth the way I did when we were at the club. As much as I wanted to lift myself and connect, I knew it would complicate things more. His fingertips dug into my hips possessively, and that move alone made my mouth part and brace for impact. His head dipped, my vision faded, but the front door shutting had me jumping at least a foot backward and out of Luke's arms.

Saved by divine intervention. And my dad.

Considering how small the room seemed just a minute ago, my dad entering made it feel ten times smaller. Luke and him both clearing their throats at the same time made it damn near suffocating.

"Wasn't aware we were having company," Dad said as he placed his briefcase on the countertop beside our food. His tone left little doubt that Luke was not welcome. This was the boy who had me in tears for weeks, after all. Seems my mom wasn't the only one who wanted to protect my heart from a Drake.

"I was actually on my way out," Luke lied as he picked up the lost key from the floor. He opened my palm, placed the key into it, and closed it again. "Just didn't want Lacey to ride out her first storm alone since coming back. Thought we could catch up."

So, he did remember our hurricane. I squeezed the key, accepting it as a small amount of newfound trust between us. He could have kept it and made my life hell this summer. I lifted the corner of my mouth in gratitude. All things considered, my evening with him wasn't horrible. The app could stay for now.

I just needed to ensure we kept our distance physically.

# chapter seven

## LUKE

The limo was quiet the entire way from the Hamptons to Long Beach. I hoped for Jack's sake that my dad didn't work from the car in silence every morning. Jack and Lacey shared one seat while I sat beside my dad. All I wanted to do was be alone with the girl across from me, but instead, I tried avoiding staring at her exposed legs for too long while I pulled at my tie. I'd been in a suit for an hour and already wanted out of it.

Lacey looked like she was made for this life. Those sexy legs were crossed elegantly, peeking out from a sleek black dress that said she was all business. Her red-heeled foot bobbed, and I wasn't sure if it was nerves or boredom from the drive. While I was fixated on her, her attention was focused on spinning her bracelet. When the car came to a stop beside Drake-Mason Pharmaceuticals, she took a visible but silent breath. I could feel her nerves and excitement from my seat.

I was the first to exit—partially because I was eager to have the day over with, but also because I wanted to open Lacey's door. It might have been the driver's job, but not today. She was the only reason I was even here right now. I was supposed to be working my job at a local bar today, but when my dad mentioned the tour for Lacey, it was the first time I had ever shown any interest in his work, or in his words . . . my future.

"Thank you," Lacey said barely above a whisper as she took my hand, only to release it immediately upon standing.

The glance she shared with her dad told me he still wasn't over my showing up the night before. I couldn't blame him for not liking me. However, there were several reasons for him to not like me, and I wasn't sure which one was at the top of the list. It was one thing to greet me at the breakfast. It was another to spend time with his only child—the girl I was making my priority this summer.

"We'll meet you up there, Lucas. I need to stop by the lab and chat with Jack."

I pulled at my tie, convinced it was becoming tighter the closer we got to the door. "Whatever."

Once Jack and my father had wandered off, it was just Lacey and me standing in the lobby. I was busy smacking every up arrow in a long line of elevators while Lacey looked like she was a child experiencing Disneyland for the first time. She stood in the middle of the room, slowly spinning to take in every part with a broadening smile as she did.

"When was the last time you were here?"

The tip of her tongue glided across her upper teeth as she looked thoughtfully at the lobby ceiling. "The time you swam in the fountain and security had to take you upstairs dripping the whole way. Your dad was so pissed."

I rubbed at the scruff on my chin while cringing and groaning. I had to have been nine; making Lacey eight. We had a lot of fun in these halls. Lacey's giggles filled the lobby, accompanying the chime of a waiting elevator. It was empty, and when the doors closed behind us, no one else had entered. We had a long wait ahead of us to the top floor where the C-suite offices and main boardrooms were located. I settled in by leaning into the back corner, continuing to adjust my tie. We were about ten floors up when I realized I'd missed something Lacey had said. Too lost in my thoughts, I lifted my stare from the floor, finding her more enthused than she should be.

"Hey." She beamed. "You're looking ridiculously handsome and uncomfortable in that suit."

I stuck two fingers between the tie and my throat and yanked downward. "That's because I am."

"Wow. So full of yourself this morning, knowing you're handsome . . ."

Before I could offer a comeback, she shoved her clutch into my abdomen, forcing me to hold it. She carefully loosened the knot in my tie, allowing my collar to become more forgiving. It barely mattered—her ocean-blue eyes were enough to cut off my air supply. It was the second day in a row they were daring me to make a move, but just like yesterday, she was swift to take back her purse and step away once she was satisfied with her work.

"Where did you learn how to tie a Windsor?"

"I had a boyfriend who wore suits every day," she said with disdain. "He couldn't tie one for shit."

Wow. I never thought a word could kick me right in the chest. Boyfriend? I pushed my hands into my pockets. I still had roughly thirty floors to wonder who the lucky guy was. Obviously they had dated long enough to live together. I wanted to know everything and nothing all at the same time. I kept my mouth shut and eyes down, knowing I didn't want to be asked about Tiffany in return.

"Awfully quiet over there," Lacey remarked, crossing one ankle over the other. "What's on your mind."

"Right now?" I teased, eyeing her toned legs. "Those red heels are hot."

The lip bite was cute. She tried to ignore the compliment, but I wouldn't let her this time. She looked hot and deserved to know it. I also wanted her to know I was looking.

"No comment?"

"Rachel was right," she said.

"About?"

"She says that guys have a thing for certain colors. Usually the color of their vehicle. Women are supposed to buy lingerie in that color. In your case, red is supposed to be an aphrodisiac."

Well, when she put it that way, yes. My imagination flooded with images of Lacey in cherry-red lingerie. My thoughts had never turned dirty so fast. My boxers tightened at the thought of her wearing the lingerie *and* the heels at the same time while doing ungodly things in this elevator.

My throat cleared. "Yeah."

As the elevator continued to climb, Lacey lifted one foot and pulled one heel off. Followed quickly by the second. Confused, I wondered if she was about to hit me with them for confirming I was turned on by them. It was the way she was watching the last few numbers blink on the panel while moving to the area directly in front of the door that told me what she was actually doing.

Game on.

I nudged her shoulder, trying to knock her off balance just enough that she would have to step to her right. She pushed me back a step. The last two floors were a constant battle of trying to budge each other to be the first out of the elevator. As soon as the door chimed, my arms wrapped around her, lifting her from the ground and setting her behind me so I could get ahead. I bolted through the parted doors before they had fully opened, leaving Lacey laughing hysterically in my dust.

"Damn it, Luke!"

I weaved my way through empty halls, knowing we were both heading for the same office. I couldn't see Lacey, but I could hear her bare feet hitting the familiar carpeted floors we had run down as children. This was our game, and Lacey usually won, but not this time. With my momentum, I could barely stop myself as I came to the threshold of Alice's office. I was catching my breath, grinning like an idiot, and holding my hand out like a child. That's when a red shoe hit me in the back of the head. I ignored it.

"Lucas," my father's elderly secretary sighed, "what are you doing?"

I held my hand out farther, waiting for the goods. No words were needed. We all knew the top drawer was stocked. While Alice slid the drawer open, Lacey—now just as out of breath as myself— made her presence known by shoving her shoulder into mine.

"Cheater." She scowled, holding out her hand beside mine.

"Oh my goodness!" Alice stood and dropped a handful of candy into Lacey's hand first. Lacey stuck her tongue out in my direction as she was wrapped in a hug. "Honey, look at you! Could you look any more like your momma?"

"See, Luke, Alice recognizes me."

My eyes rolled with her comment. I would never live that down. I wasn't sure who I was more jealous of right now—Alice getting to hug Lacey, or Lacey holding a handful of candy when I clearly won the race.

"What a lovely surprise before I retire. I miss you two playing up here. Now you both look so much like your parents. This is really taking me back."

Lacey and I both ignored the comment. Being like my dad was nothing I strived for. I had spent my life avoiding the Drake shadow. And Lacey, while she looked just like Mary, also appeared pained as she forced her lips to curl upward. Weren't we laughing just a moment ago? While this place brought back many memories for the two of us, I was sure it was bringing back even more of her mom.

After Alice finished gushing over Lacey and finally forked over a handful of mini–candy bars, it was time to join our fathers in the CEO office. Alice's phone lit up to ask if she had found us, and she assured them we'd be in soon. Lacey put her heels back on, including the one she'd struck me with, thanked Alice for allow-ing us to run the halls one last time, and congratulated her on a well-deserved retirement. As I followed Lacey out, Alice called my name. I promised Lacey that I'd meet her there and took a few steps back, not quite entering the room.

"What's up?" I asked.

"I'll be training Tiffany soon. I thought you should know."

Alice would not beat around the bush with that news. I should have known my dad would still give her an internship, even though we were through. I hadn't answered any of her messages since she arrived in New York. I didn't want to be cruel, but I also didn't want to give her false hope either. We were done.

"Is she here today?"

"Goodness, no." Her hand waved the thought away. "Enjoy your day with Lacey. Seeing the two of you together was the best morning I've had here in a long time. Be good to that girl. She's been through a lot."

We shared a goofy, all-knowing smile that had me bobbing

my head yes as I left the office again. There was no hiding anything from Alice. My attraction to Lacey was obviously plastered on my forehead. Thankfully, my ex was not here today to see it. At least with Tiffany working eight to five every day from Long Beach, I had a minimum of nine hours with Lacey where she couldn't interrupt. Keeping away from her while home was another story. If Tiffany learned where I was working this summer, I'd be done for.

I rejoined Lacey in my father's office. As Jack and Drake sat across from each other at a small, glass conference table discussing having the lab's fume hoods recertified, Lacey sat beside them quietly, twirling a blue Jolly Rancher like a dreidel. I took the chair beside my father and slid a chocolate bar across the glass. Lacey stopped it with her hand and an infectious snicker. The Jolly Rancher was launched using the same method, a little too hard, and landed in my lap.

"Now that Lucas has decided to join us, we can get started," Drake said, always needing to take a jab at me. I wasn't sure what needed to get started; all we came for was a stupid tour.

"It has been long overdue for the four of us to be in this building. From your births, every employee to walk these halls has understood that the two of you would become the major shareholders, and thus, would someday run this company. Time has flown, and now we're a few short years away from you both inheriting your shares."

I sank in my seat and dropped my head against my propped fist. I was already bored with the spiel I'd been receiving since the day I was born. Meanwhile, Lacey took in every word as if it were gospel.

"Jack and I have been discussing many things over the last few days. One being the reopening of the lab, but also considering the requirements of the positions you'll hold, which led us to a conversation regarding your educations."

As much as I wanted this discussion to turn into us no longer being required to have a pharmacy degree, I knew it would never fly. I never complained about the business minor, because I could use it outside of this building.

"Drake-Mason has already paid for Luke's tuition at North Carolina, and we feel the same privilege should be extended to you, Lacey."

I never realized my tuition was being paid by the company. Offering the same to Lacey after five years was some typical Drake bullshit if I had ever heard it—anything to save himself a buck. As teens, she and I had always talked about attending Chapel Hill together. When I heard she had started at Ann Arbor, I figured it was her way of avoiding seeing me.

"That's sweet of you, Mr. Drake. However, I didn't get accepted, even with a 4.0 GPA. Ann Arbor was my second choice, and I don't hate it."

*And I had a 3.5 . . .*

"Not a problem. I've been on the phone with admissions. If you'd like, they'd be happy to accept a credit transfer from Michigan. They were very pleased with your test scores, and you've been top of your class for four of your five years. The choice is up to you if you want to transfer."

I could see her fighting back happy tears, biting at her inner cheek. "Thank you, I would love that."

"Your mom would be proud to hear that."

It never failed that Dad could turn the discussion around to Mary. If I had been sitting across from him, I would have sent him a glare to stop. He never seemed to notice that not everyone brought her up constantly the way he did. I couldn't care less that Lacey was following in her mother's footsteps. However, I was pleased at the thought of us being in North Carolina for school at the same time.

"That leads us back to the two of you taking over this business someday. Jack and I both agree that the two of you showing your faces around here doesn't hurt. We don't want to toss you into roles you're unprepared for. So, this summer you'll both take college-credited internship roles with the company."

I stood so fast my chair hit the wall behind me. "What?"

"Sit down, Lucas," Dad barked. "Beginning Monday, you'll be interning in marketing. Lacey, I hear you have a knack for numbers—something we need around here. We'd love for you to begin in finance."

*No.* I had plans. I needed to work this summer if I was going to get out of ever working in this godforsaken building. I had two positions lined up, and by the end of the summer I was going to be a full year closer to walking away from *his* dream to start mine.

"Lucas, I said sit."

"Fuck off," I muttered. I strode to the door, feeling three sets of eyes on my back as I slammed it behind me.

"Lucas!"

I hung an immediate left, knowing it would take me to a rarely used stairwell from the top floor. My heightened pulse was already pounding through my temples. I had been mad at him many times in my life but never so mad that I thought I might pass out. He literally had me seeing red. I sat on the landing with my feet on the first stair, dropping my head into my hands to take a breath. The last time I was this mad at him was the day I took it out on my best friend. And when I heard the door open behind me, followed by the soft tapping of her heels, I knew I had to check that anger right now. Because I was not losing her again over something my father did.

She sat beside me. The red heels were kicked off, and she allowed them to tumble down a few steps as she wiggled her pink-painted toes. Usually my dad would have followed, scolded me, and I'd give in to whatever he was demanding of me, but I didn't have it in me today. Lacey being beside me was new, and even though she was silent, it was comforting to be allowed to breathe.

"Since we're getting comfortable . . ." I unwound the tie that had been choking me all morning, pulled it over my head, and tossed it as far as I could throw it. It went farther than the shoes, but not by much.

"Are you okay?" Lacey asked, placing her palm on my shoulder.

My eyes pressed tightly shut, and I shook my head *no*. "I hate this place, Lace. I hate the building. I hate pharmacy. I hate my dad. Every single day I see myself becoming more and more like him, and I can't escape. I don't want you to think this has anything to do with you—going to school together, working the summer together, or even running this place together. You're the only part of it I *can* handle. I can't handle being the next William Drake."

"I so get it," she said, fumbling with the seam of her dress. "Well, sort of. I think I'm the opposite, though. Everyone compares me to my mom. I act like her, I sound like her, I look like her. If I could be her, I would in a second."

I didn't like the sound of that last part, but to Lacey, her mom was her world. She always had been, even when Mary was alive. I had little respect for Mary, but I could respect Lacey's love for her.

"But I can't be her," she continued. "No matter how hard I try, I will never live up to Mary Mason. Mom got into Chapel Hill on her own. She didn't throw money at them. They wanted her because she was smart. She was born for Big Pharma, and I . . ."

"Was clearly born for numbers," I said with a snicker. "You

impressed my dad with something I didn't even know about you. That's hard to do."

Her frown let up, and just briefly, I saw a smile. "I work in a bank. I enjoy numbers. But I like pharmacy too."

"Mm-hmm." Something told me the last sentence was a lie, but I let her continue.

"So, I get it," she said, finishing her thought, ignoring my comment. "Everyone wants you to be your dad. Everyone wants me to be my mom."

We sit in silence for what could have been minutes or an hour; who knows? No one came looking for us. My dad probably knew I would act like that. My plans were destroyed, and part of me wondered if he knew about them all along. The only person who had known was Justin, and he wouldn't say anything to anyone. I was risking not only my reputation but the reputation of the Drake name, for what that was worth anymore. I had lost respect for it long ago.

"I don't think I can go back in there. I think I'm just going to call Justin and get out of here. I didn't mean to mess up your tour."

Lacey pursed her lips, setting the tip of her pointer finger on them and tapping them. "What if we both left?"

"And went where?" I was amused at the thought, knowing she wasn't serious. She was looking forward to spending the day in this hellhole.

"Who cares!" She practically bounced in her spot. With her eyes widening in excitement, I could have sworn they became an even brighter shade of blue. "We can Uber back and get your Jeep. Let's just take a drive and see where it takes us! I have a purse full of Jolly Ranchers and uncomfortable shoes. We'll escape the Drake-Mason shadow for a day. What do you say?"

My dad was going to be furious about this, which made the

idea more appealing. Plus, I was getting exactly what I wanted. I got a day with Lacey, and one that was all her idea. She *wanted* to spend the day together.

"Okay, pretty girl. Let's take a road trip."

# chapter eight

## LACEY

I had to be out of my mind. Instead of staying away from Luke, I was running off with him for the day. The moment we were in his car, I tossed my shoes into the backseat. Luke's dress shirt was unbuttoned at the collar with sleeves rolled up his arms, and his tie was now somewhere on the pavement of the NY 454 instead of the stairwell at Drake-Mason. The moment it was in the rearview mirror, he was liberated.

After Luke and I had agreed to silence our phones for a day of peace, I quickly sent off a text to Rachel, telling her I was fine and with Luke. I was sure my dad would track her down to figure out my location—somewhere I didn't even know yet. Her response was to ask if I had gotten off yet. I didn't respond and turned the phone off. It wasn't a discussion I'd be having while sitting beside the guy who made it a problem.

"So, where am I heading?" Luke asked, breaking our silence.

Seeing him grinning the way he was made him that much more gorgeous. I didn't know his dad had become so insufferable over the years, but now I could see just how much it affected his mental health. I was certain I was the last person to whom he wanted to admit his hatred of Drake-Mason, but I was glad he did it. This was a completely different Luke than the one from a few hours ago. And a happy Luke was an easy one to crush on.

And having that crush was perfectly fine—so long as I didn't act on it.

"Somewhere with good food."

"Hungry?"

"I'm *always* hungry," I said, already wishing we had stopped for snacks. "It's a standing joke with my friends. Hangry Lacey is a 'good' time."

"Are you going to miss them? And Ann Arbor? I swear I didn't know the company was paying for my schooling. I figured my dad was."

I still hadn't wrapped my head around it. Chapel Hill had been the dream for as long as I could remember. Drake made it seem so easy after I spent the first month of college crying over the fact that I wouldn't graduate from my mom's alma mater.

"It's not like I can't still talk to them from Chapel Hill."

"And what about your ex?"

Ahh, there it was. I giggled while pulling out change for our next toll booth. "How long have you been dying to ask me about Knox?"

"Sounds like a douche."

His jealousy had me cackling. Knox, in fact, was a douche.

"Let's just say he's a part of Michigan I won't miss. He probably won't even notice I've left."

"Wish I could be that lucky with mine," he muttered, gripping the wheel tight. "We should probably discuss Tiffany."

Tiffany. My smile vanished. I didn't want to talk about Knox, but I sure as hell didn't want to talk about any of his exes either. She was an ex now . . . was she an ex when I slept with Luke? Why the hell didn't I ask if he was seeing someone?

"I was engaged," he began, not making me feel any better. "It's been over for a while, but my dad hasn't accepted it. We aren't the only ones with an internship this summer. Tiffany is taking over for Alice."

Even though my damn heart was in my throat, I was bobbing my head. This was fine . . . no . . . this was good, even. Better than good. Luke has an ex-fiancée. This is where stalking him would have come in handy. With his eyes barely on the road, he continued to look my way while I inwardly died a little. It was a blow but something I needed to hear.

Good God, I never knew I could hate someone so much without even knowing them.

"As I said, more than over."

"It wouldn't matter if it wasn't," I said, now sure I was dying. "We both have exes. Most people do. It's not like we're dating, or even thinking about doing so. I'm sure she's nice."

"She's not."

*Oh good.* I could feel better about not liking her.

"Well then, we fire her as soon as possible!" I giggled through every word, seeing Luke smile at the thought. I mean, I was joking, but I really wasn't at the same time. I was just glad to see he liked the idea as much as I did. "Can we change the subject now? I want food."

"Yes. What would you like?"

"Food."

His attention shifted away from the road. "What *type* of food?"

"The edible type."

"I forgot just how stubborn you can be."

My arms folded over my chest. "I'm not *that* stubborn."

His brows lifted.

Maybe I can be a little stubborn. "I don't know. Good food! And a lot of it."

Luke rubbed his chin while continuing to man the wheel with the opposite hand. It took a minute, but eventually he seemed pretty damn pleased with whatever decision he'd made. He quickly shifted lanes and took the exit for Philadelphia.

"I know exactly where we're going."

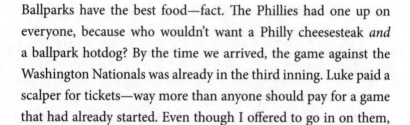

Ballparks have the best food—fact. The Phillies had one up on everyone, because who wouldn't want a Philly cheesesteak *and* a ballpark hotdog? By the time we arrived, the game against the Washington Nationals was already in the third inning. Luke paid a scalper for tickets—way more than anyone should pay for a game that had already started. Even though I offered to go in on them, Luke insisted on paying for the day. I think he still felt bad about his schooling being paid for.

By the time I had put on a Phillies jersey over my dress and a ball cap, with a foam finger tucked safely under my arm and two handfuls of food, it was the bottom of the fifth. I'd never been to a game before. While I was never into sports, my dad rarely missed a Mets game on television. And I remembered Luke and his dad attending Yankees games when we were kids. I didn't understand any of the rules, but that was fine. This was already a blast, just trying all the various food options. Even with my cheesesteak in hand, there was a mound of fried, spiraled potatoes smothered in cheese that was definitely on my to-try list before leaving. You could never go wrong with cheese.

The game . . . was terrible. However, our seats weren't bad. Eight rows behind third base gave us a fantastic view of the few plays being made. Even though this day was about getting Luke out of his head, I was having more fun than I'd had in a long time. We had food, we had beer, and a horrible game that was still tied at zero.

I offered Luke some Cracker Jack, which he accepted, tossing it into the air to catch in his mouth. I found myself engrossed in the way his jaw moved as he chewed—there was something sexy about the bone structure of his face; especially when he was happy. I didn't enjoy the way he always caught me watching, though. When his body turned to face me and not the diamond, I was certain he was on to me offering him my food on purpose.

"How long did you live with him?"

Not what I was expecting. "You really want to talk more about Knox?"

"No. But yes."

"Almost two years. He cheated. We don't speak. Why did you end your engagement?"

"She wanted my name and lifestyle. Not me. Unfortunately, we speak. I'm trying to change that this time."

"This time?"

His head shifted uneasily. "Not our first breakup. It's the last."

I shouldn't have asked. The more I learned about Tiffany today, the harder it was to convince myself this wasn't a crush. What if they got back together, and I was stuck in an internship this summer with the two of them? Drake-Mason was an enormous building, but eventually we would run it together. Could I watch him with someone else? This morning, I convinced myself that having

Tiffany around would be a good thing. Now, I didn't want to see them together. I couldn't have it both ways, and my mom's words kept repeating in my head as a reminder of what he had done to me. He tossed me out of his life so easily . . . was he doing the same to his ex?

My head was spinning.

"Hey." He gave my ball cap a little tap. "What's on your mind?"

I wasn't going to admit what was in my head when I couldn't make sense of it myself. "We didn't get a hotel room yet," I said, pulling my phone out of my purse. "Probably a mistake on a game day."

We scanned my phone for a good option for the night. We wanted somewhere close since we'd been drinking. When surrounding people began cheering, we figured it was because something had actually happened in the game. We looked up to find nothing had changed on the field itself, but the scoreboard was showing various sections of the park, and ours was now the focus. While the group behind us was standing with beers raised in the air, screaming to be seen by the cameras, Luke and I waved from our seats. We laughed as the camera zoomed in on the two of us, likely because we were the only two morons still sitting and trying not to be on camera.

But then that damn screen changed.

A rocket showed up in the screen's corner, and when it was done zooming around our faces, we were caught in a pink heart that matched the color of my face. When I thought it couldn't possibly get worse, the words *Kiss Cam* scrolled across the top, and it sounded like there wasn't a soul in the park that wasn't chanting "kiss her."

It felt like someone in the camera booth had it out for us. Luke and I were sharing small, awkward glances and forcing giggles that were just as awkward. But one of those glances lingered longer than the rest, and that's when I knew I was done for. He leaned in, cradled the back of my neck, and hungrily took my lips with his—leaving me breathless with roughly forty thousand strangers cheering us on. There was something about the boldness of the move, and the accompanying electricity, that had my entire body buzzing. In a complete moment of weakness, I kissed him back.

The kiss basically summed up our entire day. It was unexpectedly fun, sweet, and completely against our parents' wishes. Eventually reality was going to set back in. I pulled away first, still embarrassed by the camera and sliding into my seat to avoid it. One last shared look with Luke told him that I couldn't allow it to happen again. He sighed as he turned his cap so the beak was forward and tilted it downward. His green eyes were now hidden from me, making me feel even worse.

I tried to ignore the disappointment on his face as he returned to watching the game. More than that, I tried to ignore my own disappointment. Because this kiss was even better than our first. It wasn't part of a game to throw karma in his face.

This one felt real.

# chapter nine

## LUKE

The number of beers we had drunk left us no option but to walk to the hotel after the game. We made an evening of it, hitting up some local bars, eating dinner from street vendors, and hanging out with a group of locals celebrating a home-team win. I didn't know how Lacey could eat the way she did and still have a mouthwatering figure, but I loved that she didn't hold back when hungry. She was comfortable enough with me to steal from my portion when she wanted to try something new. She was so different from Tiffany, who would have spent the entire night bitching about what I ate while she wouldn't finish a salad. I liked that Lacey just didn't care.

We picked up our room key with no luggage other than the clothes on our backs and Lacey's purse. It was tucked under her arm, and in each hand she held a bottle of wine that she'd purchased at a liquor store beside our hotel. It was the first time we'd been alone all night, and we still hadn't mentioned the kiss. As much as she wanted to hate it, her eyes told me she didn't. I sure as hell didn't hate it. I only hated the way she was holding back from me.

Lacey kicked off her heels as soon as we were in the room. She handed me a bottle before screwing the cap off hers. "Cheers."

I tapped my bottle against hers and watched her knock it back. It was impressive. I wasn't sure how she could hold her booze like that but figured it had gone the same way as all the food we'd eaten today. The bottle was placed on the dresser so she could focus on removing her jersey.

"Don't let me wear this home tomorrow. My dad would never forgive me."

The jersey was likely the least of her worries tomorrow. My dad was probably going to kill me, but I couldn't imagine hers being much happier. I saw the way he had looked at me when he came home the other night, and I was not welcome. Today was added to the list of things I'd have to redeem myself for with Jack; even if it was Lacey's idea to take a road trip.

I hated the idea of tomorrow. I was going to have to rearrange my entire summer. I didn't have the money I needed to just tell my dad to take his company and fuck off. I was going to need more than a bottle of wine tonight to take away the edge of his wrath in the morning. I started that process by sipping from my bottle while Lacey emptied her entire purse onto one of the two beds to find a toothbrush she'd tossed in there. Seeing her pull an entire blood pressure cuff from a clutch was possibly the most impressive thing I'd seen all day.

"What's with that?"

"What's with what?"

"You keep a blood pressure cuff on you at all times?"

Lacey shrugged like this wasn't something anyone would find

odd. She shoved it back into the bag with everything else, minus a travel-size toothbrush and toothpaste. She stopped short of the bathroom to toss open the curtains. I knew we had to be somewhere near the pool, because the scent of the chlorine was overpowering, but what we each thought was going to be a window was actually a sliding door that led to the outdoor pool. And it was empty of guests.

Sold.

"Luke!" Lacey shielded her eyes as I unbuckled my pants and let them fall to the ground. "What the hell are you doing?"

"What does it look like?" I asked, removing my shirt next. "I'm going swimming. Come with me."

A second hand covered her face. "You're in your underwear!"

I stood there for a minute, finding the way she blushed adorable. "You are seriously getting embarrassed now? I'm still covered. My dick has been in your mouth."

Her head dropped back, and she groaned to the ceiling as if it would stop me. "I knew you would throw that in my face, eventually."

I wouldn't be throwing my dick in her face unless she wanted it there. However, I definitely wouldn't mind if she did want it again. No one was using the pool. It was late, outdoors, and for late spring, it was unseasonably cool out. Obviously, I would have preferred a hot tub but didn't see one as an option. Hopefully the pool was heated.

"I'm just saying, you've seen more of me than this. And I've seen a lot more than whatever you have hidden under your dress. I'll be in the pool."

I tore off my socks and stole a towel from the bathroom. Lacey looked every which way but at my boxers, with her cheeks remaining the color of the burgundy comforters on our beds. My bottle of wine came with me. I was perfectly capable of drinking alone out there.

The pool area was still devoid of people when I entered. I scanned the other windows and doors surrounding me, but all their curtains were tightly shut. Even if they weren't, boxers were really no different from swim trunks, anyway. My towel was tossed on a deck chair, but the wine remained with me. The first step into the water was a bit of a shock. It wasn't heated. However, with each step I took, my body adjusted to the cool water. I only set down my bottle on the cement around the pool to dive under completely.

Part of me didn't want to resurface. It would be easier to stay under the water than to deal with the reality of working at Drake-Mason this summer. I had no control over my own life anymore. Even my relationships were dictated by my dad. The only thing worse than working there this summer was working with Tiffany. Pursuing Lacey was not part of my dad's plan, but it was part of mine. She was someone whom he would get no say over, and if he did, I had enough leverage to throw it back in his face. I learned from the best, after all. And the best was what William Drake always considered himself.

My lungs were aching. I had no choice but to push my feet against the bottom of the pool and come to the surface. I pushed back my curls and wiped the water away from my eyes to see a blurry brunette standing above me in a robe. Even blurred, I could make out that she was nervously biting at her thumbnail.

"Thought you were staying in the room?"

"You cannot just leave me in there to drink alone, ass. It's depressing."

*Welcome to my life.* I floated on my back and waited as she stood there, timid as a mouse. The Lacey I had come to know since returning home was not shy.

"You getting in?" She didn't immediately answer and kept looking around us, probably to make sure all the drapes were closed, which they still were. "Lace?"

"Turn around."

"Seriously?" I asked, returning to my feet. "I'm not a complete perv. Have a little faith in me. Whatever you have on underneath is okay."

"Fine," she muttered, untying the robe.

I was not prepared for what she had on underneath. I took it all back instantly as I saw her standing in the same lingerie from the store, but now in cherry red. I could see her taut nipples through the fabric now, and fuck. . . . She'd nearly killed me with the heels this morning, but this was enough to cause a heart attack. As I stood there eyeing every single curve of her body, my heart was going to do just that or beat its way out of my chest.

"Lucas!" she yelled as she entered the pool.

I turned around. There was no way not to gawk at what she was wearing. "It was blue before."

"Yes. That one is at home."

"That's red."

"Good job, Luke."

"That's . . ." I looked over my shoulder to see she was now in the water. The material getting soaked just made the aching in my boxers worse. But my interest was piqued. "That's the color of my Jeep. Did you buy this before or *after* your little conversation with Rachel regarding wearing the color of a guy's vehicle?"

"You're ridiculous." Her eyes narrowed. "Maybe I like the color!"

"I'm sure you do." I laughed, feeling like I had finally gotten somewhere with her. Not only did she kiss me back today but she'd bought lingerie that was for me to see. "Tell me, what color vehicle did *Knox* drive?"

She found that question just as amusing as I did. She giggled as she answered, "A silver Prius."

"Small dick, too, eh?"

"You're terrible."

"Not a no."

"Anyway, I thought you weren't going to be a perv."

"Well, it's hard not to look at you when I'm talking to you."

She waded in the water for a moment before swimming behind me. I didn't understand what she was doing until her arms were wrapped around my neck and her legs around my waist. If she didn't want me to be a perv, pressing her breasts against my back wasn't the way to go, but I would allow it. It was permission to touch her again, and I was going to take advantage of it. With both hands, I hiked her up my back by her thighs and held her there.

"This way we can talk without you seeing that I'm practically naked."

"I can *feel* what you're wearing. That might just be worse, but I can behave myself."

"Good."

She rested her chin on my shoulder and it took everything in me not to turn and kiss her again. I didn't, but I wanted to. As I walked us around the pool, I wondered if another kiss would make or break whatever this was.

"Can I ask you something?" she whispered beside my ear and wrapped her arms around me tighter. "Something we said we wouldn't talk about?"

"You can ask me anything. What would you like to know?"

"If you hate pharmacy this much, why didn't you pick a different major?"

If only it were that easy.

"It's been a long time, but I'm sure you remember how my dad is. Do you really think I got a choice? The only choice I was ever given was accept my fate at Drake-Mason or be disowned. My only money was his. It's not like I had a job in high school. Your GPA was better than mine, and I got into Chapel Hill, Lace. Drake doesn't give anyone a choice. It's his way or no way."

"What about your inheritance, other than the shares? The Drake oil money?"

"I get it in two years. The only way around it is a parent's signature, which isn't coming from Dad and can't exactly come from a mom who ran off when I was sixteen."

Even though I said she could ask me anything, I wasn't ready to tell her my plan for getting out of Drake-Mason. The fact I even worked was embarrassing when people knew I grew up, and still was, *privileged*. The money I was making was good but put a lot at risk. As much as I would have loved to share that part of myself with Lacey, I couldn't trust she'd keep it to herself.

"Can I ask you something now?"

"Sure," she agreed.

"Do you like pharmacy? Or do you do it because your mom liked it?"

"I . . ." She stopped herself.

It was a serious question, and I wanted her to see that I was taking it seriously. I didn't want it to sound like I was dissing her mom. I dropped her thighs and gently removed her arms from around my neck so I could turn and face her. Doe-eyed, she looked up at me while struggling to answer.

"You can tell me the truth," I said, pushing my arms through the water. "It's just us out here."

"I don't hate it. I like parts of it. I like the math."

"But do you like *pharmacology* math? We both know there is a big difference between the two. It's a tiny part of pharmacy.

What about the chemistry? Patient care? Law?"

"*No one* likes pharmacy law." Her eyes rolled with her attempt to make a serious answer playful.

"Lacey . . ."

For the first time tonight, Lacey deliberately made eye contact with me. And with pursed lips, she shook her head *no*. Turned out we had a lot more in common than I thought. We both needed today. With a halfhearted attempt at a smile, I assured her the secret was safe with me.

We swam around in silence for a few more minutes before deciding it was too cold to continue. I got out first and looked away as I held open Lacey's robe for her. We both shivered when we hit the cool air of the room. While Lacey again retrieved the toothbrush she'd abandoned, I started the water of the shower. I stood with my hand beneath the stream as Lacey brushed her teeth.

"You can shower first," I said, shaking my hand free of the droplets when it was warm enough.

She finished at the sink and bobbed her head. As she dabbed her mouth with the hand towel, our eyes connected in the mirror. I'm not sure how long we stood there, watching each other. But when the mirror fogged, she finally turned around. My heart was back to pounding against my ribs, and I used the robe's belt to pull her closer to me. The way she watched my lips, waiting to see what they would do, had me wanting to use them all over her again. But when my head dipped to claim hers, her face turned away.

"Luke, we can't."

"Can't," I repeated, now holding her hips. "Why?"

"I just . . ."—she stepped out of my hold and pulled her robe tighter—"I think we should be friends."

*Ouch.*

People really used that line?

"I think we both know we're more than friends. We always were. You can't lie to me and say you didn't feel something with that kiss today. We both did."

"I didn't say I didn't."

"Why are you so determined to not let this play out, then?"

For the first time today, Lacey would not be honest with me. She wasn't even going to answer the question. This was more than me shutting a door in her face or ending our friendship. Something was holding her back, because if she felt the same way I did, which I was assuming she did, she wouldn't be able to ignore this. The red lingerie was case in point.

"What aren't you telling me?"

"Nothing," she said with a shrug. "I just think it would be better to be friends. We're going to work together this summer, and possibly run a company together someday. Staying friends is the smart move."

And there was the lie.

"Keep telling yourself that." I left the bathroom so she could shower, slamming the door behind me.

After I dropped Lacey off at home, I couldn't bring myself to go back to mine. I wasn't sure what had me more riled up, my dad and this whole Drake-Mason bullshit, or that Lacey and I weren't speaking over something incredibly stupid. We'd barely exchanged ten words with each other the entire way back to Long Island. Instead, I placed a call to the club I'd been hired at for the summer and informed them of my situation. They were understanding of me not being able to pick up as many bartending shifts during the day and added me to more evenings. It was risky, but I had no other choice.

My next call was to Justin. I'd picked up my first evening shift, and I was going to need a change of clothes. I wasn't even ten minutes into the shift when he showed up with a bag in hand. His amusement at what I was currently wearing was bound to be fair game for some hate.

"The Phillies? Seriously?" He asked, placing the bag on top of the bar.

"Lacey and I went to the game."

"About that . . ." he said, taking a seat at the bar.

I knew where this was going. I disappeared, and my dad's first call was to Justin. I grabbed a glass and placed it beneath the tap. I knew this conversation was going to require beer by the look on his face. Whatever it was he needed to discuss, he wasn't looking forward to breaking the news. If I wasn't currently on the other side of the bar, I probably would have ordered one for myself.

"He called you." I pushed the drink toward him.

Justin surveyed the bar. There weren't many people here in the afternoon, thankfully. I wasn't sure if he just didn't want other people to hear us or if he wasn't comfortable being in this *particular* establishment. Not only did I have a reputation to uphold but so did he.

"I wasn't the only one he called."

"Oh yeah?" I racked my brain. "Who . . ."

But then it hit me. My dad had called Tiffany. I groaned. I took a sip of Justin's beer to take the edge off and gave it back to him. So, not only was my dad now looking for me . . . so was my ex. This was the last place I needed her to find me.

"She didn't call you?"

"I send all her calls to voice mail and delete them without listening."

"Well, she showed up at my place. So, she's around."

Great. I could bank on my father having her over for dinner in no time. Of course he called Tiffany when I ran off with Lacey. I was sure that was a whole other discussion waiting to happen with my ex. I needed to keep those two apart at all costs. If Tiffany knew I was spending time with Lacey, she was going to insert herself into the mix.

"What's going on with you and Lacey?"

"Nothing. She officially friendzoned me." I tossed a rag over my shoulder and took the bag from the bar. Peering in it, I saw everything I'd need for a shift tonight and tucked it under the counter. "I know she feels the same. We kissed at the game, man. I don't know how she could even say we should be friends after that."

"Maybe she knows the truth," Justin offered. "Because I'm sure you haven't told her yet. You're both hiding shit."

"You know why I can't tell her about that day."

"She's a big girl now. I think she can handle it."

No. This was the worst time for her to find out why I ended our friendship the way I did. I would take that secret to the grave. I messed up with her once. I wouldn't lose her again over the same bullshit. I went to reach for Justin's beer, but he slapped my hand away and picked it up for himself.

"You're never going to know until you tell her. Don't mess it up by hiding something she's going to hear from someone else. You can't tell me we were the only ones who knew. With the two of you working at Drake-Mason, it's only a matter of time."

"I can't."

"You've been in love with that girl your whole life, Luke. It needs to come from you."

There was no way I could tell her the truth now. I had waited too long. In the short time since she'd been back, we'd already gained back so much ground. I couldn't mess this up again.

"Sounds like you've finally decided to tell Rachel Meyer you've been in love with her your whole life. Congrats," I countered teasingly.

Justin tipped his glass in my direction with a wry smile. "Touché and a big fuck you, sir."

That's what I thought.

# chapter ten

## LACEY

The drive to work was silent. My dad thought it best to travel apart from the Drakes after disappearing with Luke for twenty-four hours. We still hadn't really talked about it, but I could tell he was pissed at me for pulling a stunt like that after being offered tuition and a spot at UNC. It had been a week. It was stupid of me, and it ended exactly as I knew it would—with me holding back and not giving Luke any sort of reason he'd understand.

"You're supposed to report to the finance department. Do you know where that is, or do you need me to take you up there?"

"I can find it," I said with my head pressed against the car's window.

"Lacey . . ."

Here it was. I was about to have the first father-to-daughter talk ever at twenty-two. A little late in my book. Mom already had the *no Lucas Drake* talk with me, and it had stuck, so there was no need to worry.

"We aren't dating."

He audibly exhaled. "I think it would be best if you two put some space between you this summer. You came for Rachel, and I've seen Lucas Drake more than her."

That was because she was trying to get her ex's dick hard—not a conversation I was about to have with my dad. And anyway, I'd already put space between myself and Luke. A huge one. One that had kept me up all damn night for the last week. This was supposed to be our day. This was our first day at Drake-Mason, and we didn't even ride in together. Hell, we wouldn't even be working on the same floor. And, even better, he would be on the same floor as his ex-girlfriend. And that thought made me feel ill. I hadn't even met her yet. She'd at least get a hello out of him. I had texted him as soon as I'd woken up and never got a response.

"He just needed a day out. It won't happen again," I concluded.

My dad dropped me off at the main entrance of the building while he went to find parking. I swung the door open, wanting to be early to meet whoever was going to train me. Luke stood beside an opening elevator. He took one emotionless glance at me and stepped in. The doors shut behind him—I assumed he pressed the button to close it immediately. He really couldn't ride up with me? I knew we'd be working on different floors, but he could have stuck with me.

I took an elevator with a group of strangers and exited on the twenty-eighth floor. I was greeted by a stark white wall with a FINANCE sign and an arrow pointing to my right. Easy enough. The corridor changed from a hall to an already-buzzing department. Compared to the C-suite floor, this one was dated. The overhead lighting was faded and buzzed louder than the elevator music playing through crackling speakers in the ceiling. There was also an overwhelming scent of coffee, which I had a feeling was the source of many of the stains on the worn carpeting. To my right was a sea of cubicles and to my left was a string of glass-walled offices, similar to what I was used to seeing on the top floor.

My pink Post-it note instructed me to find office 501. I counted down until I was standing in front of a dark office. At first, I figured my trainer just wasn't here yet. But then I noticed an envelope hanging from a blank nameplate beside the door with my name on it. I pulled it free and opened it to find a note from Drake.

*Lacey,*

*Your nameplate is on order. If you need anything, please let my secretary know by dialing 001. You'll be meeting with Mitch O'Brien, and he'll meet you here at eight a.m. sharp.*

*I wish your mom were here to see this. I know you've made her proud.*

*—W. Drake*

I had my own office. I warily took a step in and flipped on the light. The space was a vast blank slate. There was a large oak desk, a couple of chairs, and a filing cabinet. It was the wall of windows that caught my attention. I hurried across the room and drew the vertical blinds until the room filled with natural light. From here, I could see down to the busy streets of Long Beach.

"Most interns don't get offices," a voice said from the doorway, startling me out of my trance. "You must be pretty impressive, new girl."

I wasn't expecting what was behind me. Tall, dark, and handsome was a thing, and he was leaning his shoulder against *my* door frame. His arms were crossed playfully, and his eyebrows raised.

I think he was waiting for me to explain myself, but I was still stunned by this office myself.

"I'm Mitch." He took a step into the office and unfolded his arms to extend a hand. "An interning CPA with a cubicle."

I walked around the desk and accepted his handshake. "Lacey. Pharmacy student."

"Pharmacy?" he quizzed, looking behind him as if he was the one on the wrong floor. "You know this is finance, correct?"

"It's a long story."

"Well, Lacey-with-a-long-story," he said as he took one of the open seats in front of the desk, "you lucked out with this particular office. There's another open one at the end of the hall that looks over a seniors' yoga studio. It's, well, some days it's impressive, but most it's kind of gross."

We laughed in unison. "I won't complain, then."

Not that I would have. We were both aware this office was more than what I deserved. He may have been partially joking, but Mitch seemed a little burned that he'd been here longer and didn't have as nice a setup. The fact he didn't already know my long story told me he wasn't told my name, which wasn't something I was going to brag about in this building.

"Anyway, I'm here to give you some instruction on what you'll be assisting me with this summer."

"Great," I agreed, taking a seat in the most comfortable office chair I'd ever had. This seemed to be the only new piece of furniture in the room. "Put me to work."

Mitch sat. "Don't get too excited, new girl. You haven't heard what you'll be doing yet. I can't say it's very exciting."

I didn't care what I'd be doing. I just wanted to get into the job to rid myself of first-day jitters. It worked. Once Mitch started explaining his own role with the company, it made sense. Just as

Drake had said during breakfast with my dad, he had hired interns to find every penny Drake-Mason was leaving on the table. There were many projects happening within financing to achieve this, but Mitch's goal was to find and close out old accounts.

Like any other company fighting to survive, Drake-Mason had bought out a number of pharmaceutical companies over the years. Their focus was on the up-and-comers, snapping them up before they could gain any ground in the world of Big Pharma. With those buyouts came old accounts and soon they owned a pyramid of companies that weren't well-managed.

My job was going to be assisting Mitch in finding and closing random accounts for each of the pharmaceutical companies Drake-Mason had purchased over the years, but also doing research into what businesses had been acquired or sold off by *those* companies. While he joked and said that most days he felt like he needed one of those wild murder-mystery diagrams with all the red strings on the wall to figure these out, I had a feeling he wasn't wrong. When he showed me a list of hundreds of accounts, I was ready to dig in. He could joke, but the future of my mom's company was on the line. In all likelihood, employees didn't know just how bad this place was hurting.

It was midday before I got any hands-on training. We huddled around my single computer monitor, eating our lunch and practicing what to do with an account once I'd found it. As we ate, Mitch helped me fill out the necessary forms to close it out.

"Once you review the last activity on the account, fill out this template I've set up on your computer, asking what it was used for, the account holder names, last date of known activity, and if there's any money owed or if there's actually money in the account. I'll work with the CFO to bring it to a zero balance. If it has a zero balance already, which most do, you fill out this other form. That one is sent to William Drake, the CEO, to close."

"Got it." It seemed easy enough.

Mitch leaned back into his chair and tossed the crust of his sandwich onto an empty wrapper. "So, you're a *pharmacy* student . . . ?"

I knew it was coming. He was going to want the details of my "long story" at some point. It was past one in the afternoon, and he'd mentioned this office at least ten times in his attempts to get it out of me.

"That I am," I answered.

"Please tell me you've worked with money before. How did you get stuck in finance for an internship? I'm not trying to be an ass about it. You seem intelligent, and I'm genuinely curious. Every other intern on this floor already has their degree."

"Short version . . . I've worked in a bank the last few years. Started on phones, then I moved to being a teller, and now I work as a virtual loan officer when I'm not in class. I love crunching numbers."

Mitch grinned. "Pardon my language, but thank fuck."

We were in the middle of sharing a hearty laugh when Luke clearing his throat caught us off guard. We both looked up to find he had joined us in the room, although I wasn't sure how long he had been standing there. He was leaning into the door frame with his hands tucked into his pockets. My stomach did that immediate Luke-induced flip when I saw him and heard him actually speak to me. I smiled like a teenager with a crush.

"Hey, FB." I attempted to joke with him. "Did you get a room with a view too? Mitch here says I'm spoiled."

Luke didn't give Mitch so much as a second glance as he crossed his arms. "Yeah, mine is similar. Because I really needed an office to sift through old marketing materials. And the location is prime—right beside Drake and Tiffany."

I sighed. He knew he'd hate this, and he'd been right. At the very least, I got to play in finance—something I loved. This was his worst nightmare, and even I hated the thought of him being within eyesight of his ex.

"Anyway, I was going to see if you wanted lunch. But"—he pointed to my food and glanced at the man beside me—"I see you got sandwiches with *Mitch*."

Mitch shifted uncomfortably beside me, knowing he was now caught in the middle of something.

"You weren't talking to me, Luke. You couldn't even take the elevator with me. I really didn't think lunch was an option."

"It's fine, Lace. I'll just . . . I'll see you around. I guess."

He turned away, and I was on my feet as soon as he did. "Luke!" I yelled loud enough to be heard in the hall. "Lucas William Drake, please stop and talk to me!"

He was gone before I got to the door. I was pretty sure he knew every nook and cranny of this place after practically being raised in it, and I wouldn't find him while he was on his lunch. His office was the last place he'd go for that.

"*Drake?*" Mitch asked when I reentered the room. "As in Drake-Mason?"

Bingo. The man-child who had just stormed out of this office was none other than Mitch's future boss. I nodded to confirm.

"And you are . . . Lacey Drake?"

I would have laughed if it didn't sting like hell. Once upon a time, that name was written in pink hearts all over my diary. Now we bickered like a married couple. Adorable.

"No." I sighed and dropped back into my seat. "I'm Lacey *Mason*."

I had never been one of those people who watched a clock during a workday, but I was counting down the minutes until five. I still had an hour to go and wanted nothing more than to talk to Luke. Just like this morning, we wouldn't be making the commute home together. And if I was going to talk to him, it needed to be here.

Staring at a clock that wasn't moving, I picked up my phone. I dialed the three-digit extension Drake had given me, knowing exactly where it would go.

"Thank you for calling William Drake's office. This is Tiffany. How may I assist you?"

I hung up immediately.

"Ugh!" I dropped my head to the desk. I hated myself for doing it, but my nosy side needed to know.

I gave up waiting. I grabbed my purse, turned off my computer for the night, and locked up all the folders of accounts I'd been sifting through all afternoon. I flipped off the light and made a mental note to ask for a key to the office door. It would give me an excuse to grace the top floor with my presence.

I used the stairwell Luke had escaped to when it was first announced we'd be taking these positions this summer, remembering that Alice's office was out of its sight line. While I was bound to meet Tiffany eventually, today wasn't the day. Her voice was enough for one day. I didn't need the visual of the two of them together in my head.

By the time I'd reached the C-suite floor, my feet were throbbing in my heels, and I was completely out of breath. It had taken up a nice chunk of the time I had been wishing away. Luke sat at a desk very similar to mine. His feet were crossed on the top of it, and he was leaning back so far in his chair that it looked like it could break at any second. There was a black Sharpie in his hand, which he was using to doodle on some sort of old magazine.

I didn't have to announce my presence the way he did in my office. He knew I was here and was choosing to ignore me. That was fine. He could listen.

"So, what did I do wrong this time?" I asked, taking a few steps into the office to see he was drawing mustaches on old marketing ads. "You cannot be mad at me for eating lunch without you when you saw me this morning and wouldn't speak to me. You haven't spoken to me since dropping me off at home. And even then, we were barely talking."

"I needed to come up here on my own this morning," he said without looking up from the magazine. "I knew today was important to you. I didn't need to ruin it with my attitude."

"And throwing a tantrum in my office was what exactly? Mitch is training me."

"I said nothing about him." Luke tossed the marker on the desk. "I'm just trying to get through one goddamn day of this place. You get to play with numbers, just as you like. Me? I'm being forced to learn the history of this place as if it's supposed to make me feel bad for despising it. All while sitting in offices we both know we don't deserve."

"I get we have silver spoons when it comes to this place. But if you hate it so much, then do something about it!"

"I'm fucking trying, Lacey!"

My eyes went wide at his outburst, and my lips snapped shut. Luke's chest rose and fell just as fast as his nostrils flared. Now I was getting the impression that being here today wasn't his only problem. I was.

"You want to be just friends? It's fucking hard when you don't understand that for a kid with a silver spoon, I've never gotten anything I've wanted. This is my life. You entering it and being here with me this summer doesn't magically change it. You're just someone added to a list of things I've always wanted and will never have."

My eyes burned. "You chose that. You ended a friendship that I'm trying to have with you now. Whatever you felt with that kiss, let it go."

"I'll let it go when you say you don't have feelings for me."

The first tear escaped, and I couldn't stop it. Having feelings and acting on those feelings were two different things. I could have feelings for Luke. But letting down my mom just to have him prove her right was something I feared above all else. He did it once before. From the sound of it, he was doing the same thing to his ex now. This wasn't just hard on him.

"See what I mean?" he asked. "I don't think I can be just friends with you when you can't be honest with yourself or me. I have enough on my mind with this place I don't have time to overthink that you might actually want me too. So, as nice as your offer to just be friends is, I'm not looking to make friends right now. But thanks anyway."

*Ouch.* It was the equivalent of having a door slammed in my face. Luke just shut me out, and honestly, I thought it hurt bad the first time. It was nothing compared to it happening a second. But this time, I knew it was my fault. Especially after sleeping with him.

"Right." My damp eyelashes fluttered as I turned to escape his office. "I'll just, let you get back to your summer, then."

"Wait." Luke stood quickly. "Lacey, wait! I'm . . ."

I shut the door behind me. There was no way I was going to listen to him apologize.

# chapter eleven

## LACEY

The car ride home with my dad was brutal. For a man who rarely cared to have a genuine conversation with me, all he wanted to do was discuss my new job. All I wanted to do was bury myself in a hole and not come out until the end of summer.

The process started as soon as I was within the four walls of my bedroom. My work clothes were now on the floor and kicked into a corner of the room. The pantsuit was replaced with a baggy tee and an old pair of shorts I'd once worn for a school crafting session where I'd mistakenly sat in a blob of white paint. With my freshly washed wet hair piled on top of my head and a pint of Ben & Jerry's in my hand, I was ready for a binge-watchable season of *American Horror Story*. I hadn't cried since fleeing Luke's office, but I felt like I could start again at any second. I was hoping scaring the shit out of myself would stop it.

I had multiple missed calls from him that I wasn't ready to

answer. I felt horrible for pushing him the way I did, but I was also angry at what he'd said. One moment I wanted him; the next I wanted nothing to do with him, or this place, for making me feel like I was fifteen all over again. Then I heard my mom's voice in my head telling me this was for the best. But if it was, why did it hurt this badly?

The first episode was just nearing the fifteen-minute mark when the doorbell rang. I figured Luke would try this method. He couldn't break in with another spare key if Dad was home. Based on how he reacted the last time, Dad also wouldn't let him into the house. I thought my dad had already left for the evening—for dinner with an old friend from the lab. So, to say it was surprising when Dad opened my bedroom door and peeked his head in to say I had a visitor was an understatement. Even more surprising was to see it was Justin.

Justin waited for the bedroom door to close before turning back to me. "We need to have a chat."

"We do?" I asked, pausing my show. I got back into the bed and picked up my ice cream. I wondered if he was about to admit he had feelings for Rachel. I could totally get on board with that discussion.

"Yeah. We do." Justin opened my closet doors and began sifting through my clothes. Hanger by hanger, his facial expression showing his judgment of each piece of clothing I owned. "You and I haven't really talked since your return. You and I are going on a date to catch up on things."

"Things," I repeat. "What things? Are you high right now?"

He stopped midway through a row of dresses to laugh. "I wish."

"Then what the hell are you doing?"

He pulled out a solid-black dressy romper on its hanger and held it up. "Wear this."

I placed my partially eaten pint of ice cream on the bedside table and stood to accept the hanger from him. As much as I wanted a reason to wear the superadorable outfit he'd chosen for me, I was pretty sure Justin was losing his mind. He was now on all fours, shuffling through my shoes at the bottom of the closet.

"Uh, Justin . . . ?"

"Jesus, Lace. How many pairs of shoes do you own? You don't even live here. How many are you hoarding back home?" He picked up a black stiletto and tossed it over his shoulder, making me catch it with the tip of my finger.

"Careful!" I cradled the shoe. "I don't have kids; I have shoes. And they need to be loved just as much!"

"You're odd."

"Says the guy digging through my closet! I'm not going on a date with you. I have plans tonight."

"Oh yeah?" Justin turned to sit on his ass, holding up the matching stiletto. "What do you have going on tonight?"

I grabbed the shoe from his grasp and held it with its twin. "TV and ice cream."

"Sounds pitiful. Now go put all that on and do something with your hair."

I narrowed my gaze and placed my hand on my head. He was pushing his luck. "What's wrong with my hair?"

Justin leaned back on his hands. "Have you seen it?"

No, but his grin was telling me everything I needed to know about it. I took everything with me to the bathroom and kicked the door shut to get ready. It didn't seem like he was going to give me a choice—I was going on a date with Justin.

I got ready as quickly as I could, straightening my hair and trying to offset my reddened eyes with smoky shadow and a little wing to my liner. I kept the jewelry simple—just a chunky silver bracelet. While Justin had no intention of telling me where we were going, he insisted at least ten times that I remember my ID. Obviously, alcohol was going to be involved on this *date*, and I was so down for that. The only other hint I got was in the car when I asked if we were heading to the city, because I had to work in the morning. He assured me this place was within the county limits.

It had just gotten dark when we arrived at a club with a neon blinking sign. Similar to Blue, this club's name was Purple. Unlike Blue, the building was hidden in the middle of nowhere, slightly rundown, and did not have a line around the block. Only a few women stood outside with their IDs in hand, ready to be checked by a bouncer. Justin parked but didn't make any sort of move to leave the vehicle.

"Are we going in there?" I asked skeptically.

His head shook *no* as he removed the key from the ignition. "I want to talk first."

"About?"

"Luke."

I cringed. I should have known this had something to do with him when the phone calls stopped, and Justin was at the door. Clearly, he called his best friend. Hell, I'd messaged Rachel about it. This was not what I had in mind for the night.

"What he said to you today was totally uncalled for. You're both upset about it, but that's not exactly why you and I are out tonight. He was trying to stick up for himself. He feels bad about how he did it."

*By tanking a friendship again?* "I doubt that."

"See," Justin said. "That's the attitude he feels the need to guard himself against. That comment right there is not his problem, it's *yours*. You have an idea of him you can't get past."

I jammed my finger into my chest. "I don't have a problem being friends with Luke."

"Friends?" he asked with a tilt of his head. "Lacey, we both know why you aren't letting yourself be more."

I bit my cheek. Luke wasn't the only person he had been talking to. Sometimes I forgot just how close Rachel and he could be. Justin understood my mom didn't love the idea of me with Luke, and before I could wonder if he had passed that information on, he assured me he hadn't.

"That's not for me to tell him. You need to, though. Be honest with him so that he feels comfortable being honest with you. I get that you two were once best friends, but you've been gone a long time. You don't hold that title anymore. I do. You cannot come back here and assume he's a spoiled, rich brat—like he sometimes was when your mom knew him. He is flawed, troubled, and most days just fucking sad."

My chest weighted. "Because of Drake?"

"Part of it," Justin agreed. "There is so much about him you don't know. He is terrified to tell you because he's afraid of losing you again. You're judging him solely by the boy you once knew and the night you came home. The time between is when Luke became Luke. It's time you met that guy."

"I have," I muttered, spinning my bracelet on my wrist and feeling the guilt Justin was laying on thick.

"You don't. He hasn't let you. Luke has a really shitty life, Lacey. He had multiple jobs lined up this summer to escape the very place he ended up. Then you come along, the girl who gets him out of his head, and you say he's not trying? That's not fair. So, yeah, he got mad today."

"Multiple jobs?" I said. Luke hadn't said anything about working this summer. "Doing what?"

"He told you. You didn't listen." I knew by the tilt of his smile that he was up to no good. "You're in for a treat tonight, Lacey Jo Mason."

Justin exited the vehicle first and held my door open as I stepped out. He confirmed my notion that somehow Purple was a sister club to Blue, but the two shared few similarities. After showing our IDs and stepping inside, that couldn't have been truer. In fact, I wasn't getting a club vibe from this place at all. We walked into a very normal-looking bar area.

Yes, the place was decorated primarily in the color purple, and the drink menu above the bar had a lot of purple-themed drinks. But the place was lacking any sort of dance floor. The room was absolutely packed, and everyone seemed to buzz with excitement to get back to their tables—most two-fisting tonight's drinks.

Justin grabbed my hand and dragged me toward the bar. "What do you want to drink?"

"Nothing." I was too busy trying to take in my surroundings to start.

"Lace, trust me—get a drink. You're going to need it."

That didn't make this place sound any better.

My shoulders lifted and fell. "Rum and Coke?"

Justin lifted two fingers to the bartender. The man winked at me as he pulled two glasses from beneath the bar top and filled them. Even that one wink made the whole vibe of this place feel off. I took a step closer to Justin as he paid. A voice came over a loudspeaker reminding patrons that the show would start in five minutes and to find seats.

"A show?" I asked Justin.

"Mm." He handed me my drink.

I followed him through an arched doorway that led to a room filled with round tables packed with people and dimmed lighting that made the purple-lit stage a prominent focal point. All the stage held was an empty chair. That's when I noticed the theatrical attire donned by the people surrounding us. Like feather boas and tiaras on women—only women. Justin was the only guy I could see.

"Justin?" I eyed the room again. "Where are all the men?"

His laughter was an answer. Every table was filled with groups of women—women who were ready and waiting with a stack of singles in their hands. This was a strip club. The show we were about to see was a striptease.

"You're gay!" I pulled at Justin's arm with delight. "This all makes sense now! No wonder you haven't tried to get with Rachel."

"What?" A horrified Justin was quick to look away from finding a table and down at me. "I'm not gay! Do I appear gay? No!"

Someone dressed in drag laughed, but they weren't mad. They were enjoying Justin's minor defense of his sexuality, while giving off some serious rainbow vibes of their own. This was great.

"I mean," Justin said, backtracking, "I have nothing against gays. Or lesbians. Right to choose, love is love, pride, do whatever the hell you want . . . all that shit. I love pussy!"

I cackled before wrapping my lips around my drink straw. The queen beside me glanced from Justin to me with raised brows. It only made Justin more defensive.

"Not hers! She's a friend! Stop judging me!"

"Honey, nobody in here believes you're gay for a second," they said, trying to stop themselves from cackling along with me.

"Thank God," he said, deflating his chest.

He took me by the hand and pulled me to the nearest free table while I was still wondering why he brought me here, of all places. What little light was left in the room disappeared, and a single spotlight appeared on the stage. Justin gestured to the cocktail in my hand.

"Drink up."

"Why?" I asked. Though I trusted him enough to know to drink from it when told.

"Oh ladies!" A female voice taunted as the beginning of Ciara's "Ride" began to play over the speaker. "It's the moment you've all been waiting for!"

Justin grabbed my arm and tugged it so that I met his stare. I had never seen Justin look so panicked, including his earlier run-in with the drag queen. "Don't make me regret this, Lacey. Don't judge him."

"Him who?"

But I saw who before Justin could answer.

I spit my drink clear across the table. Luke stood beneath a spotlight in a white tee and a torn-up pair of whitewashed jeans. He lifted a black ball cap from his head, allowing his curls to fall free, and made the cap practically dance its way across his shoulders. It rolled from one arm to the other as women screamed and waved their arms.

Justin tugged my arm to retake my attention. "He told you the truth. He wants his own dance studio. He was accepted on scholarship to Julliard, and once Drake found out, he put an immediate stop to it by threatening his trust. He's been saving ever since, under his dad's radar. No one knows about this *particular* job except me, and now you."

I had no time to even think about what he had just told me. My head pivoted back to the stage, seeing a smile on Luke's face that I hadn't seen since we were kids. He didn't have to hide it from me. I would have never judged him for this, especially seeing the difference in demeanor between this morning and now. He was blushing more with each catcall. This was a completely different person—in the best way.

"Ladies! Luke needs his dance partner for the night! Who's it going to be?"

Justin stood, sending his chair nearly toppling backward. With his middle finger and thumb between his lips, he released a whistle that drew the attention of not only every person in the room but also the man on stage. Luke held his hand just above his eyes to see beneath the spotlight, narrowing in on his best friend. Justin grabbed my arm, lifting me to my feet with a single jerk. With his free hand, he motioned to me with his thumb.

Luke's smile vanished in an instant, replaced with utter terror. I would never tell his dad, but I could practically see the thought running through his head. I needed to ease his nerves, and fast. I stuck my tongue out at him and burst out laughing as soon as I did, because he had the same response to it. He was still the Luke I knew, just happier and free.

Justin still had my arm tight in his hold, and once again he yanked it into the air. "She volunteers!"

*Wait. What?* "Justin!" I hushed him and yanked my arm downward.

It was too late. Luke had already jumped from the stage to the floor below and was weaving his way through the sea of tables. Women reached out and felt his arms and abdomen as he maneuvered his way through them. But all of his attention was on me. And I was so okay with that.

The spotlight followed him until he was standing directly in front of me. He paused with the hottest smile I had ever seen on him, before lifting me into the air. I instinctively wrapped myself around him, folding my arms around his neck and my legs around his ass. It wasn't the first time he had held me in this position, and it was just as fun as the first.

"Fancy finding you here, pretty girl."

I bit back my giggle as he made his way back to the stage. He took stairs this time, and with each step I was molding into him more. The start of the song had been on loop until now, and as Luke arrived at the center of the stage, with me in his hold, the DJ allowed it to play out in full. Luke dipped me so far that my hair brushed against the floor, and I shrieked. When he brought me back, I was higher than before, with my face hovering barely an inch above his. I was breathing hard, but I could feel his heartbeat matched with mine.

"Trust me," he whispered so close to my lips that I could feel his breath.

I nodded.

Luke released me. My heels hit the stage. While I regained my balance, the room erupted in screams and squeals. He'd torn off his tee and was now displaying his perfect abs for everyone to gawk at, myself included. Dollar bills were already being tossed to the stage as Luke dipped near its edge and allowed some women to touch him.

I might have been jealous, but these ladies had no idea how good he could feel.

As Ciara's voice filled the room, Luke returned and wrapped one arm around me with a hand firmly spread across my lower back. He took my hand with his free one and moved my body with his. With every move he made, he led my body to mirror it. I was his puppet, and my mind was swimming with how similar it was to him in the bedroom.

Luke turned us and made his way to the empty chair. It was his ass that hit the seat, but he brought me forward to straddle him. His smirk was playing dirty as he took my hips into his hands. My whole body flushed. With each beat of the chorus repeating "like a freak," Luke would lift my hips and bounce me back into his hips. I knew what he was doing. Just like the song promised, Luke made it look like I had control to ride it.

My damn lady parts were crying. I hadn't had an orgasm in almost a month. The last one came from this man, and it was very similar thrusting that did me in. Every bounce edged me closer.

He stood fast, knocking me off the orgasm-inducing rhythm, and lifted me again. Now I was occupying the seat. I didn't think I could turn a brighter shade of red, but I did when Luke stripped off his jeans, leaving him in nothing but his boxer briefs. Women chanted his name like he was a damn superstar as he wiggled his ass and shimmied the denim to the ground. He gave them a show near the stage's edge while more money continued pooling at his feet.

He turned back to me with a devilish stare. Meanwhile, I was looking around the stage for some other prop, wondering what the hell he was going to do to me now. I wasn't sure how much my deprived body could take. My hands were grabbed and yanked, standing me upright.

"Let your heels slide," he told my neck.

I found out what he meant before I could even form words to ask. My wrists were clenched. One second, I was standing, the next, I was sliding between his legs with my back on the stage. He had me just where he needed me—helpless. Luke was smug as he knelt one knee to my side, followed by the other, but they didn't stay there. No, I knew before he even made the move what was coming next. One of his knees nestled between mine, followed by the next, sending my legs parting with him in the middle.

My leg was grabbed by his firm hand and wrapped around his back. Every single naughty memory I had of us—all the ones I was trying to hide away—were now back as he rolled his hips into me. I hoped I was the only girl in this room to know this is how he really fucked—hip rolls and all.

Luke rolled us, and I was back on my knees with him between

them. Ciara's melody continued as he placed me back on the stage. He twirled me, spinning me on my ass before doing another dance around me for the audience. I was just a Lacey puddle on the stage floor, surrounded by more money than I could fathom.

Even through the screams of the audience, it wasn't hard to miss the wolf whistles from Justin. He may have been Luke's biggest fan. I mentally thanked him for putting me in a romper and not a dress tonight.

With the assistance of an offered hand, Luke helped me up as the Ludacris rap portion of the song began. He spun me all over the stage—twirling me, grinding into me, performing more dips. He made it look like I could dance, which is a goddamn miracle without an absurd amount of alcohol. When the song finally ended, I found myself oddly disappointed. Not because he stopped dancing with me while practically naked in front of a room of strangers. But because these five minutes of seeing Luke genuinely happy were over.

He didn't let go as we stood together for the entire room to see, both sweaty and panting for air. "Wanna get out of here?" he asked. "We should talk about . . . *this*."

"Definitely." I had a lot of questions.

# chapter twelve

## LUKE

As adorable as Justin's little date with Lacey was, I took over and
sent him packing soon after our dance. Still, I owed him one hell
of a thank-you. The last person I had expected to walk into Purple
was Lacey, and to say I was panicked was an understatement; but
with a single silly face, she made my anxiety vanish.

I showered at the club, collected the night's earnings, and left
with the hottest girl in the place. First, we stopped for ice cream,
and then we enjoyed a Jeep ride back to the Hamptons on a beautiful night. I still felt like shit about what I'd said to her earlier. And
even though Lacey had assured me it wasn't a big deal, I knew it
was. I was good at keeping people at a distance, and Lacey was not
someone I wanted to do that to again.

Most of the ride home was occupied with endless questions
about being a stripper. I knew they were coming. I hadn't exactly
wrapped my head around this career path either. It was a job. And

it was dancing. Those were the only two things in my head when up on that stage. Obviously, it wasn't my first choice. I was taking what I could get. Same as I was doing with Lacey. First choice wasn't to be her friend, but I could do that for now because the endgame was so much bigger.

"I think I should drop you off here," I said, pulling into the drive at my father's place. "Your dad already has it out for me, and I'm sure seeing you upset after work today didn't help. You left with Justin, so me dropping you off won't be good for him or me."

The Jeep came to a full stop. Lacey, completely relaxed in her seat while scanning through the radio stations, looked up to examine the surrounding area. Her pout was proof she hadn't realized we were this close to home yet. I didn't want tonight to end either. I could honestly say that it was the best night of work in my life.

"Walk me home?" Lacey asked, unbuckling her seat belt.

There was no way I was saying no to her. Any excuse to spend more time with her was a risk I was willing to take. I got out first and helped her step out of the vehicle, and then supported her while she removed her heels. They would not fare well on the sand. Soon we were on the beach with our toes in the Atlantic, walking toward her house as slowly as we could go.

"I'm sorry I didn't believe you." Lacey took my hand. The move shocked me a little, but I also wouldn't argue. I squeezed her dainty hand as our feet sank. "You said you wanted to open a studio, and I knew you were in pharmacy school. I thought you were trying to throw me off because of your money."

My head bobbed. I understood, but it made it hard to tell her the truth later when I knew who she was.

"Although," she giggled, using her free hand to stop her hair from blowing into her face, "that was some serious cash on that stage tonight. Holy shit."

"It pays well," I agreed.

I spun her slowly, wanting to dance with her up and down this entire beach. Her laughter mixed with the sound of waves was a childhood memory I could never forget. When she came back to me, she let me slow dance without music right in that spot. She didn't pull away, but I could see the debate playing out in her mind.

"What are you thinking?" I asked, even though I felt I knew the answer.

"A lot of things."

"Such as?" I spun her again, knowing it would bring back her smile. And it did.

"Do you miss your mom?"

The question nearly knocked the wind out of me, but I tried to regroup quickly. That wasn't where I was expecting the conversation to go. I assumed the question wasn't about my mother as much as it was about missing *a* mother, which was something we had in common. It wasn't the first time I'd been asked, and usually it was a straight no. Tonight, however, honesty was my policy.

"Sometimes." The word hit me right in the chest.

"What do you miss about her?"

That question left a lump in my throat. There were a lot of things I missed about her, but it was hard to say them out loud. It was hard not having someone rooting for me at games, or coming to competitions for dance. It was four years before my dad even realized I was in dance classes, and he'd pulled me out as soon as he did. There was no one to talk him down from this one-way path he had me on. The hard part was not understanding why my mom didn't take me with her. I knew he made her miserable but did I?

"I miss having someone on my team. I wish she knew I was on hers."

Lacey fell silent as she took in what I'd said. Lacey had been on my team then, but I'd messed it all up, and I knew that's what she was thinking. I'd had bad days with my mom, too, and it was Lacey who heard about those. But at that age, every kid has issues with their parents. Even she did. Lacey's dad could be overbearing and absent all at the same time. Her mom being gone either made that better or worse.

"What about you?" I asked, knowing the subject was a hard one. "Did your dad become more active in your life after your mom's accident?"

Lacey sighed so loud I could hear it. "He did what he needed to do. Are we friends the way my mom and I were? No. The accident just made him more aware that he needed to parent. He's not a bad dad. He just doesn't know what he's supposed to be doing. Teenage girls need their moms, and he couldn't be her."

I could see her getting upset, and that wasn't my intention. I pulled her into my chest and stopped our swaying. Over her shoulder, I saw a light come on in the house she was staying in. Jack was home.

"Sorry." She swiped away a stray tear. "I miss her a lot. Especially now that I'm back here. I'm on the beach, walking the same halls, and the spot where she had her accident is so close to it. I hate not knowing where that spot is, but I also don't want to know."

I knew where the accident happened. It was in a parking ramp beside the building—my dad wouldn't set foot there to this day. His driver dropped him outside every single day just to avoid it. He rarely talked about Mary's accident, other than she had a medical emergency while leaving work and crashed her car. It caught fire—he never told me that part, but I read about it and saw the pictures of the aftermath. The less Dad spoke about Mary, the better. Even though I didn't want to, I needed to let Lacey know she could come to me if she wanted to talk about her mom.

"Do they know what caused it?"

"Possibly a stroke. She had horrible hypertension. They thought if she had gotten out of the car, she would have survived it. There was a guy from Drake-Mason who saw it all happen, and he tried so damn hard to get to her. He ended up getting burned pretty bad."

Out of everything she had just said, I was stuck on her mom's hypertension. The night of our road trip, Lacey had dumped a blood pressure cuff out of her purse. I found that weird at the time, but now it made my stomach sour.

"You have hypertension," I stated, now understanding. "The cuff . . ."

"It's nowhere near my mom's numbers." Lacey was playful when she pushed my shoulder. But it didn't ease the worry. "Hers stemmed from preeclampsia from when she was pregnant with me. It just never went away. My grandma faced the same scenario. I check mine all the time; I'm fine."

I hoped her blood pressure was inherited from her dad's side of the family.

Lacey tugged at my shirt. "I'm fine," she repeated. "Now, come on, friendly boy. Finish walking me home. It's getting late, and we have work in the morning. If I'm the grumpy one tomorrow, it'll be all your fault."

We couldn't have that. There was nothing I could do about my internship. I needed to make the best of it. There was little doubt that Lacey was that. I needed to make use of my time at Drake-Mason to work on whatever I wanted this to be with her. There were a lot of things holding us back from that right now. And as we approached the beach house, one of those things stood with his hands on the deck railing overlooking the beach. There was very little amusement on Jack's face upon seeing me with his only daughter. I couldn't blame him after upsetting her this evening. Justin was now next on his shit list.

"I should get up there," she said, taking a noticeable step away from me toward the stairs.

"Wait." I reached for her hand and pulled just enough so that she turned. With watching eyes, we both let go right away. "About those lunches at work . . . that's our time together. Okay? We won't see each other unless we carve out time for it."

The stunning smile she gave me before leaving was confirmation that an hour of her day was now reserved for me.

# chapter thirteen

## LACEY

The accounts assignment was supposed to be easy. The amount of work on my desk disagreed. Just when I thought there couldn't possibly be any more, Mitch would show up with boxes covered in thick layers of dust and musty from sitting in some storage room for the last five to fifteen years. There was quite the range. Not every box had what I was looking for. But if it so much as looked like it was associated with the finance department, it seemed to land in my office. Of the six boxes I'd gone through over the last few weeks, I'd only found four accounts to investigate. Two were already closed, one I did close, and the last had me on the struggle bus all morning. It was making my head hurt more than I cared to admit.

The account was active. Now it was my job to pinpoint why, but that was the problem. Money from an undisclosed location was being put into this account monthly—exactly one thousand dollars on the first of every month. From there, it was withdrawn on the third of each month and went to . . . ?

"Lacey, are you even listening?"

"What?"

I looked up from the map I had drawn, which was basically a lot of blank bubbles with arrows and dates. Luke's eyebrows rose high, and he removed the pen from my hand. I hadn't even noticed I was continuously clicking it until the noise was gone. Luke's sandwich was already gone and mine was still fresh in the foil wrap.

"Why don't you just hand it off to Mitch? You're obsessed."

"I'm not." I tucked the map into an empty yellow folder and shoved it into the filing drawer of my desk. I pulled my lunch closer. "What were you asking about?"

"The box I brought up here yesterday. Did you look at it?"

I sighed and slumped in my chair. "I forgot all about it."

Luke stood. Thank God for his rolled sleeves—the muscles in his arms bulged as he retrieved a box from the corner of my office. I bit into my tuna salad on rye and tried not to make it obvious I was drooling for him and not the sandwich. Every single afternoon I craved this time together, and it wasn't for lunch. Luke was playing the friends game cool, and now it was me who knew it wasn't possible. I was still sexually frustrated, and I was one move of his hand running through his blond curls away from having him take me on my desk.

"I found these and knew you wouldn't want me to throw them out."

He placed the box on my desk. I stood and sifted through it. He was right. The box wasn't marketing materials—it looked like it came straight out of my mom's old office. There were a few awards with my mother's name on them, her framed pharmacy diploma, and a bunch of old Drake-Mason directories. While they had listings of staff and their phone numbers, they also had inter-office pictures, company picnics, and even pictures of Luke and me running the halls. They were more like yearbooks arranged by department instead of graduation. Each page I turned was better than the first. Luke stood behind me, one hand in a pocket and the other pointing out pictures I might have missed or reminding me who some of the people were.

"Look!" I pointed to a picture of my mom and his dad, eating lunch together just as we were doing, with big toothy grins.

"Yeah."

Luke didn't find it as cute as I did. He reached over my shoulder and turned the page for me. Fun hater. When he tried to flip the page a second time, I stopped him by throwing my palm down to the page. A name caught my attention.

"Wait."

"See someone you know?" he asked.

"Kinda." I pointed to a man who was much too young to be as bald as he was. He stood in a lab coat holding a bunch of balloons for some sort of party going on in the background. "Frank Leonard," I said the name beneath the photo aloud while tapping it. "That's the guy I told you about. The one who was burned trying to save my mom."

"He was young." Luke mirrored my thoughts. "That's too bad."

It was. Her life ended that day, but even though his didn't, it sort of did. I had never met him. My dad visited him in the hospital to thank him and said he barely recognized him. It was the last we spoke of him, but we rarely spoke of anything from that time, so that wasn't saying much. Seeing the man who almost gave his life for my mom brought closure to the part of my mind that had wondered about him all these years. This was only one directory out of several. I hoped I'd get to see more photos similar to these.

"Thank you for not throwing these out."

"You're welcome." Luke placed his hand on my shoulder and gave it a squeeze for comfort. "Now, about tonight."

"No." It was a word I had been repeating all week.

"We don't have to say it's for your birthday. Just a group of friends getting drinks at a strip club on a night without strippers."

We could say it wasn't for my birthday all we wanted. I knew better. There was no way this man had not bought me a gift. And knowing Luke, it was going to be perfect. I was going to get all melty, the way I did for him, and I'd cave. Just looking up at him now and seeing the way he looked at me had me wanting to get up on my toes and close the distance between our lips. I hated knowing what I was missing. Every second I spent with him was a countdown to the inevitable. This wasn't even a crush anymore. My feelings for this man were becoming intense. Ever since we danced on the beach. He had to be feeling it too.

"Please?" he whispered. His hand dropped from my shoulder to my lower back.

*Melted.*

"Another one!" Mitch's announcement had Luke taking a step back and me wanting to follow him. Mitch entered the office with another file box and dropped it onto the pile that sat against the wall. While he looked damn proud of himself for the find, I was cursing him in my head. I needed to shut my door on my lunch breaks.

"Mitch, tell Lacey she needs to accept the fact she's turning twenty-three and that it should be celebrated with beer."

I glared at Luke.

"Happy birthday!" Mitch's hands landed on his hips.

"It's not my birthday. Tomorrow is my birthday."

"Ahh, an Independence Day baby?"

"We called it Lacey Day when we were kids." Luke picked up the other half of my sandwich, knowing I wouldn't eat it, took a bite, and swallowed. "She didn't enjoy sharing the day with America. We had to make it all about her. Now she won't even celebrate at all. We have the day off. We should celebrate it over the three-day weekend."

"Well, tomorrow Hurricane Tiffany is supposed to hit," Mitch said. "Can't blame you for getting the celebrating out of your system early."

I choked on air while Luke's stare went to the ceiling. "Every day of my life is Hurricane Tiffany," he muttered.

I still hadn't had the pleasure of meeting her, and there was a reason for it. As much as I was trying to avoid Tiffany, I knew Luke was avoiding her just the same, and making sure that we didn't meet. She was somewhere on the top floor right this minute. Apart from hearing her voice the one time I called, there was another when she called this office on behalf of Drake, looking for Luke. I lied and said I hadn't seen him as he sat across from me. He didn't know it was her I'd spoken to.

A three-day weekend with a storm. That meant I wouldn't see Luke. Why did that sound so horrible to me? Not seeing him was seriously bothering me more than a damn hurricane. And why did it have to be named Tiffany?

"You already look panicked," Luke joked, believing my panic was storm related. "Come on. We'll duck out early. Justin and Rachel will meet us. You won't even know there's a storm coming."

Doubtful, but fine.

# chapter fourteen

## LACEY

Without a main attraction on its stage, Purple was just like any other bar. Well, maybe with fewer dudes. It was still surprisingly packed for a Thursday night. Luke snagged a table while I used a restroom stall to change into a navy, knee-length cotton dress that was off the shoulder. It was comfy for a relaxing night out.

It was really the first time the four of us had spent time together since we were kids. And that was the theme of our night. We sat around and retold every memory we could think of and laughed until we were all practically crying. It didn't feel like a birthday, thankfully. That was until Rachel reached below the table and lifted a bag decorated in multicolored polka dots.

I groaned. "I said no gifts!"

"Open it!" Rachel squealed.

The bag was long and narrow. Until I picked it up and felt how light it was, I figured it was a bottle of wine. The weight was throwing me as I lifted it up and down. Even though Rachel and I had stayed friends, we hadn't exchanged gifts since we were kids. I couldn't think of what she would get me.

"Something to help you out!"

Whatever it was, it couldn't be good.

I picked out a piece of sparkly tissue paper, seeing two items. Both of which were not exiting the bag. I shoved the tissue back in. A DVD with a huge dong on the cover, and a vibrator.

"Rachel!" I scolded.

"You said you didn't have one!" She continued to giggle so hard she was slapping her bare knee and leaning into Justin as she tried to breathe. "Girlfriend, you gotta get off. It's been months!"

"Rach!" My embarrassment continued as I stuffed the tissue paper into the bag as if it could make the items disappear. I shoved the bag to my feet. Luke attempted to snag it, but I kicked it backward with my heel. If I was lucky, we'd all forget about it by the end of the night.

Luke dipped his head beside my ear. "Months?" he questioned playfully and so loud that it was not a whisper, as intended. He was clearly already buzzed.

"Yeah. Apparently, you're the only man who has ever gotten Lace o—"

My hand flew to her lips to stop her from finishing the sentence. "Rachel Jeanine!"

"Stop being so uptight, Lace. That gift will help."

It wouldn't.

"Thanks," I said sarcastically. This was exactly why I *didn't* need to come out tonight.

"No problem. Always willing to help out your lady bits. Happy birthday!" She turned to Justin and elbowed him. "Dance with me."

We'd ordered mozzarella sticks, and Justin was too busy

working on those. He bit into one and shook his head *no.* "I don't dance."

For someone who had a crush on Rachel, he was passing up a major opportunity to be alone with her. She was back with her ex, who had refused to come out with her tonight. No one was sad about it. Justin, however, was not taking advantage of the situation. She nudged him again, this time tilting her head in Luke's and my direction.

"Time to *dance.* I don't care if you stand there with me twirling around you. We're leaving the table."

It took a minute, but it clicked. Justin stood. He took one last mozzarella stick and his Guinness. From his back pocket, he tossed a pink envelope to the table. It was a Zappos gift card to add to my shoe collection. A man who listens . . . Rachel was missing out.

Then it was just the two of us at the table. I stared awkwardly at my drink, wishing it would refill itself. I had a buzz, but not one great enough to shed the Rachel-induced embarrassment. A small gift bag appeared in front of me.

"My turn," Luke said, ignoring the elephant in the room.

I picked up the bag and dug through the tissue until I felt a box the size of my hand. It was some type of jewelry. I bit my inner cheek and slowly opened the suede box to find a gold charm bracelet. My lungs inflated at the sight. It was beautiful and way too much.

Luke's arm left the back of my chair, and he took the bracelet with both hands, unclasped the chain, and wrapped it around my wrist. "An ice cream cone, for a night where you let me show you the real me without judgment." He picked up each charm with the pad of his pointer finger. "A baseball, for your first game. A pi symbol, for your love of math. A flag, for Lacey Day. A sandcastle, for the first day we met on the beach. And last, a *P* and a *G*, for Pretty Girl."

It was without a doubt the most stunningly thought-out gift I had ever received. I looked up from the bracelet to find Luke observing my reaction. I knew whatever he gave me would make me melt, but this was more than anything I could have imagined. The invisible wall my mom had placed between us crumbled. My mind was scrambling to pick up the bricks and put them back. But with him looking at me like I was the only person in this bar, I couldn't figure out why I should.

"Luke, this is beautiful. Thank you."

"Happy birthday, Lace."

It was me who reached out. Me, who clutched his shirt and pressed my forehead to his chin, feeling his breath move the wispy hairs that had fallen loose from my ponytail. His arm wrapped around me, placing his outstretched fingers on my back.

"You're so frustrating."

"I know." His smile brushed the skin of my temple.

"This gift is a more than a friend gift."

"I know," he repeated.

"Lacey." Rachel's voice cut through whatever trance we were under, sending both of us retreating to our personal bubbles. She held her hand out for me to take. "I need to use the restroom. Come with me."

It wasn't a question of if I wanted to. She was worried. Not about anything Justin had done, as he was currently standing behind her with the same expression. Luke said something about getting more beers before leaving the table. I let Rachel drag me to the restroom at the other end of the bar. As soon as the door closed behind us, her palms were in the air.

"I'm in love with him."

My hand covered my mouth almost as soon as I said the words. I was pacing the room. Rachel grabbed my wrist to stop me. She lifted it to see the new jewelry I was certain was never coming off.

"Whoa. He did good."

"Right?"

Too good. Everything about him was too good. Men like this weren't supposed to exist. So why was this the boy my mom feared for me? He broke my heart once, but he was a kid. Justin was right. This wasn't the boy I'd left years ago.

"I was going to kiss him again," I confessed to Rachel. "I wanted to kiss him again."

"I know. That's why I stopped you."

"Am I making a mistake?"

"No." She waved off the notion. "Lacey, Justin and I are both on the Luke and Lacey train, but I know how much that promise to your mom meant to you. And Justin thinks—and I agree—that you and Luke should talk first. Sober. You both keep so much in. Make sure this is really what you both want before taking that leap."

I took a deep breath. She was right. We were both drinking, and this wasn't something to take lightly. There was still so much about Luke I didn't know. But I wanted to. And I needed to be honest with him about my mom's wishes holding me back. While I was close to telling him when he walked me home on the beach, I didn't.

My head bobbed in agreement. She talked me down. Meanwhile, the door to the bathroom had swung open. I was half expecting Luke and Justin to be sending someone in to see what was taking so long. Instead, a blond woman entered and moved between us to get to one of the three open sinks. She shook her hands out with nerves before splashing water on her face.

"Sorry," she said into a paper towel. "My ex is out there, and I'm finally getting the nerve to talk to him. Please ignore my spazzing."

I laughed sympathetically; as did Rachel. The lady's room of a bar was always the best place for healing. Lord knew I needed it too. But she was making me look sane right now.

"Was he an ass?" Rachel asked the stranger. "We have a friend who works here. We can get him tossed if he's a problem."

"Oh no!" She waved her hand, shooing the idea away. "It was me. I messed up. He's perfect. Sweet, hot, rich . . . everything. I was an idiot."

"You both need some lady-ball courage tonight," Rachel said. "Hike up your tits and tell those guys out there how we really feel!"

"Yes!" the girl cheered as she moved back to the door. "Nice meeting you, ladies! Good luck tonight!"

It was back to being the two of us. While Rachel's little motivational bathroom speech may have left the other woman pumped, I was back to panicking. Rachel wrapped me in a hug. I needed it.

"Come on," she said, letting go of me. "He can't take his eyes off of you. There's nothing to worry about. What's one more day?"

One day. While we had plans to meet up on the beach for the fourth of July festivities, we didn't know for sure if the fireworks would go off as planned. Mitch might have been the first to inform me that there was a storm coming tomorrow, but now the hurricane was the topic of discussion for everyone. While it was supposed to be small, somewhere around a category one or two, it would be roughly the same as the one I was caught in as a child. One day could turn into the entire weekend, because if that wind picked up, my ass was staying inside.

We returned to our table to only find Justin mindlessly scrolling through his phone. "Took you guys long enough," he said without looking up. "Luke's getting beers."

"He was getting beers when we left." I plopped back into my seat.

"I'll go look for him," Rachel offered. "He probably couldn't carry them all."

Luke bartended for this place on weekends. I doubted carrying four bottles of beer was an issue. I scanned the room. It had been over fifteen minutes since he'd wandered off, and now Rachel was standing at the bar, placing our order alone. I looked over my shoulder at the entrance, and my heart plummeted into my stomach. With arms crossed over his chest, jaw clenched, and a shoulder leaning into the wall, Luke looked livid. And I understood why. The blond woman from the bathroom stood next to him, doing a lot of talking with her hands.

"Justin?"

"Hmm?" He finally looked up from his phone.

"Who is the girl standing with Luke?"

I turned my head to look over my shoulder again. Justin mirrored the action briefly and turned back to me. He didn't have to say it—I knew who she was. The bathroom encounter wasn't the first time we had spoken. I really underestimated that storm warning.

"Shit," he muttered, tossing his phone on the table. The word didn't make me feel any better. "Lacey, I need an honest answer from you. Do you have feelings for Luke? Not this playful bullshit. Do you see yourself having a future with Luke?"

I bit my cheek and twirled my new bracelet as I peered back at Luke, telling Justin exactly what he wanted to know. These feelings were becoming heavy.

"Then Tiffany is your worst fucking nightmare. She gets to him, weasels her way back into his life, and fucks with his head. She's a younger, female version of his dad."

Somehow I knew that.

Rachel arrived back at the table first and immediately knew

something was wrong. When she saw Tiffany, she realized the pep talk in the bathroom had been a mistake. By the time Luke returned, he wasn't the same. In fact, for the rest of the night he was pretty quiet, except for ordering more rounds for the table. Tiffany was nowhere to be seen, and as horrible as it sounded, I hoped her night didn't go as planned for Luke's sake.

Justin and Rachel left around midnight, but I vowed to stay with Luke. I was worried he'd try to drive home. We stayed until closing, then moved outside as we waited for our Uber.

"I'm practically sober now," Luke slurred. It was the first time I'd seen him drunk.

"That's is a lie, dude." I pushed his shoulder until he stepped back and was being held up by the exterior wall of Purple.

"Truth," he said.

It wasn't the truth. He was now stripping on the wrong side of the wall. He unbuttoned his shirt until it fell open and leaned forward to take it off, swinging the material over his shoulder after he did. His perfect abs were there for my viewing pleasure. And I ogled the shit out of them.

"What?" He chuckled. "I'm hot."

*No shit.*

"Just keep the pants on, FB."

"Will do," he assured me. "You know, I like our nicknames for each other. They're cute. Tiffany calls me Drake—as if I needed another fucking reminder that I'm becoming my dad."

It was the first time he'd brought up Tiffany tonight since talking with her. He kicked a rock into the street. I was hesitant to bring up the fact I'd seen her, but Rachel reminded me to be open with him. He needed to be open with me about her.

"Do you think she's going to tell your dad?"

He looked up and frowned, realizing that I'd seen them. "No.

I don't think she knows I work here. I think we cut out early, and my dad sent her after me. Sometimes I think his driver follows me around when I pull shit like that."

I didn't know whether to be thankful she didn't know Luke stripped here, or dumbfounded that Drake would have his own son stalked. The more I learned about him from Luke's point of view, the more I disliked him. I couldn't blame Luke for wanting to be nothing like him.

"I'm sure she doesn't call you Drake to piss you off. Maybe she just likes the name."

"Well, she could have had the damn thing if she didn't feel the need to side constantly with my dad."

I bit my lip. Luke's eyes widened, understanding he'd made it sound like part of him still loved Tiffany. He loved her enough to propose. But his head shaking *no* was more assuring than anything.

"I have other plans for that name, Lace. Stop worrying about Tiffany." He slid down the wall and stopped. There was so much surprise on his face that I thought maybe he'd seen our Uber, but he quickly crawled forward a few feet on the sidewalk and stood again. "Drunk people piss on bar walls," he whispered, brushing off his back as if he'd gotten some on him.

He was all over the place, but it had me laughing on a night I thought was doomed once his ex showed up. My buzz was already wearing off, but Luke couldn't even stand without swaying. Shifting my purse and gift bag farther up my arm, I reached into the pocket of his pants and retrieved his keys to pack them safely into my purse.

"Lace?" he said as I zipped the bag.

"Hmm?"

"You gonna use that later?" He tapped the gift bag and leaned back into the wall he'd just crawled away from. He could barely keep his eyes open.

"Maybe," I joked, knowing he wouldn't remember in the morning.

"Can I help?"

"I think I can manage it myself."

He pouted his lips. "Really?"

"Yep. I've got it."

"Lace."

"FB."

"What if it needs batteries? Oh!" His eyes grew wider. "Or is it one of those Tamagotchi vibrators with the cord?

I cackled and leaned into the wall beside him. "You mean a Hitachi? Luke, a Tamagotchi is that little egg-shaped toy on a key chain. It was supposed to be a digital pet. Remember? You kept killing yours, because you forgot to feed it."

"Ohhh." He overexaggerated the word as he set his head on my shoulder. "I do remember that. Mine was blue."

"Correct."

"Yours was pink."

"Also correct."

He looked up at me with a grin. "So, about that vibrator . . ."

"Luke, you are *so* drunk."

"Yes," he agreed.

"I know what I'm doing down there. I'll be fine."

"Lies. Only I can get you off, remember?"

My face flushed to a warm shade of pink. "I remember." And I was hoping he'd forget in the morning.

"Have you tried thinking about the night we were together? I do. And the red lingerie. You can't just wear that for me and then *not* wear that for me, you know? You'll kill my nuts, and I've become very attached to them over the years."

I had officially decided drunk Luke was my favorite Luke, even if he had me just as embarrassed as Rachel had tonight. I wasn't sure how many beers he'd had, but it was enough that his filter was gone. I wished my phone was charged enough for me to record some of these for Justin and Rachel.

Headlights beamed down the quiet roadway. Our Uber driver stopped beside the curb. I helped guide Luke to the car and had to push him into the backseat. I joined him there and gave our driver Luke's address first. Then I leaned into the door and shut my eyes, feeling the exhaustion of the day.

"Lace, wait."

"What?" I turned my head back to Luke, who could barely keep his own eyes open.

"I love you, Lacey. You're going to have the best birthday ever tomorrow. I promise."

I swallowed his words down. *Did he just say he loves me?*

"You won't remember any of this tomorrow," I said with a shake of my head.

"Sure I will." He closed his eyes but kept a cute smile on his face. "I could never forget a moment with you."

Then he fell asleep.

# chapter fifteen

## LUKE

"Lucas." A hand shook my shoulder. "Luke . . ."

My eyes flickered open, but I was convinced I was in a dream. Sitting on the edge of my bed was the most gorgeous alarm clock I'd ever seen: Lacey. Unfortunately, searing pain in my skull brought me right back to reality. My hand slapped my head, and I lifted the covers back over my face. Lacey giggled as she pulled them back down.

"I brought you Aspirin and Pedialyte."

I groaned. "I'm dying."

"I figured."

I sat up and took her hangover remedy. Last night hadn't hit her as hard as me, as she appeared to be unfazed by the beers she'd had. There was no way I hadn't doubled her intake. I was going to pay for it this morning.

"You're up early."

"Rachel and I got a spot on the beach. Justin went to get us some greasy sandwiches, but the traffic is already nuts."

Greasy food sounded perfect, but it could wait. Lacey was practically in my bed right now. I set my beverage on the nightstand and looped one arm around her waist to pull her in closer. She squealed and giggled but caved and curled herself into me. Last night was a lot between her birthday and Tiffany hunting me down. I wanted her to know that I still had every intention of making today about her. Every single moment we had shared since her return had come to this day. I was so in love with her I couldn't see straight, and last night was the first time she'd let her guard down to show me she was feeling the same.

I spun the bracelet on her wrist, enjoying the fact that she was still wearing it today. She had paired it with a black swimsuit cover-up and a sun hat that was now somewhere on the floor. As much as I wanted to see what was under the ensemble, I kept my hands where she could see them. We needed to talk before making any sort of move. I needed her to say out loud that she was feeling the same. And although Justin wanted me to tell her the truth about the day my mom left, I wasn't ready, and neither was she. It would ruin her day.

"Happy birthday."

"Thank you."

If the door to the beach house hadn't opened, I could have stayed right where we were all day. Justin yelled about having breakfast on the beach and shut the door again. Lacey sighed, and while doing so, clutched me tighter. His timing was terrible.

"We're going to talk today," I told her.

Her smile was playful as she sat up. "About?"

She knew what it was about and had me mirroring her expression. I took it as a yes. We were definitely on the same page. I wanted to kiss her right now, and I was sure she'd let me. But if we didn't get down to that beach, our friends were bound to show up looking for us.

"I suppose I could make time in *my* day to . . . *talk*," she teased.

I sat up as she stood. And when she played with the hem of the cover-up she was wearing, I sat up even straighter. My brows lifted as her clothing also did, and they stayed there. Lacey had been holding out on me. I grabbed the blankets and pulled them over my lap as the room filled with her giggling. She stood in her fire-engine-red bikini, her confidence making her sexier by the second. With the bend of her body, my head cocked, taking in her peach-shaped ass as she retrieved her hat.

"You're killing me, pretty girl."

"I don't know what you're talking about."

"Red!"

"Is a brilliant color." She snapped upward with a wink. "I look forward to our chat, FB. I'll see you on the beach."

She was gone before I could suggest we give up and have the chat as soon as possible.

The wind didn't help my volleyball game any. Truth be told, it was never my sport, but now I had an excuse to fall back on. It also gave me excuses to fall onto the sand, taking my teammate down with me. And she didn't fight it. The day was filled with so much sexual tension there were times it physically hurt to watch Lacey strut around the beach in swimwear meant for my eyes only. It didn't stop others from looking, but whenever she got hit on by some rich loudmouth dickhead, it was me who got those sexy little winks.

Our opponents, on the other hand, weren't sharing our good moods. Rachel had promised to bring Chris along, making Justin the fifth wheel. None of us had had the chance to meet the man Rachel swore she loved, and she had every intention of showing him off. Justin, trying to keep up, brought a date. Then Chris canceled, using the impending storm as an excuse. Every chance Justin got while out of Rachel's earshot, he made comments about how much he despised Chris—ranting about how he could never make time for her friends. When Justin's date grew bored with the conversation about Rachel's love life, she wandered off down the beach with someone else. Now the two were stuck with each other, without their dates, and sharing equally shitty attitudes. The two really needed to just bang it out already. The more they drank, the more Lacey and I hoped for it.

By the time the sun was setting, we were tired, slightly sunburned, and feeling no pain thanks to a keg the group beside us had shared. Our chairs were planted around a small fire, our cooler was recently restocked, and life was good for a night. While our little gathering wasn't the norm on this beach, with others having parties and indulging in the luxuries of living in the Hamptons, I preferred this. The storm just needed to hold off a little longer, but it wasn't looking good on that front. I wasn't the only one who had noticed the drastic change in the wind and waves in the last two hours.

"You okay?" I observed Lacey as she focused on her phone and not the surrounding celebration.

"Just checking in on my dad."

It wasn't the answer to what I had asked, so I took it as a no. The lights were still off at Lacey's place, meaning Jack wasn't home yet. He was working on a holiday. And not just any holiday— he was working on his daughter's birthday. He and my dad were more alike than I'd thought.

"And?"

"He almost turned around and went back, but he's close to home."

"We could have a sleepover at my house," I teased.

She was playful as she rolled her eyes. But I saw the smile telling me she didn't hate the idea. Lacey tucked the phone under her thigh for safekeeping. She grabbed the bag of marshmallows and popped two into her mouth, causing her to look like the cutest chipmunk I had ever seen. I was surprised she didn't choke on them when a loud snap of thunder cracked above us. It sent her flying out of her chair and into mine. While the situation wasn't ideal, having her in my arms absolutely was.

"It's not even raining yet."

She smacked my shoulder. "I know!"

Her skin was warm and smooth against my palm as I rubbed her outer leg. While she lifted a brow at the move, she didn't fight it. "We haven't had our talk," she said. "Don't get too cocky."

"Ready when you are."

"But we haven't even done sparklers yet."

I could live without the damn sparklers. I could skip the entire fireworks show. But I saw her disappointment already. For someone who didn't want to celebrate her birthday, she lived for it the same way she did when we were kids. Keeping one arm around her, I leaned over the armrest of my chair, searched the sand beneath it for a few seconds, and finally retrieved the box of sparklers. She practically bounced in my lap at the sight of them.

She only left my hold to light two of them using our fire and to offer some to Rachel and Justin. Justin passed. Rachel took two for herself and was disappointed she had to set down her Solo cup to hold them. While Justin was annoyed with how drunk Rachel was getting, he wasn't about to allow her out of his sight until he knew she was safe at home. Unlike Chris, who didn't care how she got there. Luckily, her house wasn't far.

Lacey studied her sparkler and carefully lit a new one with the one that was almost out. The look she gave me when she looked up from the firework would have knocked me on my ass had we been standing. This look told me no talk was needed. I needed to kiss her right now while we shared this moment together—in the very spot where we'd met as kids. I leaned in.

"Luke . . ." Justin warned.

I halted my movement, keeping my eyes on Lacey. "Justin, I swear to God, not now."

He would not stop this kiss.

"Seems like a good time to me," Tiffany announced from behind my chair.

My connection with Lacey ended as she deflated in my arms and stared off into the fire, blinking rapidly for a few seconds before getting up from my lap entirely. I closed my eyes and took a deep breath to calm myself. This was the epitome of a fucking nightmare. Not once did I tell my ex where I'd be spending this holiday. Not once did we spend this day together while on this beach. My father, knowing exactly whose birthday it was, knew exactly where I'd be right now.

"Hey!" Rachel lifted her Solo cup into the air. "It's the restroom chick from last night! Hey, girlfriend!"

"That's Luke's ex," Justin whispered.

"Oh." Rachel giggled. "That's not good."

*No shit.*

I'd told Tiffany last night that I was celebrating a friend's birthday. It was the only way to get her to back off. While I'd been avoiding her for weeks at Drake-Mason, I knew we had to have a serious discussion about just how over our relationship was. I also needed to schedule a day where I could pack up my shit and move out of our place in North Carolina. But now wasn't the time for that. I also knew I needed to have a discussion with her about Lacey, because Lacey being home and working at Drake-Mason was something I'd chosen not to share with Tiffany, and now I was about to learn just how big of a mistake that was.

"Can't even look at me?"

I could, but she wasn't the priority right now. Lacey was. And while she wasn't letting on just how pissed she was, I could sense it. Especially when she reached for her swimsuit cover-up and put it on, hiding her red bikini.

"I'm with my friends, Tiff." I reached for a beer from our cooler. As I did, rain droplets pelted my bare arms.

"I see that. We haven't been properly introduced."

I continued to ignore her. Between Tiffany and this storm, Lacey was done. She was packing up her shit faster than I could grasp what was happening. And while I figured out how to fix this, my best friend was playing wingman.

"Lacey, don't go yet," Justin said without leaving his seat.

He sucked at wingman duty.

"Lacey?" Tiffany said. "Lacey *Mason*?"

Just when I thought this couldn't get worse, it did. Lacey stopped folding up her chair. I could think of a million reasons why I needed to stop this conversation from happening, but one was front and center in my mind. I stood. This time, it was Tiffany I turned to face, and I held out my hand to tell her to keep her mouth shut.

"That's me," Lacey agreed. Her foot hit the bottom of her chair, causing it to collapse. She tucked it beneath her arm.

"Wow." Tiffany folded her arms over her blue bikini top. "I had no idea I was talking to *the* Lacey Mason last night in the bathroom."

"Listen, you twatopotamus." Rachel stumbled through the sand, sending half her drink flying out of her cup. "I don't like the way you're talking about my friend!"

Justin was quick to wrap an arm around her stomach and drag her backward. "You know what? I was wrong. Time to go."

"I'll walk her home." Lacey volunteered. "It's on my way."

"Lace!" I grabbed her wrist to stop her from walking off. "It's about to storm. Let Justin take Rachel home, and I'll take you."

She pulled her wrist free. "You have company."

"Yes," Tiffany agreed. "He does."

I ignored Tiffany and this time gently took Lacey's upper arm. "Please?" I begged.

Lightning cracked again, this time sending Lacey an inch higher into the air. She looked up to the sky as rain droplets covered her cheeks. At least I was hoping they were rain droplets. Her head shook *no*.

I released her, angry with myself for being in this situation. I could not piss Tiffany off out of fear that she would retaliate using Lacey. I could not piss Lacey off any more tonight by walking off this beach with Tiffany. I was stuck. I needed to let Lacey cool down. I took a step back and watched her link arms with Rachel to keep her from falling over.

"Justin . . ."

He nodded before I even got the question out. "I'll make sure they get home."

Great. That left me with one problem. And she was the last fucking person I wanted to deal with tonight.

# chapter sixteen

## LUKE

The fireworks were canceled. While I texted one girl, begging her to come back, another followed me from the beach back to the house. Over the last few months, I'd gotten used to the way she followed me around, barking orders about how she had planned our lives around the Drake-Mason dream. Tonight, as she followed me, Tiffany was eerily quiet. She was furious, or really upset—probably a mixture of both.

"Where are you parked?" I asked.

"Why?"

"Because I'll walk you back to your car."

"What do you mean?"

*What do I mean?* The wind in the last hour had picked up exponentially. The hurricane was here, and everyone on the beach had fled home—ready to ride it out. There was no way in hell I was getting stuck with my ex.

"You may not have noticed, but it's raining. The storm you share a name with is supposed to hit soon, and I'd prefer not to worry about being stuck in it. Now, where is your car?"

"I'm not going anywhere until you tell me why Lacey Mason was sitting on your lap tonight."

I pivoted, feeling my face flush in anger. "I don't need to tell you anything, Tiff! You and I are not together. You don't get explanations about where I go, who I hang out with, or who I'm seeing!"

"You called off our engagement a few months ago, and you're already seeing her? You two haven't even spoken in years! I bet she doesn't even know why. It would be a shame if she found out."

Tiffany had never made me see red before that last sentence. Not with the bullshit with my dad, or Drake-Mason, or even with hating the idea of a studio or changing majors to the arts. It felt like a threat, and knowing Tiffany, it was one. Tiffany and Justin were the only two people who knew why I had cut Lacey out of my life, and now Tiffany was going to hold it over my head.

I stopped short of the beach house door. She wasn't passing this threshold.

"Stay away from Lacey," I warned.

"Or what?"

"Or having you fired becomes my first fucking priority." Lightning cracked above us.

Tiffany blinked wildly a few times. As we stood there, we both knew Alice's position had been promised to her for as long as she *needed* it, which, for her and my dad, meant until I married her and she'd no longer need to work. Drake-Mason was her last tie to me, my dad, and our name.

"Your dad won't allow it."

"He will if my ultimatum is me taking my position or keeping you as a secretary." I waited a moment for her to respond, but her mouth remained shut. Just the way it needed to stay. Whatever I did, keeping Tiffany away from Lacey was now a priority. "Go home, Tiff."

I didn't wait for her to reply. I locked the door between us. It would remain that way.

———

Hurricanes in New York were by no means rare. Living on the beach my entire life, I'd been through my fair share. There was really nothing you could do but wait for it to pass, and they always did. My father had called, warning me he'd be riding this one out from the city due to street closures preventing access to or exit from the Hamptons. I'd assured him I would be fine in the pool house after he'd offered me a room in the main house. I preferred the view of the storm from here.

I showered off the day's sweat, feeling the bite of my sunburn as soon as I stepped under the water. I held my palms against the tile, listening to the storm wreak havoc outside. The windows were rattling even before I got in, but now the rain was hitting the roof so hard I couldn't hear myself think. If I could, every single thought would be about Lacey. I'd tried messaging her time and time again, but without a response. She saw the messages, but she didn't respond. I couldn't blame her for it either.

It wasn't even five minutes after I left the shower when the lights flickered off. While the main house was on a generator for occasions such as this, the pool house wasn't a priority for electricity. I was prepared, though. I had well-stocked cabinets filled with food, batteries, and candles. Although my boredom would put me to sleep before I needed any of it. I dressed in the dark and paused midway through putting on a shirt when I heard banging against the door of the pool house—like something was repeatedly blowing up against it. I didn't rush to fix it, having no intention of getting dry clothes wet again for something like a rogue deck chair.

I rounded the corner of the bedroom to investigate. I wasn't expecting what I saw.

I jumped the couch like it was a hurdle at a track meet. Lacey was outside, sopping wet, and in a storm no better than the one she was trapped in as a kid. Her fists continued to pound against the door while I unbolted the lock.

I swung the door open so hard it hit the wall behind it. "What the fuck are you doing?" I asked, pulling her inside. "That's a fucking hurricane!"

Cold, wet hands gripped my neck and pulled me to her lips. The move wasn't what I was expecting, and everything I wanted. I pried her mouth open with mine, eager to taste what I'd been craving since the baseball game. And while our tongues twirled, my hands were eager to get the wet clothes off of her as soon as possible.

"We haven't talked," I growled the words into the kiss.

"Tell me she's gone," Lacey whispered, practically moaning as I began nibbling at her collarbone.

Her jealousy amused me. "Gone."

"Then fuck our talk."

I couldn't agree more. I barely had the time to do so as Lacey gripped my erect cock through my shorts. I had one hand positioned on the back of her head, pushing her into another kiss while my other hand was up her shirt, unclasping a bra and freeing it from her cold skin. Her nipples were firm and begging for my occupied tongue. It wasn't just me who was eager. Lacey came into this house on a mission and backed me into the couch until I fell into a sitting position. It was right where she wanted me.

For once, I wasn't the one being ogled as I stripped down to nothing. I sat back, watching as best as I could without light as the most stunning girl I had ever seen removed her shirt and bra. The wet clothes slapped against the wooden floor. Unable to keep my hands to myself, I slid my fingers between her skin and her jogging shorts, shimmying them to the floor as I pressed my mouth to her stomach. Her fingers tangled in my hair, gripping it tight and yanking it until my head fell back. She wanted my eyes on her as she sank her knees into the cushions on either side of me.

I always knew our connection was intense, but nothing compared to what I was feeling in this moment. If I went any longer without being inside of her, I feared my lungs would simply give up and forget how to breathe. All the sexual tension from this summer was colliding. We were growing out of a friendship we shared as kids and reaching the full potential we'd been suppressing. The realization seemed to hit us at the same time, because our new kiss deepened and slowed. Every time it stopped, it was only to catch brief glimpses of a smile that told me this was okay to continue. And continue it did. Lacey lifted herself just enough that I could push down my shorts, unwilling to lose the connection of our tongues. As she sank back into position, I finally entered her.

Her gasp rumbled against my lips. I used my arm wrapped around her back to lift and drop her slowly. Her pussy was the only warmth about her. I pushed my chest against her breasts, hoping to heat her skin. We started slow, taking it moment by moment. It didn't take long for Lacey's hips to roll faster. I knew what she was going for.

I gripped both sides of her face and pecked at her lips. "Tell me what Rachel said was true. Tell me I'm the only one who has ever seen you come."

Her head dropped back. Her mouth fell open. Her head bobbed with an unspoken yes.

Christ.

"*Luke . . .*"

It was a plea. A plea for a repeat of what we had experienced that first night. I was the only one to experience how beautiful she was as she came, and I was not taking it for granted. I was the luckiest guy on the planet right now. If it was true, and Lacey hadn't come since that night, then she was craving something only I could give her. She was fighting her own head to make it happen.

"Take what you need," I ordered. "Use my cock and make yourself come on it. Take it."

Her mouth hit mine. She increased the speed of her hips, repeating the rhythm of their roll and the friction until she couldn't take it anymore. Once again, her head dropped back, and the moan that erupted from her throat gave the hurricane winds a run for their money. Her body thrashed in my arms as her pussy clenched tightly around me. Her orgasm was powerful, and I could feel how much it took out of her after it happened.

I stood, bringing her with me. And I didn't let go of her as I lowered her back into my bed. I remained hovered over her. Our eyes danced until she pulled me down for another slow, earth-shattering kiss. With one thrust of my hips, I entered her again. This time I took the lead on our lovemaking. And it didn't stop until we couldn't stay awake any longer. But she remained wrapped in my arms as the storm roared in full force around us.

Shattering glass stirred me from a deep sleep. I tried to sit up, but Lacey remained naked and curled up in the crook of my shoulder.

The battery-operated clock on the other side of her told me we'd slept through the morning, until almost the noon hour. You would never have known from the sky, which kept the pool house darkened. Whatever had broken could stay that way. There was nothing I could do about it right now. I pressed my lips to Lacey's temple and closed my eyes again.

"I'm hungry."

I laughed, prying one eye open to find a pair of blues gazing up at me. Lacey giggled and groaned, pressing her cheek into my chest. She wasn't as out as I'd thought. My arm was asleep, but I pulled her in closer.

"What broke?"

"Probably a window." The sound of the curtains flapping against the wall was my clue. I was going to have to take them down, as they were likely soaked by now. "You scared?"

Her head shook *no*, and she squeezed me tighter. I realized that Tiffany showing up to Lacey's birthday not once but twice wasn't ideal, but I couldn't have asked for a better outcome to this weekend. We were now stuck together in this house until the storm was over. Neither of us was complaining.

"Your dad know where you are?"

Lacey stretched. "He already called, knows I'm safe, and thinks I'm with Rachel. Seriously, tell me you have food."

"I have cereal. Can't promise the milk is still good with no power. Might have to eat it dry."

"Works for me!"

Lacey left my side to spring out of the bed. Her naked frame was a vision—and a damn good start to my day. I reminded her of the glass, and she slid on a pair of sneakers I'd left by the bedroom door. It was a look, that was for sure. It had me amused as I followed her to the kitchenette. While Lacey poured us each a bowl of cereal, I cleaned up what I could of the glass and took a call from my dad to ensure him his namesake lived to see another day. The bigger glass chunks went into the garbage, while the smaller shards had to be pushed into the corner of the room using one of my T-shirts. This place had a lot of supplies for a pool house, but a broom was not one of them. I took down a surfboard that hung on the wall as decor and propped it against the area of the busted window. Lacey pushed a chair against it to keep it upright. The last thing we needed was for them all to blow out, leaving us no other option than to book it into Dad's house.

The bedroom was the safest spot. We put on some comfy clothes before taking our breakfast back to the warm bed.

"I wasn't expecting you to show up," I admitted. "I wouldn't have blamed you."

"I wasn't expecting to either." Her finger twirled around in the bowl until she located a marshmallow. "Not because of you, or your ex, but because of the storm."

"I didn't know she was coming. I swear."

Her head shook. "I know you didn't. Still kinda sucked, though."

"Yeah."

"She knew about me. She was surprised that you were with me."

I sucked in a breath before nodding *yes*.

"Why?"

"Drake-Mason has two names, Lace. She knew the company wasn't just for me. Tiffany has been around since I began college. Clearly, you haven't been. She knows we haven't spoken in years."

It was partially the truth. I would not ruin this weekend. That particular discussion could wait for another day. For now, it had worked, and Lacey seemed okay with the response. While I sat up against the headboard, Lacey returned to my side and stole a few pieces from my cereal bowl.

"It could have been like this all summer, you know?" I said, pressing my lips against her hair. "Why have you been fighting this so hard?"

She sighed, and I wished I could have seen her expression as she did.

"You broke my heart once after we were friends for almost ten years. What's to say you wouldn't do that again after a few months during a random summer?"

My chest ached thinking how badly I'd hurt her. "I would never do that to you again."

"I think," she began, "I think I know that. But you need to understand that I was a mess, and my mom had to get me through it. Going through my first heartbreak with her is one of the last memories of her that I have. Her telling me to move on from you is something that really stuck with me."

The last comment made my blood boil. It took everything in me not to respond to it. I took a deep breath and lifted her chin so she'd look at me. She bit her lip, and I knew it was to prevent herself from crying.

"I promise you—I will never break your heart again." I watched as a single tear rolled down her cheek. I collected it with my thumb. "I lo—"

Lacey's hand covered my mouth before I could say it. With wide eyes, her head shook *no*. "Don't you dare say it yet."

"Why?" I asked against her palm.

"It's too soon!" Her hand dropped and moved her bowl from her lap to mine before curling her legs under her butt to sit up straight. "Luke, you do not know how hard it was to break this promise to my mom. Those three words are another gigantic step."

A step I was ready to take.

"It doesn't change how I feel, Lace. And I know you feel it too; especially after last night."

"I know."

"Then let me tell you how much I lo—"

She stopped me again. "Lucas!"

"Lay-*hee*!" My response was muffled as her hand pressed even harder against my mouth.

Her giggle allowed the heaviness in my chest to let up. She dropped her hand. "Not yet. We can use another word."

"Such as?"

"Uh." She looked around the room for a minute before pointing to some painting of a boat at sea. "Ship!"

*Ship?* I was questioning the enthusiasm she had put behind the word. I looked back and forth between her and the picture on the wall, wondering if her hunger had gotten the best of her. She was losing it.

"Are you serious?"

"Yes! Like when you want two people in a movie to end up together; you *ship* them. I ship you and me."

"I don't think that's a thing."

"It is!" She bounced playfully and slapped my chest.

"Nah. You definitely made that up, pretty girl." I laughed.

"It's a thing!"

"It's really not."

"It is too!"

"No."

That time she hit me with her pillow. "Lucas!"

I took it from her hands and hit her back as her laughter filled the room. "Lacey!"

"Google it!"

"Fine! When I'm right, I get the red lingerie."

I reached over her to retrieve my phone from the bedside table, stopping only to kiss her along the way. As cute as it was to see her in my clothing, I regretted getting dressed. I had half a mind to forget the Google search and take them off of her. She knew where this was going, reached to the table and got the phone for me—all without breaking the kiss. She tapped it against my shoulder.

"Google it," she whispered.

I groaned and took the phone. There was just barely enough of a charge to do this. It took a while, but the app opened. It did not go in my favor. So much for the red lingerie happening. Lacey's grin already knew what I was about to say.

"So, apparently *ship* is a thing."

I waited for her to throw it in my face, but she didn't. Instead, she placed a hand on each side of my face, beaming ear to ear. God, she was stunning. My mouth curved to mirror hers.

"I ship you, Luke."

Although it wasn't the word I wanted, I felt all the same meaning behind it. I pulled her into me. "I ship you, Lacey."

That *L* word would have to wait for a day when she'd need to hear it most.

# chapter seventeen

## LACEY

Watching Rachel eat a hamburger the size of my head was not something I was used to seeing every day. In fact, I'd never seen her eat anywhere near this much food. We'd even started with mozzarella sticks, and she was giving me a run for my money. I was the ridiculous eater of this friendship and was full on half a salad. After shoving the last bite of burger into her mouth, she licked the ketchup and mustard off each finger with a popping noise.

"What's with you?"

"What do you mean?" she asked.

"Are you pregnant?"

"Hell, no." She sat back in her chair. "You need to have sex for that. Do you want dessert?"

Dessert? I felt like I was going to burst at the seams. "Where did you just put all that food?"

"I've been dieting. This has been my first time away from Chris since I started."

I didn't like the sound of that. First off, Rachel didn't need to diet. I'd been told I was thin my entire life, and Rachel and I were about the same size—except for her breasts, which were roughly double the size of mine and perfect for literally everything she wore. Second, why did Chris get any say in this diet? She was obviously hungry.

"Which diet are you doing?"

"Lacey . . ." Her eyes rolled, knowing where I was going with this.

"Did you eat breakfast today?"

"I didn't want breakfast."

That was such a lie, and we both knew it.

"He's not worth it. Starving yourself will not make his dick hard. Bingeing food when he's not looking is going to make you sick."

She didn't get the chance to respond. Our server returned to the outdoor patio with a refill of our drinks and offered the check. Rachel declined the offer of dessert minutes after proclaiming she wanted one. I wondered if she had actually changed her mind or if she feared she wouldn't have it finished by the time Chris came to pick her up. They were going to go look for a place together—something else I didn't agree with, but I was keeping my mouth shut to appear supportive. We'd spent the whole morning shopping for furnishings for a place that didn't exist yet.

"So, when do we get to shop for you and Luke?"

I lifted a single brow, my lips wrapped around my straw. Luke and I had been seeing each other for a few weeks. It was hardly time to start picking out couches and combining our food into a single pantry. Did I hate the thought of it? Absolutely not. But this summer came out of nowhere. As it was, I had a stack of enrollment forms for North Carolina, and I hadn't even touched them. Break was almost over, and I still needed to figure out how I was going to move all my things from Michigan. I had never felt so spacey and unorganized. I couldn't focus on anything but Luke—not even work.

"Has he asked you yet?"

"Asked me what?"

"To live with him in North Carolina?"

"Of course not!"

"You really don't think he will?"

I took another sip of my water. Honestly, it hadn't crossed my mind. I figured I'd be in the dorms. I didn't know what Luke's housing situation was there, and part of me didn't want to. He'd said little about his ex, but they were engaged until a few months ago. Did they have their own place? An apartment? A house? Did she move out? Did he? Was their stuff still intertwined and waiting to be separated? I probably had more questions than Rachel did. Until now, I hadn't given it an ounce of thought. Had he?

My thoughts were interrupted by an alarm—one I had only heard once before. It was hard to forget. I reached into my purse, digging for my phone. The damn thing was so loud that everyone around us had stopped talking and was waiting for me to silence it.

"What the hell is that?"

"Some app that Luke put on my phone."

"It's annoying."

That was a fair observation. And as I looked at a screen asking for a password, I knew telling her I had to wait for Luke to message me would not go over well. I held the phone between my thighs, hoping they would mute the obnoxious chirping. Everyone, including my best friend, was looking at me like I had grown a second head. Finally, I felt the vibration from a text.

It read: *I ship ___.*

*You.* I entered the word as quickly as possible. The noise stopped, and I exhaled my relief. Today's date popped up with a red block over this evening. Last time, tapping this box told me Luke was showing up at my place unannounced. Today's tap revealed an address for where to meet him with a promise for a date night in. I was relieved. While Rachel and Justin obviously knew we were seeing each other, no one else did. Two weeks of staying apart while being together sucked. The only time I really saw him was during our lunch break. We hadn't had the discussion of when we were going to tell our dads, but it also wasn't something we were eager for either. Both of us were in for a long discussion of why it was a horrible idea for business partners to date.

"You are smiling like an absolute fool. Tell me again you won't be living with him this fall."

While I might not be able to hide my stupid grin caused by the thought of spending tonight with Luke, I could order us dessert. I waved my hand at the server.

The address Luke sent me in the app was a dance studio. The place was massive, and as I walked along the sidewalk, I reviewed window after window until I saw Luke in front of a line of mirrors. He wasn't alone. Along with the sweat-covered man at the front of the room stood at least fifteen children on multicolored mats. If that weren't enough to make my ovaries explode, I wasn't sure what else could do the job. He had the kids twirling and jumping, mixed with lots of giggling. When Luke saw me through the window, he waved for me to come inside.

I hoped for the sake of all those kids that he would not have me dancing with him tonight.

I waved back, taking my first step toward the door. Stupidly, I walked directly into another woman. Her coffee nearly left her hand, but I caught it before it fell to the cement. Thankfully, not a drop was lost.

"I am so sorry!" I handed the cup back to her. "I wasn't watching where I was going."

"Oh, don't worry about it," she said. "No harm done. Standing still on a busy sidewalk is bound to get me run over. I just wanted to watch my daughter dance for the last few minutes of class."

Well, that answered that question. I wouldn't be dancing in front of a bunch of kids tonight. Thank God. Although, considering she wanted a glimpse of the class, she'd been behind a cement pillar, which I couldn't imagine having the best view.

"Do you want to come inside and watch?" I asked, motioning to the door with my thumb. "I'm heading in now."

She was quick to shake her head *no*. "I'll let Lucas finish his class. Becca knows where to find me. It was lovely seeing you."

*Seeing me?* Didn't she mean meeting me?

Before I could question the phrasing, the woman had her back to me and had joined a man similar in age. She handed him the other coffee she had been carrying before joining him on a park bench to wait for the class to end.

"Lace," Luke said, head poking out the door of the studio, "you coming inside?"

I took one last glance back at the couple, catching a similar stare from the woman on the bench. While I didn't know for certain, because it had been years since I had seen her, I had a knot in my stomach that told me who she was. Midforties, blond hair, someone who knew me when I lived here before—because I knew

I hadn't seen her at Drake-Mason—and someone who called Luke by his full name. The thought of me running into Luke's mom made me nauseous. Part of me hoped I was overthinking all of it, and it was simply a stranger.

"Lacey?"

"Yeah." I shook the thought away. Again, I felt spaced out. There was no way it was Beth Drake.

I entered the door Luke was holding open for me, stopping for a quick peck of his lips along the way. While I wanted more, PDA wasn't something I would do in front of a bunch of five-year-olds. But there was one hell of a smirk after that peck that told me that later I'd get my wish. It was a good thing I packed an overnight bag.

By the time Luke had returned to the room, the kids were no longer focused. While some still twirled to a Katy Perry song, others were chasing each other around the room, and a few had taken the chance to sit on their mats—which I found the most relatable of the three options. Luke introduced me to the group before telling me the last five minutes were free time, and they got to party as they wished.

"Luke, which one is Becca?" I scanned the room.

He pointed to one of the few children who had kept dancing. "Long blond hair in a braid. Why?"

While I couldn't get a good look at her as she twirled, it didn't ease my stomach any. While Luke was the spitting image of William Drake, there were some features he got from his mom—such as the curls in his hair. If Becca had them, her braid was hiding it.

"I met her mom outside. I know her from somewhere and can't place her. Have you met her?"

"Nah. Usually her dad picks her up."

"What's her last name?"

"Uh." He picked up a clipboard hanging from a hook on the wall. "Clark. That help?"

"No." I continued to watch Becca dance, tucking the name away in my head. "Must just be déjà vu."

"You feeling okay?"

"Hmm?" I finally looked away from the girl I was hoping was not Luke's sibling. "I'm fine. It was a long day with Rach. She had me running all over this city. I'm exhausted."

"Well,"—he began walking backward—"good thing I have a relaxing date planned, involving the couch, a movie, and lots of food."

Luke clapped and told everyone to roll up their mats and stack them, while I was thankful this man could read my mind. This was exactly the type of night I needed. While I felt like shit for telling my dad I would be staying with Rachel to discuss interior design, all I wanted was to curl up with Luke on the couch and relax.

Our date night had to wait as Luke ended his shift at the studio. While each kid packed up their things, the parents arrived to retrieve them. I stood near the door and watched, waiting for Becca's family to make their entrance.

I wasn't even surprised when, just like Luke had said, only her dad appeared.

The pool house door shut behind us. Finally, Luke and I were alone. My arms swung around his neck; his wrapped around my middle, and we both went for the kiss I had been craving. There was so much relief behind it that neither of us wanted it to end. Unfortunately, my growling stomach had other plans.

Luke laughed into the kiss. "What do you want for dinner?"

"Chinese."

"I'm down for that. And what movie would you like to watch?"

I tried to think of the longest movie possible to keep us both awake. I wanted every second I could have with him this weekend. "*Titanic.*"

"The ship sinks. That seems ominous."

"*Pearl Harbor?*" It was the first long movie that came to my head after *Titanic*. As soon as I said it, I covered my mouth with my hand.

Luke pulled away and smacked his own chest as if wounded. "That sank too! Are you telling me our ship is sinking?"

My arms wrapped around him again. "Never. I ship you so hard, FB."

"Can we pick a less dismal film, then?"

"You pick. Something long!"

While Luke chose the movie, I changed into something more comfortable. I stole one of his tees and paired it with my cotton shorts. Before leaving the bedroom, I opened the notes app on my phone. I wrote the name Elizabeth Clark and immediately closed out of it. If she was who I thought she was, being a part of Luke's life without him knowing wasn't fair. I hoped to be proven wrong.

When I returned, Luke had pulled up some Stephen King movie—which seemed to go against the nonominous theme he requested—and had a booklet on his lap, notebook on the armrest of the couch, and a pen ready to write. I took my spot beside him, leaning into his open arm and tucking my feet under my butt. The booklet was for class selections at North Carolina.

"I thought we would try to get some classes together. I know I'm a year ahead, but there are some we might swing."

I took the book from him and began flipping through the pages. This was actually happening. I was going to attend my mother's alma mater. The pictures of the campus were stunning. And while the book began with some information about the dorms, I quickly flipped past it, not wanting Luke to bring up the living situation. Maybe he hadn't thought of it either. We hadn't said the *L* word yet, and that should probably come first. I should have kept flipping until I got to their pharmacy program, but I stopped earlier.

"I might take some accounting classes." I viewed the page with envy. "For fun."

"You should. And you could take more than a few, if you wanted," he suggested. "You could change your major."

I ignored him and flipped to the pharmacy pages Luke had already dog-eared. With a shake of his head, Luke understood the conversation was over. We were going to pick our pharmacy courses. I highlighted all the classes I had already taken in Michigan in pink so Luke could compare the two.

"Lacey." Luke's fingers snapped, bringing me out of a daze. My highlighter had stopped at some point and was seeping the fluorescent ink into the next few pages. Luke's phone was pressed to his ear. "Your stomach is speaking to you. I can hear it. What does it want to eat?"

"Egg drop soup."

"My girlfriend wants the egg drop soup," Luke told the phone. "And I'll have broccoli and beef."

*Girlfriend.* My mouth curved. It was the first time I had heard the word out of his mouth—the first time we had labeled what this was. Luke was my boyfriend. I was his girlfriend.

Damn, I really liked the sound of that.

# chapter eighteen

## LUKE

Even after spending a weekend together, finding Lacey standing at the elevator on Monday morning would always be one of the best parts of my day. It was only a few hours ago that I'd kissed her good-bye so she could return home in time to get ready and drive to work with Jack. The instinct to do it again was a hard one to suppress as I joined her in waiting for the next elevator to arrive. I just might have if it weren't for crowds of others who were also waiting.

"Lacey."

Her smile said everything I needed her to feel. "Lucas."

"How was your weekend?"

"Pleasurable." She bit into her grin, joining her hands at her back with her clutch tucked under her arm. "I'm surprised to see you here so early."

"New alarm. It was very effective."

I loved the way her shoulders caved as she giggled. I was trying so damn hard not to do it myself. I could honestly say waking up with my cock in her mouth was hands down the best alarm I'd ever had. Showering together to save time . . . also beneficial—until you're not actually showering. If we could have woken this way every morning, coming into this hellhole wouldn't have been so bad.

The doors parted. I waved Lacey to enter first and followed her in along with the others. The doors had just about closed when a manicured hand stopped them, causing them to reopen. I heated up when Tiffany stepped into the elevator, knowing this was going to be a long ride up.

"Drake," she enthusiastically clamped her hand around my tie to adjust it, "I called you this weekend. Did you get my voice mail?"

I knew she had called. Lacey did not, and if her eyes had not been fixed on my tie situation, I knew they'd be wordlessly asking me why I had forgotten to mention it. I swatted Tiffany's hand away and took a step back in what little space was left.

"Deleted it without listening."

She pretended to pout. "Your dad invited us to dinner tonight. I thought you could pick me up in East Hampton around six? It gives us both time to freshen up. Unless you'd like me to go home with you tonight, and you can drop me home afterward."

That was not happening. I had a shift working at the bar tonight, and I couldn't even use it as an excuse without it getting back to my dad. I could practically see the steam escaping Lacey's ears as she eyed the back of Tiffany's head. More than anything, I needed Lacey to keep her cool, because if she set Tiffany off, I knew Tiffany could shut it all down with a single sentence.

"I'm busy tonight."

"We can move it to tomorrow, if that works better for you."

"Busy all week." I shrugged. It wasn't a lie.

"Well, we have plenty of floors to come up with a day that works with your busy schedule. We should also discuss which day we'll be going home at the end of the summer and get our flights scheduled."

Lacey took a step toward Tiffany just as the door chimed. Panicked, I placed my hand on Lacey's back, ushering her into the hall that led to the finance department. "This is our stop. I need to grab something from Lacey's office. I'll see you up there."

I kept us walking until the doors shut behind us.

"She's delusional!" Lacey attempted to stop midway down the hall.

"I'm well aware." But this was not a discussion we were having here. I kept my mouth shut and kept walking until I was in Lacey's office. She was quick to shut the door.

"Do you two still live together even though you broke up with her?"

"Technically, yes." I held my hand up to stop her from asking another question. "I wasn't exactly planning on another girlfriend so fast. I thought I had time until I was back in North Carolina to get the housing sorted. My dad and her parents both pay for the house we live in. It was bound to get messy."

"That's"—she sighed—"understandable. Where exactly were you planning on living during the school year?"

"Honestly? I hoped you and I would find somewhere near campus, but I wasn't going to bring it up this soon. I didn't know how to ask. It's an enormous step, and I get that. If you wanted to live in the dorms, or an apartment somewhere, I'd fully support that. I'd be bummed, but I'll go with whatever you want to do."

Lacey's eyes widened. "Oh."

I stilled. "Is that a good *oh*, or a bad *oh*?"

"It's . . ." She hesitated, making my insides squirm. Her lips lifting gave me hope. "I think it's a good *oh*. We can talk about it. I haven't told my dad that we're dating yet, and that needs to happen first."

Yeah. I got it. Jack wasn't a fan, and Lacey wasn't ready to break the news about us. The glares he dished out whenever he saw Lacey and me so much as greet each other were enough to hold off. But when she was ready for that conversation, I would be too.

Lacey stepped forward. She took hold of the tie that Tiffany had adjusted and gave it a tug until our lips could touch. The kiss started softly but quickly became desperate, like it always did. Lacey had me walking backward until the back of my thighs hit her desk. Even with the door closed, we were being incredibly reckless. First waking up to a blow job, then shower sex, and now she was heated again.

"Someone is horny today."

"You have no idea," she whispered. "That shower this morning was hot."

"You know." I slid my hand under her dress. My fingers traced the lace of her underwear. With one finger, I pushed them aside and sank into her. She was ready. I knew without even seeing that the lips of her pussy were still pink and swollen from our shower. "If we lived together, we could have mornings like this one every day."

She gasped when I worked my finger and circled her clit with my thumb at the same time. "You're not playing fair."

"Not playing fair would be this . . ." I stopped and pulled my hand from her dress. I kissed her cheek and turned for the door. "Have a great day at work, pretty girl."

"Lucas! You're going to pay for that," she said in a hushed tone as I opened the door to a busy hallway.

"Doubt that." I winked. "See you at lunch."

I hadn't even made a dent in the storage room. To be honest, I wasn't trying very hard. Most of the items in it were getting tossed into a garbage can. The only reason I took any sort of time to look through the old boxes was in case I found something regarding her mom that Lacey might want to keep. Which is why I was happy to find more directories hidden away. Lacey could see the building of her mom's legacy, while I saw the demise of mine. When I flipped one open to see a picture of all of our parents, including my mom, at a Christmas party, I immediately shut it. It had been years since I'd seen a photo of her, and I wasn't expecting it to hit as hard as it did. I placed the booklet, along with a few others, into a box to take to Lacey's office.

"Finding anything good?"

My dad had never come to check on me. I knew he was only here now because Tiffany told him I'd declined their dinner plans. I tossed a stack of magazines into a trash bin beside me, sending up a cloud of dust that was nearly comical. I didn't bother looking up at him as I continued to sift through more of his hoarded trash.

"If you consider fifteen years of dead skin cells good, I guess."

"There should be some things from Mary's office."

"I already gave them to Lacey." I bit my tongue to stop myself from saying anything more.

"Well, I'm glad you didn't throw them away."

As much as I wanted to, it wasn't my place to decide what happened to them. Nor were they his to keep. They should have been given to Jack years ago. He probably didn't want to be anywhere near this place again to collect her things, and my dad took it upon himself to do it.

"About dinner . . ."

"I already told Tiffany no. Stop pushing this. She and I are over."

"She's wife material, Lucas."

Wife material. That was hilarious. Wife material meant Hamptons material. She knew how to play the game. Put on a show where everything appeared perfect. Marriage advice from the guy who fucked up his own was the last thing I needed. Was my mom *wife material*? If so, it didn't give me a lot to look forward to.

"You're making a mistake with Lacey. Use your head, Lucas. You're going to be working together for a very long time."

Confirmed. He was aware of my relationship. Collin really was an excellent spy for a chauffeur.

"As I said, Tiffany and I are through. Kind regards to your invite."

"Right." He huffed his frustration, realizing he would get nowhere in this conversation when I refused to so much as look at him. He was one to talk. "Well, during your little lunch today, please inform Lacey you'll both be attending a board meeting at one o'clock. We are going over the financials for last quarter. It will be good for both of you to act like the coworkers you're destined to be."

I tossed another stack into the trash. "Whatever."

He waited another minute before disappearing.

When lunch came around, I brought two sandwiches to Lacey's office and allowed her to choose which she wanted. She went with the turkey combo, leaving me with a patty melt. She picked at the food before pushing it away.

"*You* aren't hungry? Since when?"

"I gave up on that mystery account," she confessed. "I gave it to Mitch."

We had vaguely discussed this a few times. I knew it was weighing on her. Proving to Mitch that she could close out one of these harder accounts left her extremely determined and equally tired. Her entire desk was a road map of dates and amounts that made no sense to me. In defeat, her arms scooped all the paperwork together until it was in a messy stack before shoving it into a yellow folder.

"You'll get the next one."

"It's the last one. The others were easy. If I could have figured out where that money was coming and going, it might have amounted to thousands of dollars we could have saved the company."

"It's probably for something stupid. Some supplier who prints Drake-Mason on our pencils."

Even though she laughed, it wasn't enough to stop her from filing the envelope away. I took the last bite of my sandwich while she broke off the smallest corner of the bread on hers and nibbled it. Apparently, that was enough for lunch, because she wrapped up the rest and slid it beside the unopened bag of chips.

Lacey stood. "We should get to that meeting."

"We could skip it."

"And do what?"

Oh, my head was filled with plenty of ideas. I could keep her busy for hours. "Finish what we started earlier."

"Nope." She went for the door. "You lost those privileges. No red lingerie for you."

"Wait. What?" I swiveled in my seat. "You have to be joking." But she was already gone.

She couldn't do that. She couldn't just tease that red lingerie and leave me high and dry. I jumped out of my chair. I had to run to catch up to her, but I wasn't fast enough. As the elevator door closed, she stuck her tongue out at me. I could hear her cackle on the other side of the metal door as soon as she was out of sight.

By the time I had made it to the top floor, Lacey already had a seat. While the board members had a spot at the big kid table, everyone else had a chair against the wall. And unluckily for me, Lacey chose a spot beside her dad—who I didn't know would be attending. I got stuck on the opposite side of the room beside some guy whose job was to take meeting minutes. My job was boring, but damn, that one had to be the worst. After sitting, I inched the chair a few inches to the right, leaving me with the perfect view of Lacey if I sat straight enough to see over another woman's shoulder.

After my father introduced me, Jack, and Lacey, it was straight to business. Today's meeting was about the expenses of reopening the lab and how they could recoup the money as soon as possible. As if I wasn't bored enough, they turned the lights off for a presentation by Jack. It nearly had me sleeping. I pulled out my phone and texted Lacey instead.

*Teasing the red lingerie and making me take a separate elevator as punishment for earlier is nothing. You know I'll just see it later.* I sent the message and waited.

Lacey, who was actually listening to these people talk numbers, stopped to view the lit screen. She hid a smile as her thumbs typed rapidly. When they stopped, she looked up at me and waited.

*That wasn't your punishment.*

My brows lifted high, questioning that statement. Lacey's head shook *no* before she was back to texting. I stared at my screen, ready to hear what she had in mind. Whatever it was, Lacey's devil horns were showing. The phone buzzed in my hand.

*I bet I can make your cock hard right here and now.*

I had to disagree. There was nothing she could do that would make me erect while in a board meeting with our dads. Instead of texting back, I shook my head *no* at her. It wasn't possible. She coyly picked up her phone again and sent off another message.

*That thong you want to see me in so badly is absolutely soaked.*

That was a very sexy thought. But she was going to have to do better. Tempting. *Better not get too wet over there, pretty girl. You'll have to take them off*—sent.

My phone was fast to vibrate. She must have had the text ready to reply before I had even sent mine. I read it and nearly choked on my breath.

*I thought the same thing. That's why I took it off and put it in your pocket.*

My throat cleared, and I was in a sweat to get the room's attention off of me. The presentation paused with my dad idly waiting to restart. "You good, Lucas?"

I glared at Lacey's giggle.

"All good," I said. "Continue."

As the slides began again, my hand dove into the pocket of my jacket. When the left side was empty, I tried the right. My fingers intertwined with cool, dampened lace. My girl was right, she had these fucking soaked. And now she sat across the room wearing no panties, and she was teasing me as she grazed her fingertips over her collarbone. Her tongue ran along her upper lip—the same lips that woke me this morning.

My cock went hard as stone.

I squirmed in my seat. The temperature of the room had shot up at least twenty degrees. Knowing I would disrupt the presentation again, and no longer caring, I leaned forward to remove my jacket. It would assist with the heat and with hiding a boner that would put my preteen years to shame. This girl had me in actual pain, and she was damn proud of herself. Every little move she made on the other end of the room caught my attention and caused my dick to throb with the need to be inside of her. And the longer this meeting went, I could see in her big blue eyes that she was fighting it too. She uncrossed and recrossed her legs in the opposite direction, and we both knew it was because of how wet that pussy was.

When the slides were over, the meeting was adjourned, and the lights came back to life one at a time. Lacey and I were the first ones to stand. We needed out of this room, and we needed out now.

We wouldn't make it to her office. And we couldn't use mine.

Keeping my jacket draped over one arm, I used my other hand to usher Lacey in a direction she wouldn't be familiar with, but she didn't hesitate to allow it. I had her trust that I was going to get us somewhere where we could be *alone*. We passed the C-suite offices and moved toward a long, unused corridor that led to the storage room I'd been cleaning all morning. It was perfect. No one went near it, and it had a lock on the door. And the second we were inside, that lock was engaged.

My mouth went right for her collarbone. The moan that came out of her was the sexiest noise I had ever heard. She wasn't holding back. Her chin lifted, giving me full access to the spot where she loved to be kissed most while she unbuckled my belt and sent my pants to my knees.

"Fuck me," she begged.

I lifted and bunched her dress between our stomachs and lifted her by her thighs. Two steps put her back against the wall, and a single shift of my hips put my cock deep into her wet, pulsing pussy. She didn't just want this; she needed it, and I was all too happy to give her exactly what she needed. My thrusts were rough and her whimpers were loud, and still she begged me to keep going with her mouth against mine.

I was close to flooding her and needed a plan. We'd tempted fate one too many times this summer with my pullout game, and while we usually had condoms readily available, I didn't have one on me. But I kept thrusting, knowing I couldn't stop until she was ready. It didn't take long before I was covering her mouth to mute her cries. She shook in my arms while her body held my cock like a vice. When she finally came down, I dropped her to her feet just in time for me to grab an old magazine to shoot my load into. It went immediately into the trash while both of us tried to catch our breath.

She wrapped herself back into my arms. Her dress fell back into place. I kissed her like we hadn't just had our tongues down each other's throats while fucking at work. This kiss was new—desperate. I was so madly in love with her, and all I wanted to do was say it.

"Lacey . . ."

Her head shook *no*. "Not yet. Not here."

*Well, I tried.* "I ship you. But that word is going to fly out, eventually."

Her lips curled upward cutely, and she adjusted her dress back into place, ensuring her red bra strap was no longer visible. I was quick to pull my pants back up and fasten my belt. While we weren't as put together as when we entered this room, this was as good as we were getting. Lacey bent down to retrieve my jacket we'd tossed to the floor. When she came up, she woozily took a step backward, nearly landing on her ass. If it wasn't for me grabbing her arm in time, she would have.

"Whoa," she giggled as she regained her footing, "you know the sex is good when you're dizzy after."

"You're pale." There was no color in her cheeks, even though we'd just gone at it like rabbits. "When was the last time you actually ate?"

"I had a protein bar for breakfast. I'm fine—just stood up too fast with a headache from that stupid account. But speaking of lack of food, you should see what Chris has Rachel eating. It's literally nothing. Put that bug in Justin's ear so he can talk some sense into her."

My concern wasn't with Rachel at the moment, but I would pass the message along. Lacey didn't seem worried about the stumble. She opened the door back to the hall and motioned for me to exit. As we left the room, I decided I'd be walking her back to her office.

"We're getting you food."

"I'm fine," she repeated.

As much as I wanted to argue with her, her stopping midway down the hall had me doing the same. I was too busy worrying over her to notice we were not alone. Tiffany stood with her hands on her hips—a stance I knew meant she was ready for an argument.

"I'll meet you downstairs."

"I'm a big girl, Luke. What is she going to do? Get us fired?"

She laughed, but I couldn't do the same. I knew Lacey could stand on her own; that wasn't the problem. I had gone all summer and kept these two apart as best I could. Now, it was no secret Lacey and I were together, and Tiffany was about to do what she did best. The last word was always hers, and this time, it wasn't hers to tell.

"Go downstairs."

"What do you not get about me being fine?" Lacey was becoming defensive. She started walking again.

I rushed to get ahead of her. I needed to get to Tiffany first and get her alone, and I did not know how I was going to do it.

Her head was shaking at me, and mine was doing the same right back. She was upset, and it was understandable. I threw my new relationship in her face.

"Classy," was the first word that came out of her mouth. "I can't believe you."

"Tiff . . ."

"That apple didn't fall far from the tree." She pointed directly at Lacey. "For someone who said he didn't want to end up like his dad as an excuse to end our relationship, this is a fucking comical turn of events."

"Tiffany, enough!" My voice dared her to say another word, but she'd said plenty. Lacey wasn't speaking, but I could hear each breath she took as the wheels in her head turned. This was a train wreck, and it was my fault.

"Luke," Lacey whispered. "What does she mean by that?"

"What?" Tiffany stepped forward. "You think you're the first Mason to sleep with a Drake? Mommy started that trend years ago."

"Shut up." Lacey took a step forward, and I pulled her back by her arm.

"Are you really that dense?" Tiffany laughed. "That's why his mom left. Because yours couldn't keep her legs shut. Luke walked in on them and told his mom. She bolted the next day. The same day he unfriended your ass."

My eyes shut, wishing I was anywhere but here. I should have told her. My first instinct was to say "I'm sorry," but nothing came out. My head shook, my mouth opened, and I still couldn't say it in front of Tiffany. When my lids lifted, I knew just how badly I had fucked up. Lacey already had tears clinging to her lashes.

"Is that true?" Lacey asked as her face flooded. "Tell me she's lying."

She knew it was true. She just needed me to say it.

"I'm sorry." The words were too late. "I should have told you a long time ago."

Lacey pulled out of my grasp. The impact of her hand on my cheek was so hard I saw stars. The smack echoed in my ears. My eyes watered with the instant pain. As much as it hurt, I knew she was hurting a million times worse.

"Lacey . . ." I tried to take her hand. She immediately snapped her arm closer to her body.

"You promised you wouldn't break my heart again."

I did. And I did it knowing that one day she would learn the truth. If not from me, she was going to hear it from someone. But hearing it from the mouth of my ex was the worst possible scenario. I couldn't make that up to her. There would never be a right time. I finally had the girl of my dreams and telling her I shut her out because of her mom would not help. It was going to send her fleeing in the opposite direction.

Which is exactly what was happening as I watched her storm away from me.

# chapter nineteen

## LACEY

I hailed a cab. The first one didn't stop. It whizzed past me, pretending not to notice me jumping up and down for a ride. The second one didn't have a choice. I all but threw myself in front of it. The driver's curses could be heard from outside the vehicle. But once I was inside, one look in his rearview mirror told him I wasn't mentally stable right now. Tears had reached my neck, and they weren't about to stop soon.

The ride was a blur. I had the driver take me as far as he was willing to go before ordering an Uber for the remainder of the drive. I thought about a million things and nothing at the same time. All I knew was that I couldn't face my dad while looking like this. We had driven together this morning, and there was no way to keep my composure long enough to get home. I wanted my pajamas. I wanted my bed.

I wanted my mom. I needed her to tell me this was all a lie.

My clutch hadn't stopped making noise from the time I left Drake-Mason, and I knew every single one of those messages and calls was from Luke. Even with no intention of answering, I brought the phone with me into the bathroom and placed it on the vanity while I stripped down to nothing. His scent was all over me, and I couldn't think straight between that and the ache between my legs from where he had penetrated me a short time ago.

Immediately after stepping into the shower, the tears started again. I could barely catch my breath between the sobs. My knees shook until eventually I gave up and sat, wrapping my arms around my legs and letting the stream hit my face to take the mess away. I had no energy left in me to even pick what I was most upset about. Everything felt like a lie. My mother lied when she told me how much she loved my dad. She lied about every late night at work. Every missed dinner. And Luke? He knew and blamed me. He lied about why he shut me out, and of all people, he told Tiffany the real reason instead of me. That should have hurt the worst.

He didn't even follow me.

I told myself not to expect him to. I told myself over and over that what he told Tiffany was a lie—an excuse for why his mother left him when she was rarely around. But each time I told myself this, I knew it was denial. Luke would never make something like that up. His reason for lashing out the day my mom and I showed up made more sense.

The shower went cold, which I didn't even know was possible in this house. By the time I dressed in a pair of sweats and a tee, it was nearly dinnertime. My dad was going to be showing up soon, and I had nothing in me to face him and not give away just how fucking sad I was. My mom was his world. She was mine. And now I was questioning if we were hers.

I swiped past my missed calls from Luke and tried Rachel,

knowing she was with Chris. Even though she didn't answer, I still packed a bag. I couldn't be here. I couldn't be with Luke right now. I needed time to wrap my head around the bombshell that had been dropped on me. My headache from earlier was surging through my temple as I walked out of the house. I was seriously regretting not bringing my car here. Walking distance left me one option. At the very least, it was probably the last place Luke would come looking for me.

The last time I had knocked on this door, I was ten years old. And I hadn't thought about what the hell I would say if a parent answered. Thankfully, I didn't have to wonder for long. I knocked twice before Justin opened the door. His face told me he already knew why I was there.

"Did you know?" I asked, feeling stupid. I was sure everyone knew except me. I was blindsided by my obsession with the woman I thought I knew everything about. I hiked my bag farther up my shoulder.

"I was with him when he found out," he admitted, holding the door open wider. "They didn't know we were home, and Luke was going to ask if he could spend the night here. They were . . . intimate."

I pressed my eyes closed to escape the image. "Justin . . ." I sighed.

"I couldn't tell you that, Lacey. They weren't my parents. I told him to tell you. He was scared and still is. The one person he told, fled and left him to make sense of it all. You really think he wanted to try it a second time with you?"

Hot tears burst from my eyes. Arms wrapped around me. Justin allowed me to bury my face in his shirt and freely sob for minutes—until snot was coming out of my nose. He rubbed my back until I was calm and then pulled me inside.

I had a place to escape to for the night. My dad assumed I was with Rachel, and I hoped Luke did too. Luke's best friend was one of the last people who I had thought would be helpful right now. But he let me talk for hours. I'm not sure how many rants and tangents I went on about my mom, my dad, Drake, and Luke, but Justin listened to every single one without judgment until I finally fell asleep on his couch.

The cushion beneath my legs dipped from someone sitting. I jolted upright to find Rachel holding a coffee and a bagel. With a groan, I dropped backward and rolled to face the back of the couch. All I wanted right now was an aspirin and water. My body felt like it was day two of a hangover I didn't deserve.

"You and I are going to have words about you getting a sleepover with Justin before me."

For the first time since yesterday, my lips tried to form a smile. They failed, but there was hope. "So, you admit it; you like Justin. Where is he, anyway?"

"The shower. And I like Chris. Justin is nice to look at. I'm not here to talk about them."

"Did you know too?" The question seemed stupid at this point. I had to be the only person in this town who didn't know my mother was bedding William Drake. Her silence confirmed. "Did Justin tell you?"

"No. I overheard my parents talking about it years ago. I didn't know that Justin or Luke knew."

"So, you found out after his mom left?"

Her head shook no. "A few years before."

My stomach soured. I was sorry I'd asked. I sat up but drew my knees closer to my chest to rest my head on them. Years. They'd screwed around for years, and everyone knew but me and my dad. There was no way he was aware of this—or he would have left her long ago. He wouldn't still be putting flowers on her grave every birthday and mourning the love of his life to this day. My heart was broken for us both, and I couldn't even tell him.

"Lacey, are you okay?"

*No.*

I took a deep breath. It made me feel worse. My head was killing me, and now I was certain the room was spinning out from under me. I didn't know I was falling over until Rachel screamed for Justin and leaped from her spot to stop me.

"Lacey, look up," Justin demanded.

*How did he get here so fast?*

I did as I was told. Light flashed, causing me to squint and turn away. He held his hand up in front of my face.

"How many fingers am I holding up?"

"I don't know."

I tried to move off the couch and realized I wasn't on it. I was on the floor beside it. I'd blacked out. It couldn't have been long, but it was long enough that Justin had arrived at my side in a towel and Rachel was already on the phone.

"Don't call Luke!" I warned.

"She's talking to an ambulance. Don't worry about her. Can you sit up?"

I rolled to my hands and knees. I was fine. I was going to show him just how fine I was by getting to my feet. I didn't need a damn ambulance. I put my hands on the edge of the couch, just in case I needed the help, and lifted myself one foot at a time.

"What the fuck was that?" Justin said, still holding his towel with one hand and dripping everywhere.

I held my palm to my forehead. "Can you get my purse?"

"You're not going anywhere."

I knew that. "There's a blood pressure cuff in it. Can you get it, please?"

Justin told me to sit while he went to retrieve the bag from his room. I didn't. I was too busy being stubborn and proving to him I was okay. Every move I made was being relayed to whoever was on the other end of Rachel's call. I closed my eyes again, taking on my headache one steady breath at a time. All I wanted to do was go back to sleep.

With Justin's return came the familiar ripping noise of Velcro. His own stethoscope was hanging from his neck against his bare chest. I had confidence Justin knew how to work this and could handle me just holding out an arm for him to take over. He started with my heart rate, holding two fingers against my wrist while looking off at an obscenely large clock hanging over the couch as a decoration focal point.

"Stay still," he whispered, still watching the clock.

"I am."

"You're not. Sit down. You need to stop swaying."

"I'm not." I opened my eyes just in time to watch the room go from vertical, to horizontal, to dark.

"Lacey! Lacey, wake up!"

# chapter twenty

## LUKE

I sighed at the dark office. I was stupid to believe Lacey would come back to work today and risk seeing me. The lack of any kind of response to my endless texts and voice mails made it clear—she had no intention of speaking to me any time soon. It was nearly midnight when the calls began going directly to voice mail. It didn't mean I stopped trying. I'd already sent her two texts this morning. None of them said how sorry I was or the reasons I held back from telling her the truth for so long. It was something I needed to tell her in person; as I should have done years ago.

"She's not here yet, eh?"

Mitch arrived on my right. He lifted a mug to his lips that read *I Am an Accountant*. Any other day it would have made me laugh, but not now.

"She called in sick?" I looked at my watch. "It's almost ten."

"I've heard nothing. I was pretty stoked to tell her I had a breakthrough in our account. I finally found a name on the with-drawals. I think it's related to an ex-employee who was injured on the job. Looks like some sort of compensation payout. If you see her, have her call me. I know it was eating at her."

Even though I agreed, I wasn't sure she was going to give me the option to tell her the good news. Mitch always put a damn smile on her face. And I was the guy who fucked up left and right. I pulled out my phone and sent another text, this time asking where she was and telling her I wanted to talk face to face. I was sure she was with Rachel—someone who was also refusing to answer texts. If I had to, I would show up at Rachel's place without an invitation.

It was going to have to wait until later tonight. This was sure to be the slowest workday of my life.

To pass the time, I actually did what was expected of me. I worked tirelessly to finish emptying the storeroom. I had piles of things for my dad to go through, more items for Lacey that had belonged to her mother, a few items that were worthy of an eBay auction, and a lot of trash.

My phone never left my side. Not once did it ring. Not once did it buzz. My heart broke a little more with every minute that passed. I hadn't cried since the day my mom left, and multiple times throughout the day I felt myself on the brink as I overthought everything that had happened this summer. We didn't find each other again to end up as nothing more than estranged coworkers. I couldn't let that happen.

I tied off the last garbage bag, tossed it into the pile outside the door with the others, turned off the light, and headed for my office. It was lunchtime, and I had to find something to do with myself during the hour I reserved for Lacey.

"Surprised to see you here today," my dad said through the partially shut door of his office.

I stopped and pushed the door open farther with my shoulder. "I didn't realize I had the choice to not be."

"Well, you and Lacey both ran off early yesterday. In fact, Tiffany and Lacey have both decided to not show up today. It seems to be the norm. You realize, human resources tracks your attendance for your record. We have to send those records in order for you all the claim college credits."

I didn't run off. I went home, hoping Lacey would come find me there after letting her blow off steam. "I don't know where Lacey is. I told Tiffany to get fucked and never show her face here again."

"Lucas!" he growled, standing.

We'd had enough arguments for me to know he was about to slam the door and lay it on thick. I beat him to it. I slammed the door behind me so hard that I heard its glass pane crack. Part of me wished the whole damn thing had shattered into a million pieces because that was how I felt right now, and it was him who got me here.

"Ask me why!" I yelled, with every ounce of air in my chest. "And then think really fucking hard about what I just said. I don't know where Lacey is."

"I'm not interested in a catfight!"

"Lacey ran off because your little secretary—the one you just *had* to have working here in order to make my life miserable—told her about you and Mary!"

My dad's hard features softened as his chest rose and fell. We never talked about it, but he knew I knew. I was the reason his wife left. I told my mom, hoping she would finally leave and take me with her. She didn't.

"My sex life is none of your business and not for you to discuss with the women you sleep with."

"Are you fucking kidding me right now? I was engaged. Do

you really think I would lie to her when she asked what happened to Mom?"

He walked back to his seat and threw himself into it. He rubbed his face with his hands before dropping them both flat against the glass desk in front of him. He was seriously just going to act like I hadn't said what I said?

"I told you this Lacey business was no good for you."

"I'm in love with her."

"Lucas." My dad's head snapped upward, wide-eyed and ready for round two.

"Is that really so hard to comprehend?" I would have laughed if I weren't hollow inside. "You want me to be this version of you. I fall for a Mason girl, and now you don't like it?"

"You're going to run a business together."

"Like you and Mary did?"

I used to fear his glare, but now I could see he was just as empty as I was. I was more like him than I knew.

"Mary is gone, and we are done talking about this. You need to focus on what's important. For me, that is you and this business, and you keeping the business running smoothly long after I am gone. As your parent, I'm telling you this dance business you think I don't know about, and the running around with Lacey, it all needs to stop. Focus on school. Keep your work life and personal life separated. Don't make me do it for you."

He always knew everything. If Collin could constantly know where I was, I figured my other jobs were no secret either. A threat against the life I was building was always an argument away.

I stood taller. "I will walk away from this company."

"And I will donate your Drake inheritance to this company out of spite and keep your shares. You will be billed for the tuition this company paid with the intention you would be hired."

My head shook. He was a bastard. Every single time I thought I had a way out of here, he was ready for it. I didn't need to argue about the tuition—somewhere there would be a document he'd had me sign with this exact stipulation. William Drake always played two steps ahead. By staying with Lacey and not taking this job, he could bankrupt me.

I was ready to argue until I was blue in the face, but my back pocket rang. Hoping it was Lacey, I pulled my phone free. What little optimism I had faded when I saw Justin's name flash on the screen. I silenced it and put it back into my pocket.

"What's it going to be, Lucas? This fling of yours worth it?"

I opened my mouth, but my phone stopped me a second time. It buzzed with a text first and then rang again. It was Justin again, and now something felt wrong. He would take the hint and leave a voice mail any other time.

"Rain check," I said, turning on my heel, exiting the room as my dad called after me.

I went for the stairs. I wasn't waiting for the damn elevator to tell me what my gut had been doing all day. Something was wrong. His text said for me to call him back right away, but my stupid ass couldn't make a call in the stairwell. I exited to some random floor I had never been on and stood in the middle of a busy hallway of people who probably knew me even though I didn't know them. I punched the Redial button and paced with each ring until finally I heard Justin.

"She's at Southampton Hospital. Room five hundred and three."

"What happened?" My panic intensified. "Is she okay?"

"She's okay. You need to get here now, though."

It was the lunch hour. Getting back to the Hamptons wasn't going to happen quickly. I'd be lucky if I could get a cab or an Uber right now.

"Luke?"

"Yeah." I clutched my hair in a fist. "Do I need to get Jack?"

There was a pause that was making my skin ache. "I don't think that's a good idea. Lacey was very against it when I brought him up."

"What the hell happened?" I yelled louder, now causing a bunch of strangers to watch me have a mental breakdown in front of them. "Give me something here. You can't just tell me she's in the hospital and not tell me why."

He sighed heavily. "Luke, I need you to meet me in the obstetrics unit. They are trying to get her blood pressure under control."

My heart sank to my stomach.

# chapter twenty-one
## LACEY

My hands were shaking in my lap. One hand now had an IV inserted into the back of it. My arm was bruised and sore from many failed attempts to find a usable vein. My lack of hydration over the last two days had caught up to me. Which was the reason Justin was handing me another cup of water. The room was silent, and that was okay. I was so far into my head that I couldn't speak, even if I wanted to.

The water went on the bedside table beside the other five now-empty cups. I read the label of my IV to pass more time, hating that I knew what it meant. Labetalol/sodium chloride. Not the first choice for any normal patient with hypertension. However, I was no longer considered normal. Labetalol was the first choice in beta-blockers for hypertension in pregnancy. I sniffled, feeling panic fill my chest for the nth time since waking up here.

*I am pregnant.*

"Lacey, try to stay calm."

My tethered hand came to my face so I could cry into it. In a matter of twenty-four hours, my life had spiraled. I was healthy. My mom was my idol. I could face my dad. I had Luke. And now I had nothing. There was only one person I wanted right now, and I wasn't sure I was ready to even look at him, let alone tell him this. He thought his life was fucked before? We aren't even through college, and we were eight weeks along.

Justin stood and nudged me with his elbow. I slid over just enough in my bed that he could join me. With one arm extended, I curled into the space he'd opened and laid my tear-soaked cheek against his chest to cry. I would have taken Rachel, too, but she left to go get me some things from home.

"Deep breaths," he instructed. "No stress. Remember?"

There was no way I couldn't be stressed right now. I had just been diagnosed with the same disease that killed my mom. Hypertension always scared me, but now it was threatening my life. How simple and quick it was for the body to black out. Yesterday, I wished I had my car with me here in New York; now, I was thankful I wasn't behind the wheel like she was. Between stress, an unplanned pregnancy, and dehydration, my blood pressure was at such a dangerously high level that I could have given myself a heart attack at twenty-two. How was I supposed to not be stressed? Justin was literally keeping me sane right now.

I took deep breaths, wishing I could fall back asleep and wake up from the nightmare of the last day.

"I want to talk about Luke."

My head shook *no* against his chest.

"Lacey . . ."

"I can't." My voice cracked. "How am I supposed to even tell him where I am right now? I slapped him yesterday and meant it."

"Stay calm. Okay? I have to tell you something, and you need to stay calm."

That wasn't a good start. I sat up, sniffling, watching Justin fade into a blur. "You didn't."

"You blocked his number. I unblocked it. Please talk to him. He's so scared, and you're keeping him out when you need him most."

As my head shook *no*, my phone sprang to life, blaring a familiar alarm. The only way to stop it was to read the text that would shortly accompany it. I'd avoided those texts all day. Now Justin was handing me my phone with a lit screen and a text notification. My mother's name would end the alarm.

I swiped tears from my eyes and entered the word *Mary*. The app opened with a block of time set to now. My shaking thumb tapped on it.

*I'm here. I know you don't want to see me, but I left you a voice mail on the way here. You can delete all those others, but please, please, listen to the one I just sent. Then decide if you want me to come in or not.*

The voice mail icon showed a red circle with a seven within it. I was hesitant to press it, but I knew Justin was still sitting on the edge of my bed to make sure I did. From the list, I selected a voice mail left only a few minutes ago and pressed the phone to my ear.

"Hey," Luke's warm voice spoke softly. "It's uh, me. I guess I knew you wouldn't answer. I had to try. I'm just begging you to please listen to what I have to say before you hang up and delete this."

I could hear his nerves. As Luke paused, Justin left the bed and returned to his seat. I grasped the phone harder, waiting and needing his voice to come back.

"Lacey, I fucked up. I will apologize to you until the day I die for Tiffany being the one to tell you about your mom. I told her the reason my mom left, and she used it spitefully. I can't take that back, but I wish I could. I never wanted to tell you. That secret destroyed me for a long time, and I didn't want that for you. I never wanted to ruin the image you have of your mom. You had two parents who loved you, and you should not let it change your opinion of them."

I was back to sobbing. But I was nodding my head to agree, as if he could see me. I tried to quiet myself so I could still hear what Luke was saying. I understood why he kept it to himself. I now wished I didn't know about our parents, but I also wished he didn't either.

"This is not the reason I am calling you. Lace, I broke the second you walked away yesterday. I'm not whole without you. I haven't been since you left seven years ago, and I can't lose you again. I know you have something to tell me, and I'm ready to hear it. Okay? I'm ready for that news you just received. Because Lacey, I have something to tell you too. It's important. So, listen closely."

My head nodded again as a sob escaped my throat.

"I'm in love with you, Lacey Jo Mason. I fell in love with you the first day I met you, and never stopped. Let me prove it to you."

"I love you too," I whispered to the phone, even though he couldn't hear it.

"And don't for a second believe that I don't remember telling you the night we were drunk in the car. I meant it then just as much as I mean it now. I ship you, but I love you more than anyone else in this world. I'm here. Please let me in."

Justin stood and left the room. I knew it was to go fetch his friend who was waiting somewhere in this hospital. Even though the call had ended, I held the phone tight to my ear, letting it replay as I wept. When the door actually opened to reveal Luke in the flesh, I finally allowed the phone to slip into the sheets.

He hesitated a moment before walking completely in.

"Hey, pretty girl."

I lost it. But Luke was there to engulf me in his arms and press his warm lips against my temple as I clung to him for dear life. I didn't realize how scared I was until the fear of losing him lifted. I could sense his own relief as he kept kissing my cheeks and wiping away my tears with the pads of his thumbs.

"I didn't know." My head shook with his hands on each side. I needed him to know that this wasn't some sort of trick, and that I wasn't hiding this pregnancy from him. "I didn't know."

"I know, Lace," he said. It was the reassurance I needed. "It's okay. We'll be all right. I love you."

"I love you too."

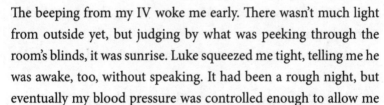

The beeping from my IV woke me early. There wasn't much light from outside yet, but judging by what was peeking through the room's blinds, it was sunrise. Luke squeezed me tight, telling me he was awake, too, without speaking. It had been a rough night, but eventually my blood pressure was controlled enough to allow me to sleep. This was the quietest this place had been since arriving. Even the hallway outside my open door was silent.

"Doing okay?" Luke whispered, still sounding sleepy himself. "Need anything?"

I shook my head and nestled in close. I felt good. My headache was gone, and I was no longer woozy. My stress could have been a lot better, but that wasn't going away any time soon. For now, I had what I needed. I had Luke.

We'd had very little time to talk last night. When Rachel and

Justin returned, they did their best to keep my mind eased by playing cards and watching TV with us. I knew they were both worried, so I didn't have the heart to tell them I needed alone time with Luke. And by the time they left, we were exhausted.

Luke placed his hand on my belly—one looking no different from a night I'd eaten too much—and used his thumb to rub small circles atop my gown. He watched as if it would somehow react, but I knew he was just deep in thought.

"Eight weeks," he said. "That's the night at Blue. It feels like so much longer than that."

He was right. There was no other night that it could have been. Luke kept saying this was okay, but was it? I didn't come here this summer expecting to have sex. My birth control was trashed as soon as my breakup with my ex happened. While we used condoms as much as possible, we had just learned a real lesson about being reckless with them. Talking about living together while in school was a huge step, and now a baby was being added to the mix. Our feelings for each other were strong, but Luke looked terrified right now.

"Are you okay?" I wasn't sure I wanted to hear the answer, but I needed to ask.

"Yesterday, my dad told me that everything he's done has been for me." His lip twitched, threatening tears. A deep breath stabled him. "How is that possible? Yesterday, I knew I never wanted kids—I had shit examples for parents. But right now, I feel like I'd do anything for a baby the size of a peanut. I would never put our baby through the shit he's put me through."

"Maybe in his mind, Drake is doing what he thinks is right. He wants you to succeed."

"No. He's selfish. Every move he's made has been about him. And when he doesn't get his way, he becomes a bully. I promise I will never become him. I will never put money before us. Things are going to get messy, but you and this baby come first."

Something was wrong. Luke's lids hung low, unwilling to meet my eyes. We hadn't discussed our parents' affair. Or how we were going to tell our dads the news. I wasn't sure if his sorrow was even about that. I placed my hand on his cheek.

"What happened?"

"Nothing."

"Luke." I recognized the lie instantly. "No more secrets. What's wrong?"

The hesitation to tell me wasn't making this any better. He shifted on the bed, this time giving me much more attention than a few minutes prior. Whatever he was about to tell me would not be good.

"My dad knows."

"Knows . . . ?"

"All of it. About me saving money and working at the club and the studio. About us."

"Oh." I stilled. If he was this upset about him knowing, I could only assume Drake's reaction wasn't good.

"He, uh,"—Luke cleared his throat after it cracked—"threatened my Drake inheritance. He said he'd invest it into Drake-Mason instead and make me pay all tuition back to the company if I didn't end this. Lacey, I would never choose that over you."

How could he do that? How could he after what he and my mother did? Maybe we could have hidden this relationship long enough for Luke to get his money and never speak to his dad again, but now that wasn't an option. We couldn't hide a pregnancy. My dad wouldn't like this, either, but . . .

"I didn't know your dad hated me that much."

"He doesn't. He just knows I love you, and he knows how to

hit me where it hurts. He's making me choose. And I've chosen."

My eyes flooded. "But that makes this my fault."

"It's his fault, Lace. He's bitter because his life didn't go the way he wanted it to."

And which way was that? Was it with my mom? Or his wife? I wasn't even sure how I was supposed to look at William Drake again after learning about this affair. And now knowing he would disown his own son because of me?

"I want to know everything you know about my mom."

Luke's head shook no. "Just let it go."

"How long?"

He sighed. "A long time."

"A year?"

His lips remained shut.

"Two? Three?" My blurry view widened when he remained silent. "Over four years? How long did you know?"

"I told my mom as soon as I found out. According to the paperwork from the divorce, it claimed he was unfaithful for five or more years."

I wanted to be sick. It now made sense why she didn't want me to crush on Luke. But over five years? That put us back to when we lived on the beach. So many nights of working late were now emerging in a different light. Was she working? Or was she with Drake?

"Lacey, do you think your dad knows? He hates Dad."

"No way," I was quick to answer. I was more than sure of it. Any hostility he had toward Drake was strictly about closing the lab. "He might hate your dad, but he worshipped the ground Mom walked on. He can barely hold a conversation about her without getting emotional. Luke, he can't know. It would crush him."

"He hates me too."

My nose scrunched. "Hate is a strong word."

"He hates me."

"He doesn't . . ."

"Oh yeah?" He placed a fingertip back on my belly. "How is he going to take this?"

My head dropped to Luke's shoulder.

Another answer I was sure of . . . "Not well."

# chapter twenty-two

## LACEY

It only took one more day for me to be discharged. I was running out of excuses for not being at home or work—which was now a lie about me taking off work for a few days to visit a New York City spa with Rachel due to stress. HIPAA wouldn't allow the hospital to tell my dad anything about my health, but me being on his insurance was now a threat. While Luke battled with the billing department to not take my insurance and allow us to pay in cash, I was having my last physician consult before being allowed to leave. And just when I thought our situation couldn't be any worse, he mentioned two words that threw our entire plan of telling our dads once we were settled in North Carolina into disarray.

Bed rest.

I was being placed on light bed rest at eight weeks. Between hypertension and having periods the last two months, we were now labeled a high-risk pregnancy. It was hard enough hiding from my dad for three days. There was no way I was going to be stuck in a bed for the rest of summer and have him not notice. This meant I couldn't go into Drake-Mason each day, and it meant no spending time with Luke—who literally was not welcome. We needed a new plan.

"Are you doing okay?" Luke's right hand left the wheel to rest on my thigh.

It was probably the fifth time he had asked since leaving. My eyes were closed, and my head was resting against the passenger seat. Nothing about this last week was okay. Everything was a disaster. And to top all of this off, the one thing that was replaying in my head was not the fact that our parents had an affair and tried to keep it from us for years, or that we had no way to hide this pregnancy when neither of our parents wanted us in a relationship. No, it was on Luke's inheritance going down the shitter, and his dad's willingness to bankrupt him. Even today, we used some of the money he'd been saving to pay the hospital bill.

"I just have a headache."

"We should go back."

"It's just a normal headache." I pried one eye open enough to see the worry etched in his features. "What the hell are we going to do? I can't sit still long enough to be on bed rest."

"Well, you're going to." He was quick to answer as he changed lanes and beat the heavy traffic. "You can't play around with this, Lacey. You can't stress over anything. We need to keep that blood pressure under control. Your dad needs to know."

I understood his worries. He was right. My dad did need to know about the hypertension. This is what killed my mother. Still, my numbers were nowhere near what hers were. I was obviously stressed while learning the news of her affair, and there would be nothing else that could set me off that way.

"The entire drive to work, I sit. I sit all day at my desk."

His head shook the whole time I spoke. "I'll get Dad to let you work from home. You said it yourself: there's not much left to do. He won't question why you don't want to be there. It's okay to hate the guy, Lacey."

It wasn't the worst plan. I would have a talk with my dad about my blood pressure being on the high side, and how working from home would be less stressful for now. But there was no plan to fix Luke's dad cutting him off. I may not look pregnant now, but it was only a matter of time. So, even though I was agreeing to this, I had another plan. And maybe being away from Luke while he worked all day was going to allow me the time I needed to pull it off.

I opened my phone to find the name I had hidden away in it a few short weeks ago.

Luke drove me home and physically waited until he saw me get into the bed. The number of eye rolls I gave him couldn't even match the number of times he told me to stay in it. While adorable the way he pampered me before he left to return to Drake-Mason for the second half of his workday, leaving me snacks and a few bottles of water, the second I was alone, I was pulling out my phone again. He promised to bring my work home, but this was more important.

Elizabeth Clark.

If my gut was right the night of our date, Luke's mom was closer to him than he believed. I was now a knocked-up, bedridden girl on a mission to save my boyfriend's dream of escaping the Big Pharma lifestyle. The FBI had nothing on me when it came to my stalker abilities, and this was the best use I had for my time. It took me exactly fifteen minutes to find the address. It was now confirmed. Luke's mom was not only still around but Luke had a half sister, and she was in his classes.

Her social media was locked down, leaving me no way to reach out to her other than the address that was now stored in my Maps app. It was barely noon. I'd only been in the bed for twenty-five minutes, and my feet were already hitting the floor. I wasn't stressed, but I made sure the blood pressure cuff was in my purse. I felt fine. A ride into Farmingdale would not hurt. I wouldn't even be on my feet for the next hour or so.

The Uber showed up in less than a half hour. And almost before I knew it, I was sitting curbside next to possibly the cutest family home I'd ever seen.

They had a goddamn white fence and a puppy playing in the yard. It didn't seem possible that this could be the same woman who walked away from Luke so many years ago. Part of me wanted to see that she'd failed in some way, as a punishment for leaving her child behind. She had another child who deserved better.

I slowly unlocked the gate as my driver pulled away. I stood on a welcome mat while feeling anything but welcome. I compared the address to the one on my phone one last time before tapping my knuckles against the stained, wooden door. My only anxiety in this situation was that she would open and slam the large door in my face, but I supposed it wouldn't be the first time.

It opened. I believe most of the shock was on my end, because I could see just how much of Luke there was in her features. And now I knew I was looking at a woman I'd seen so many times as a child. While she wasn't around much, this was definitely the same woman who fed us ice cream sandwiches on hot beach days. As angry as I was with her for leaving him, there was some sort of comfort in that.

"I know I didn't introduce myself at the studio, but I'm . . ."

"Lacey." She finished the sentence with a bob of her head.

I tucked my hair behind my ear. "You remember me?"

"You look like your mom."

A few weeks ago, I would have loved hearing that. Knowing what I did now, I wondered if it would make this conversation harder on us. My mom was the reason she left. I was so eager to get here I didn't even think of that. It didn't matter. This still needed to happen.

"Sorry," I muttered, staring at my feet on the welcome mat.

"Don't apologize." She motioned for me to step into her home. "Your mother was a beautiful woman."

I accepted the invitation quickly, before she could change her mind. Two steps landed me in a family room filled with over-stuffed furniture and a television hanging from a wall that was otherwise filled top to bottom with family photos in various-size frames. My nerves, combined with my need to be nosy, landed me directly in front of them. There were at least thirty photos of her with her new husband and their daughter, Becca. From family vacations and holidays to dance recitals, their entire life played out on the wall.

I lifted a finger and pointed behind me after turning to face her. "Not one picture of him?"

Her mouth opened and closed again. After a brief pause, she pointed to a wine rack on the wall of her open kitchen. "Would you like a glass of wine?"

Wine sounded wonderful. Unfortunately, that wouldn't be an option for a while. This pregnancy thing was new, and while our best friends knew, I didn't feel comfortable sharing it with just anyone. I shook my head *no*. Instinct had other plans, landing my hand on a belly that showed nothing yet.

"Ahh," she said with a knowing smile. "No wine, then. Water it is."

I took a seat on the couch. Elizabeth returned with two glasses of ice water and handed me one. The whole situation felt weird. I still smelled like the damn hospital; I had to look like a disaster, and now I had shown up and basically told this woman within five minutes that she was about to be a grandmother.

"How far along?"

"Eight weeks." I sipped the water. "That's not why I'm here, though."

"I didn't know if you recognized me that day outside the studio. I can't lie, I was a little worried you were going to go directly in and tell him I was there."

"You could have gone in yourself."

Her eyes glassed over as she shook her head. She reached for the tissue box beside her chair and instead of grabbing one tissue, took the entire thing. She pulled a few out before extending it to me. Yeah, I was going to need them too. No doubt. I took three for myself and clutched them in a fist.

"I always knew you two would end up together after all these years. You were inseparable. When we managed to pull you apart, you were all he'd talk about. These last few years, I've worried about his happiness, but seeing you again, I knew he was going to be okay."

"That's not fair to him," I said, feeling hot. I told myself not to become overly defensive, because I had a motive for being here. "You're a part of his life, and he doesn't know it. He believes you want nothing to do with him when clearly that's not the case at all."

"Does he know you're here?"

"No. He has no idea I know where you are. I'm supposed to be on my first day of bed rest, and instead, I'm here to find out why you really left him when you still care for him. You should have approached him a long time ago. He should know that little girl is his sister."

"I didn't think he would want to see me again."

Her sniffling was breaking my heart. She had dropped her head and was now weeping. I should have told Luke where I was going, because he needed to see that he had a parent who loved him. As stupid as Elizabeth was, she missed Luke, and it was written all over her face.

"He was the sweetest kid." My throat caught the next sentence, and I had to swallow hard to clear it. "How could you leave him with Drake? He thought you were going to take him with you."

"I couldn't." She wept and dabbed her eye with the tissue. "My life was a mess. William was controlling every part of it, and I knew if I took Luke with me, I was never going to be free of him. I had to put my mental health first. I had every intention of going back for him, but weeks turned to months and months to years. I was afraid that if I went back for him after that long, he'd reject me."

She ran her hand through her hair the same way my boyfriend did when frustrated. I didn't know if bringing it up would make her feel better or worse about leaving him behind. Elizabeth's lip continued to quiver as she shredded what was left of the tissue in her lap.

"William could be scary. Especially when threatened. I would have never gotten away with taking Luke and fighting William in court. I didn't have the money; I was mentally unfit to be a parent, and he scared the hell out of me. I swear the only reason he wanted kids was for that damn Drake name to carry on. He may have loved me at first, but the end of that marriage was rocky. There's no telling what he would have done if I ran off with his son."

"But you left Luke with *him*." The tears hit my chin before I realized they had started. "Do you have any idea how miserable he is? He has no control over his life. Any move he makes that isn't approved by Drake is the wrong move. And he uses his money to ensure Luke is dependent and loyal to him."

I wasn't telling her anything she didn't know. She was nodding, because it was the same thing she had experienced. "I had to get out of there. I couldn't take him with me. That will forever be the worst day of my life. It wasn't easy."

She made it look easy. She could have reached out to him in a hundred different ways, and she chose not to. In the end, it wasn't my choice to forgive her. I really had no say in it at all. The only opinion that would matter was Luke's. I wanted to understand how she could leave him when a mother's instinct should be to protect. But it just sounded like she wanted to protect herself.

"Are you going to tell him about me and Becca?" she asked through her sniffling. "She loves his class. If that's your intention, I just want to prepare her. She doesn't know who he is, but she really looks up to him."

"If he asks, I won't lie." I clutched my elbow hard, unsure how I would even bring up Becca in conversation. I shouldn't have to, but I'd also promised Luke no more lies in this relationship. That's something we needed to stick to. "He deserves to know the truth, but I'm also not sure he wants to hear it. He has never once attempted to find you."

She sat back against the seat and placed the tissue box back in its place. "So, why are you here if he wants nothing to do with me?"

I took a long sip of my water. This was the only plan I could come up with to help Luke. I didn't want him to suffer because he chose me. His dad always seemed to be one step ahead of him, but would he really see this coming?

"Drake is threatening to bankrupt Luke if he doesn't end our relationship and take his place at Drake-Mason."

"That doesn't surprise me," she said. "But I also don't know how I can help him."

"His inheritance." I stood, handing her back my glass. "It only requires one parental signature to make any changes before Luke is twenty-five. Drake is threatening to invest it into Drake-Mason with that rule. If you still love that boy you left behind, help him. Your signature could release his Drake inheritance early."

Elizabeth smiled through her tears and stood as well. "Let's get my lawyer on the phone. If that's true, I'll have it signed immediately."

It was the first time in days that I felt like I could breathe.

# chapter twenty-three

## LUKE

I had seriously been underestimating the amount of work Lacey did in a day. Mitch had helped me box up most of it yesterday, but today was the first time since dropping her off at home that I was going to be able to give it to her without Jack being home. The box felt like it weighed a ton and was jammed full of every paper and folder that was sitting on her desk. At least this would be enough to keep her occupied while she rested.

Since it was the weekend, she wouldn't have to touch the box at all. But sitting on top of it was my iPad. We still had lots of planning to do before our semester started in a few weeks. For starters, we needed a place to live. And now we had to come up with somewhere for three of us instead of two.

I kicked the door a few times with my foot. I had tried calling from the car, but Lacey didn't answer. Either she was sleeping, or her phone was dead again. In case of the latter, I kicked harder the second time. It would have been handy if she had let me keep the spare key.

I was just about to set everything on the ground and attempt calling again when the door finally opened. I stood straight again from my partially bent stature and found myself staring at Jack. The box slipped as I panicked and we both caught it just in time before I had let it go completely.

"Shit. Sorry!" I reclaimed my hold of it.

Jack let go with a quizzical look. "May I help you, Lucas?"

Was I supposed to be breathing? Jack never failed to make me feel unwelcome, but he wasn't supposed to be here. He was going to look at an apartment today, according to his daughter. And Lacey was correct, he was not ready to hear we were in a relationship, and definitely not ready to know Lacey was pregnant. Now I had to think and think fast.

"I have some things for Lacey," I said, wanting to keep the conversation simple. While I knew Lacey had mentioned being forthcoming about her blood pressure to her dad, and the lie about working from home for less stress, I didn't know the full extent of her lie yet. Something in the box caught the corner of my eye and made this way easier. "It's stuff from her desk, and I have some old directories and things from Mary's office. She wanted me to hold on to them, and I finally had some time today to drop them off. Thought I would help her out by bringing her office stuff."

He looked from the box to me. "She's not home."

Uh, what? Not being home was not an option. Where the hell was she? The discharge orders were very specific. She was only supposed to get up for showering and light activity . . . like opening the door for her boyfriend after her dad left the house.

"Not home?"

"Not home. As in, she's not here," Jack clarified.

"I'm here!" Lacey's voice came from behind me.

One glance over my shoulder and I could see she was aware she was busted. She was dressed for a date—not in comfy clothes that said "bed rest." My head was shaking at her, not caring if Jack saw or not. I'm sure when it came to her health, he'd finally be on my side.

"I thought you had a private showing for an apartment." Lacey looked at the watch on the underside of her wrist. "You're going to be late."

"I was just about to head out." Jack stepped farther from the door. "You didn't say you were having company."

"Because I didn't know I was having company," she lied as she walked right past me and stepped into the air-conditioning. There was a folder beneath her arm that had me cocking my head. My full name was on it. "Come on in, Luke. Want something to drink?"

I followed her, keeping my head tilted to read the envelope, while Jack reminded her that he'd be home in a few hours and how she should be resting instead of having guests. A few hours was fine. That was more than enough time for me to scare her into not leaving the house again. She didn't seem to believe this was an issue as she kicked off her shoes and headed for the refrigerator. She pulled it open and grabbed a pitcher of lemonade and a couple of glasses while I stood there and waited for some sort of explanation.

"Where the hell were you?" I finally gave up when she would not fork over anything willingly. "What part of 'bed rest' do you not understand? The stay-in-the-fucking-bed part? Or the part where you need to rest because your body is trying to kill you?"

She giggled as she poured. "You're being a little dramatic. I'm fine. I feel great. I had an errand to run, and I'm going right back to the bed. Now, kiss me, please."

She was incredibly frustrating, and ridiculously stubborn, but

I did as I was asked. I dropped the box on the countertop. As soon as my arms were free, she was in them and on her tiptoes. It had only been a day, but it was unbelievable how much I could miss her. The relief of her and our baby being safe, right here in my arms, was exactly what I needed after a rough morning with my dad. I could feel that same relief from her when she kissed me.

"I ship you."

She looked up at me with a beautiful smile. "I ship you."

While I was glad that she'd finally allowed me to use the *L* word, I loved that this was ours. "What's in the envelope with my name on it? Where were you today?"

Her smile instantly disappeared. And just as fast, she slid out of my arms. Not a good sign. Lacey picked up the envelope and hugged it against her stomach, preventing me from seeing my own name. As if that was going to make me forget I'd seen it.

"Lace? What was so important that you left bed rest?"

"Before I tell you, you need to promise that you're going to stay in this house, not get angry, and let me explain in full. We said no more secrets, and this wasn't exactly a secret because I didn't know for sure if it was her or not."

"Who?"

"Promise me." She bit at her thumbnail.

My chest felt tight. Seeing Lacey this nervous and worried that I was going to get mad was already putting me on edge. My full name was written on an envelope that looked important. It was not sloppily written on in someone's handwriting. It was typed on. There was only one person I could think of right now after hearing this was a female, and I couldn't bring myself to say it aloud because it was impossible.

My eyes stung, and I wasn't sure when the last time I had blinked was. "*Where* were you?" I asked again.

"At a bank."

"Which bank?"

"Yours."

I couldn't remember every conversation we had this summer, but I knew I hadn't brought up where I banked. The accounts I attempted to keep from my father were back in North Carolina. There was only one bank it could be. I highly doubted Drake had looked up from his work long enough to answer where my bank accounts were located.

"Lacey," I warned and took a step back like the envelope was going to bite.

She raised her hand to stop me from moving any farther. "Just listen."

My eyes finally shut and refused to reopen until she answered. It felt like I could vomit, knowing what she was about to say next.

"I was with your mom."

My chest felt like it had ripped in two. I sat my ass on a stool and dropped my face into my hands. As much as my eyes burned, I promised myself I would not cry over that woman ever again. I needed to breathe. I needed to keep calm. I needed to not yell at Lacey and cause her anxiety when that was all I wanted to do.

"She didn't want that, Lacey." My voice still cracked. "She wants nothing to do with me. That was not your choice to interfere."

Lacey's palm squeezed my shoulder before she rubbed my back. "Luke, I didn't make the choice. She did. That's why I need you to listen and keep calm."

I finally looked up. "What do you mean, she did? She hasn't tried to see me once in seven years." But the look on Lacey's face said otherwise. I may have been refusing to cry, but her lashes were coated in fresh tears.

"Do you remember our date night? The one where you had me go to the studio?"

"Of course, I do."

"I told you I had met Becca's mom. And that I couldn't place her. Luke, it was your mom I talked to outside the studio. The reason she never came in was because she was afraid."

I stilled. Becca had been in my class the last two summers, and my brain was trying to recall a single time when her mom had come to watch class. There were so many kids in the group, but Becca always stood out more than the others, and I was sure only her dad had entered the studio.

This was a lot. I sucked in a breath and held it for so long that Lacey took my hand in hers and gave it a squeeze. "She still loves you a lot. And I had a really pleasant talk with her, but I won't tell you all that she told me about why she left without you. But you need to know that she wanted you, and her fear of your dad's retaliation played a big part in why she didn't take you with her. If you want to talk to her, she is more than willing to do that. She would love it, actually. She just believed there would never be a good time to come back into your life, and I couldn't answer for you either."

My throat felt like I had swallowed a golf ball. Meanwhile, Lacey had reached across the counter and dragged the envelope closer. I had spent the entire morning arguing with my dad—about ending my other jobs, and sticking to my schooling, my relationship with Lacey . . . and every attempt to live my own life came back to his money. Money I now needed for a baby. I picked up the envelope, lifted the flap, and pulled out the paper just enough to see the release of my inheritance with my mother's signature across the bottom.

"She didn't hesitate for a second, Luke. And I know I don't get a say in this, but if anyone can understand what your dad puts you through, it's her. If this is all you want from her, that's okay. She has made peace with it. But she would love to get to know the guy that Becca idolizes."

I pulled Lacey forward and dropped my head against her chest. The weight on my shoulders that had been there for the last twenty-three years lifted. I could breathe. No one had ever attempted to help me before. Every girlfriend saw a business with dollar signs. Lacey, who loved that business, was okay with me stepping away from it because she knew I didn't love it. I was finally one step ahead of my dad. I was free of him. I had no words to thank her enough for this relief. So, I held on to her as tightly as I could. And she let me.

"Jacob."

"It's not," Lacey paused and tried to hide the cringe in her reply, "terrible."

"You're a shit liar."

Lacey giggled and repositioned her head on my chest. We'd lost interest in our movie an hour ago. Now, we found that agreeing on a baby's name was going to be the hard part of our relationship.

"Madison."

"Why do you keep picking girl names?"

"Why do you keep picking boy names?" she countered.

"Because the thought of having a girl is terrifying."

She smiled. "That's exactly what will make you a great girl dad."

Maybe. I had a list a mile long for what not to do with a son, though, and that was my life story. While I wasn't sure if I had it in me to speak to my mother, what she did for me today was parental instinct. At least one of the two had it. My biggest fear was not learning from their mistakes. With this baby, I knew a girl would be in excellent hands with Lacey. While Mary wasn't an ideal role model for a relationship, she was a wonderful mother to Lacey.

"Mia."

Lacey's attention left the movie again to peer up at me. I didn't know she could smile as hard as she was in this moment. "I love that name for a girl. Mia . . . *Eloise* Drake."

Well, we could finish one thing today. I leaned up just enough to kiss the top of Lacey's head. We had a girl's name. Maybe it would change fifty more times in the upcoming months, but we finally agreed on something.

"You know, a place to live needs to happen first." I pointed to the iPad that we hadn't touched since arriving. It was still sitting with the box from Drake-Mason. "We leave in a few weeks. We have to at least look for an apartment."

Her eyes followed and landed on the box. Her body sighed. "Do we? You won't be going to school. You can't tell me that dance studios would do better in North Carolina than New York."

"And North Carolina is the number one pharmacy program in the States. I thought you wanted to attend your mother's alma mater?"

Lacey fell silent.

During our road trip she'd admitted she didn't love pharmacy. It really hadn't come up again, except for the night we'd tried to pick classes together. She wanted to take some accounting courses. Accounting wasn't something you needed to travel to North Carolina to do, but I wanted her to say that herself.

"I want Drake-Mason," she said. While it was whispered, it was also defensive. "But I fucking hate pharmacy, Luke. I want to run a business, not learn the shit my dad does in a lab or know the inner workings of outpatient versus inpatient pharmacies. I want to make it financially stable again."

She was so hot when she was being herself.

"Well," I said, pushing her hair out of her face, "what about a CFO position? All accounting. No pharmacy. You'll always be part of the board, and that keeps you in the C-suite."

She flipped excitedly to her stomach. "We could get an apartment closer to the city."

I would have gone anywhere with her.

She flew from the bed to retrieve the iPad. Knowing I was going to remind her of the bed rest, she quickly sat on the floor and began sifting through all the papers from her desk and the old directories. She formed neat piles that made no rhyme or reason to me. While I wanted to hang out in this bed with her longer, Jack was due home soon.

"I should go, Lace. Your dad will not be happy if he finds me in this room. He hates me enough already."

"Well, you should stay to work on that. We could order a pizza, and you two can get to know each other."

That was the worst idea she'd had all night. However, it was necessary. Whether or not Jack liked it, Lacey and I were serious and starting a family. If we could get one parent on our side, maybe my dad would follow. Unlikely, but we needed to try.

"What kind of pizza does your dad like?"

"Ham and pineapple."

I wrinkled my nose in disgust as I pulled out my phone. "There is no hope for us getting along if he believes fruit goes on pizza."

Lacey giggled as she leaned her back against the wall. She continued sorting through the box while I ordered dinner. She was blabbering on about how us living together would be great for Rachel and Justin to admit they have feelings for each other—something I knew would never happen on Justin's end. But when she stopped midsentence to stare at an item from the box, I knew something was wrong.

"What is that?"

"The report Mitch wrote on our mystery account. This says he found a name, and that it's part of an injury benefit payout. But this can't be right."

"Yeah. I forgot to tell you he found who the money was going to. He didn't tell me the name."

Lacey looked up, emotionless. "He got paid for the last seven years. This says it was Frank Leonard."

Frank Leonard—the man who attempted to rescue Mary Mason from her car. That didn't seem so strange. Did it? If anything, that seemed likely.

"He was an employee," I reminded her. "He was hurt on the job, trying to save one of its founders—who was sleeping with her partner. I could easily see my dad paying that guy for the rest of his life."

Lacey's eyes kept shifting from me, to the paper in her hand, and back to the box. She was back on her knees in no time. Papers from her piles flew in every direction as she began the hunt for more information. She had my attention.

"Lacey," I attempted to calm her down.

"Luke, those payments started in June."

"So?" I dropped off the bed and to the floor.

"So, my mother's accident was in *July*. Why did your dad begin paying him a month before my mom's accident?"

She didn't give me a chance to answer. Not that I had one. Lacey picked up the box and flipped it, sending anything left within to the carpet. What she was looking for must not have fallen out, because she was clutching her head in panic.

"Lace."

"It's not here!"

"What's not here? I packed everything from your desktop. Just like you asked. Mitch helped."

"What about the filing cabinet drawer? There was a yellow folder. Do you see a yellow folder?" She swiveled around to look at the documents behind her. There was no yellow folder.

"The drawer was locked. I couldn't empty it. Lacey, calm down. June and July are easily confused. Are you sure those payments didn't start in July?"

Her head was shaking. Even though I wanted her to be wrong, my gut knew how obsessed she was with this particular account. If she believed the activity had begun in June, it did. That didn't change the fact that I needed her to be calm right now. This wasn't good for her blood pressure, and there had to be a simple explanation. She crawled to the first stack she had made—the directories.

"What are you doing?"

She didn't answer. She was flipping so fast there was no way she could actually read what was on the pages. But now I could see what she was scanning. While photos in the first few pages of these directories were fun to look at, they had an actual use. When Lacey got to a heading labeled *L*, she stopped flipping and ran a single finger down the listing. When her finger paused, I knew she had found Frank Leonard.

"Do you really think he's got the same phone number after all these years?" I asked, trying to talk her out of this. "You've never even spoken to the man. Maybe we should call Mitch first."

It was too late. She was already dialing. I was going for the blood pressure cuff when she turned on the speaker feature. She didn't even fight me; she held out her arm as it rang.

"Hello?" a scratchy voice answered, followed by a cough that sounded like he smoked cigarettes all day long.

"Uh." Lacey paused, meeting my stare. This was a horrible idea. "I'm looking for a Mr. Frank Leonard. Is this who I'm speaking to?"

"Yeah. Who's this?"

While her blood pressure was high, this was a normal number for Lacey. I tore the cuff off and tossed it to the bed behind me.

"Hello, sir. I apologize for calling you so late on a Saturday. My name is Lacey Mason. I'm . . ."

"I know who you are." He cut her off. "What do you want?"

Lacey blinked at the phone, unsure how to continue. He wasn't friendly—that was for sure. "I, uh, well, I work in accounting at Drake-Mason Pharmaceuticals. My job is to review, move, or close old accounts. We located an account believed to be linked to your disability payout. I see here the activity began in June 2011. Is that correct?"

The phone screen blinked before fading to black. The call had been ended.

"Hello?" Lacey asked the silent phone.

"Lacey . . ." I grabbed her hand before she could call him again. "I think we should call Mitch."

"Where is your dad right now?" She ignored my plea.

"Drake-Mason." I hated where this was going. "He works every Saturday."

Lacey stood and tucked the report with Frank Leonard's name into her back pocket. "Luke, we need to get the folder from my desk."

"We can't just waltz in there on a Saturday. Can't this wait until Monday when I go back?"

"No."

"Lacey . . ."

"He was paying Frank Leonard before her accident, Luke! Give me one good reason, and I'll let it go."

I didn't have a good reason. But I had a million reasons why we shouldn't leave this room right now. All of those went out the window when Lacey grabbed the keys and almost ran out of the bedroom with me still standing there, wondering what the hell was happening.

Too many events were falling into a timeline that never added up until now. I caught Mary and Dad having an affair. I told my mom . . . she left. Mary showed up later that day. I slammed a door in Lacey's face while Mary and my dad talked. Mary told Lacey that Drake men were no good after having an affair with one for years. A few weeks later, she was gone.

Even though neither of us had said it, we were obviously both thinking about it.

*What if Mary's accident wasn't an accident at all?*

*What if Frank wasn't hurt rescuing her?*

*What if my dad had Mary killed?*

While I didn't want to believe my dad was capable of something like this, I knew he was. I was on my feet and chasing after Lacey. We didn't need Mitch. We needed the police. Before anything, we needed the folder with Lacey's research—something I could get while she stayed in bed. But when I arrived outside, I added a vehicle to that list. Because she was gone and so was my Jeep.

# chapter twenty-four
## LACEY

My heart pounded as I ran another traffic light. It was the third one I was mentally apologizing for. While traffic wasn't as bad as it would have been if it were a weekday, it wasn't light either. I was weaving through cars and had lost count of how many times I'd been honked at. Meanwhile, the cell phone on the empty passenger seat hadn't stopped ringing since I'd left. No doubt it was Luke, but my eyes weren't leaving the road to confirm it.

I needed my research.

I needed to prove myself wrong. Or else my mom's accident was anything but. Everything in the folder was either a payout from a company thanking a man for his attempt at saving one of its founders, or it was a road map on how to get away with murder. While I prayed for doubt, there wasn't any in my mind—the activity started exactly one month prior to the day of my mother's death. We had stumbled on to something we were never supposed to see.

The report Luke had unknowingly tossed into the box to bring home to me was already completed. It was a copy. The next step was sending it to Drake's email—something I couldn't stop. Anyone with eyes on this report could be in danger. That meant me, Mitch, and anyone else he had brought on to help. If Drake worked all weekend, would my desk be empty by Monday? I needed the folder.

Another horn made me scream and swerve.

Through blurred vision, I could see Drake-Mason's purple-and-red sign ahead. I thrust my hand into my purse for my security badge. I didn't know if it would even let me in on a Saturday evening, but I was going to find out. I took the first open spot close to the building and threw the car into park.

While the lobby lights were on, most of the building was dark. I dropped my head back to scan the building. Two other floors were lit. I didn't need to count to twenty-eight to know my office was one of them. I was frozen in place, but still my hands shook while gripping the wheel.

"You can't go in there now," I told myself, still staring upward. "Shit. Shit, shit, *shit*."

I picked up my phone. Luke's last call was five minutes ago. Using my twitchy thumb, I selected his number to return the call. The screen went from completely black to showing a symbol requesting its lightning cable. It had been ringing nonstop for forty-five minutes and was now dead.

"Fuck it." I tossed the phone into my purse.

I would have left the Jeep running, but I wanted Luke's vehicle to still be there when I got back. I took my purse and my badge and approached the front of the building. Thankfully, when I waved the badge, the door buzzed me in. The lobby held one security guard who didn't seem to mind that I had just let myself in. His head didn't even lift from the paper he was reading. Judging by the screens in front of him, I was sure he had seen me pull up to the building.

I bolted for the elevators and pressed every single Up button available. I didn't have to wait for two of them to open. One was mine. When I heard the lobby door buzz and open a second time, I knew the other elevator would be Luke's. I heard his panicked voice calling my name, but I repeatedly hit the button that would close the elevator doors. I mouthed the word *sorry* as they shut, cutting off my view of a furious Luke.

"Damn it, Lacey! You're fucking stubborn!" The sound of his hand against the outer door was muffled as the car began its ascent.

This was going to be easy. The fact that the lights on my floor were on was just a coincidence. I was going to grab the folder, and we'd be out of here in no time. After drying the tears from my face using my shirt, I shook my key ring to find the key to my office and the filing cabinet drawer of my desk. I couldn't pinpoint why I couldn't stop crying. There were a lot of reasons— hormones, fear, frustration, but a lot of it was for my mom. Drake took her from me. The closer I got to my floor, the more certain I was. The entire summer I was reviewing an account paying to keep someone silent.

I was right. When the doors reopened, a lit hallway guided my way to my office. My office door stood open, telling me this wouldn't be as easy as I'd thought. Especially when I found William Drake sitting in my chair with the exact yellow folder I'd come for in his hands. He didn't even bother to look up when I entered; he just kept reading with one hand hiding the emotion on his face.

I never imagined I could look at someone who was made of pure evil, but here he was. Through the rage now coursing through my veins, my fear took the backseat. This man took my mother.

"You set yourself up to fail." My voice was hoarse from crying the entire way here.

"What are you saying?" he asked, rubbing his head.

"Frank Leonard. Paying him before the accident. If you had just started a few days later, no one would have questioned the account."

Drake lifted his head. "I don't know what this is."

I laughed. Somewhere down the hall, the elevators chimed. Luke would be at my side any second. But this wasn't his battle with his dad. This was mine. I was getting that folder.

"You killed my mother."

When the sentence left my mouth, I wasn't sure what I was expecting. Seeing his eyebrows sink at the same time as his shoulders wasn't a reaction I saw coming. His head shook *no*, and his stare fell back to my research.

"Lacey."

My upper arm was gripped hard, yanking my attention to Luke.

"Are you out of your mind?" He wasn't expecting to find his father in my office either. His lips immediately snapped shut. But Drake didn't seem to care that either of us was here right now.

"He killed my mother!" I yelled.

"Lucas, shut her up! I need to think."

I snapped my head back to Drake, and then I dove for the folder, but Luke looped one arm around my waist to hold me back. My arms and legs flailed as I tried to free myself.

"He killed her!" I screamed as my tears began flowing again.

"I didn't!" Drake stood and clutched his hair in the same way Luke would. "Frank Leonard did! I think! I don't know where this money came from!"

"Liar! Seven years you've been paying him!"

"Lacey, you need to calm down," Luke continued. "Your blood pressure . . ."

Drake walked around the desk and held the folder out to us. His lip quivered. "I would never have hurt Mary."

Luke's grip loosened as I reached for my work. I took the folder from Drake and wrapped my arms around it tight. I wouldn't let it go until it was in the hands of the authorities.

"Think, Lacey." Drake pointed to the folder. "Was anything about that account similar to the others assigned to you? Same bank? Town? Anything?"

My head shook *no*. Partially because I couldn't believe he actually thought he would get away with this and partially because there was nothing about this account that was like others, other than the location being New York State. I wouldn't give him any information willingly. But this one was different—it was one of the few accounts still holding a positive balance and the only account with activity other than interest. Someone was depositing into the account.

From the hallway, I heard the elevator chime again. My mind instantly thought of the security guard downstairs. Could he see Lucas holding me back on the cameras in the hall? But there were two voices and the sound of feet dragging on the carpet. Drake lifted a single finger to his lips, and we all moved out of sight from the doorway.

"She knows." A husky voice echoed through the halls. "She traced it right back to us. How did she even get my number?"

I looked at Lucas at the same time he looked at me. We knew that voice. Just over an hour ago was the first time we'd both heard it. Frank Leonard was now walking the halls of Drake-Mason. But how? Luke and I had badges to get in.

"The account is linked to the old lab." I recognized the second voice instantly. I tensed, losing grip of the reality we were in right now. "There's no way she could have figured that out. You're lucky I was still in town."

*Dad?*

"She called me directly."

"And it was the best-case scenario," my father said. "I told you—as soon as Drake mentioned he was fishing for money, I knew I had to come back."

"What are you going to do?"

"Collect the computer from her office and burn this place to the ground. Starting with that damn lab."

Luke never left my side. My world was spinning out of control, and I wasn't sure how I was still standing in one place. I got dizzy. Luke's arm may have been keeping me up, or maybe it was the horrified look on Drake's face as he took all this in too. I had blamed the wrong man. The one I accused not five minutes ago now looked just as devastated as I felt.

I took two steps toward the door. I wanted to confront my father. Luke wasn't about to let that happen.

"You're pregnant," he reminded via whisper. "I know you're mad, but please don't be stupid right now, Lace."

Drake glanced at us briefly, taking in the news. "You both stay in here. No matter what. Call the police and get security up here. Barricade the room with the desk."

"Dad . . ."

"Lucas, do as you're told just one fucking time. *Please.*"

It didn't matter. My dad entered the room and stopped short when he saw the three of us, followed shortly by someone who I could only assume was Frank Leonard—a stocky, balding man who instantly made the room smell of stale beer and cigarettes. His skin was shiny and pink—covered in scars from a fire seven years ago. Luke's hand tightened around my upper arm, and I knew it was because we were both aware of the gun that was clipped to Leonard's belt. He made no attempt to hide it beneath his plaid shirt.

"Jack," Drake took their attention. His hand lifted—an attempt to keep both men calm. "What have you done? Mary? The accident . . ."

My dad was unraveling before my very eyes. He was cold and unbothered by the fact we had heard everything that had been said in the hall. He stared at Drake with a hatred unlike anything I had ever seen. He knew all along about the affair; it was written all over his face.

". . . wasn't an accident." Dad finished Drake's thought.

My heart shattered with a gasp.

"Jack," Frank warned, his eyes shifting between the two men.

Even the man who had played some sort of hand in my mother's murder looked worried about the change in my dad's demeanor. When Frank went to rest his hand on the gun hanging from his hip, Dad got to it first. He swung it into Drake's face, and the sound of the safety clicking made everyone in the room jump. Drake's eyes filled with tears as he nodded—it wasn't fear; it was an acceptance of the truth. Luke released his hold on me.

"You took everything from me." My dad's hand shook, causing the gun to do the same. "My ideas, the lab, my wife, my dignity . . . everything!"

"I did," Drake agreed. "But Jack, you killed Mary."

"Stay calm," Luke whispered, with his lips pressed to my hair. "He has a gun. Just stay calm."

Stay calm? My dad had just admitted to murdering my mother, and I was supposed to pretend like I was fine? I could barely breathe, let alone act like there wasn't a gun pointed at Luke's dad. I wanted to be involved in whatever plan he had, because being left in the dark was not working for me.

I gulped and nodded to confirm that I would stay still.

"I had security call the police when I got here," Luke whispered again. "I couldn't take any chances with you being up here alone."

"You took everything," my dad repeated. His attention turned to Luke and me. "And this kid is just like you. Even your son believes he can take what's mine. What if I took something from you?"

Dad's arm swung. The gun was now pointed directly at Luke's face. His Adam's apple extended, and he went white as a ghost. I tried to put myself in front of him but Luke's arm would not let me move. I cried out, wrapping my arms around Luke's neck and sobbing. He was shaking in my arms but standing as still as he could. My father could not take Luke from me too. Not Luke. We'd been through too much for it to end like this. I was clinging to him for his life.

"You already took from me, Jack." Drake took a few steps and slid himself between the gun and Luke. "Leave our children out of this. You took the woman I loved. No one else needs to get hurt for what Mary and I did."

The elevators chimed from the hallway. It had to be the police. Frank Leonard didn't stick around to find out. He fled the room, and it sounded like he took the stairs as an exit. Meanwhile, time had stopped. The room was silent, waiting to see if Drake's pleas to save us would hold. And there was a moment when I thought it would. But ultimately, my dad shook his head *no*. There was no time between that decision and the pop of the gun. There was only one shot, but two bodies hit the floor.

One was mine.

# chapter twenty-five
## LUKE

Jack's white shirt splattered red with the gunshot. His arm stayed raised even after he fired. For a moment, everyone remained right where they were. Then, half of us were on the ground. In front of me, my dad clutched his upper chest, soaking his hand in the same blood that covered Jack and screaming in pain. And behind me, my girlfriend lay motionless.

"Jack . . ." I slowly lifted my hand, fearful that any sudden movement could set him off. "Jack, Lacey is sick. Her blood pressure—I need to see if she's okay."

Tears were falling down his cheeks as the gun shook in his hand. He looked from my dad to Lacey and back to me. My dad's screams were filling the room, but he was still trying to roll his way toward Lacey. I didn't know what was worse—hearing his pain, no sound at all coming from Lacey, or me being a coward and afraid to drop to them. I couldn't help either of them if I was dead.

Lacey's whole body thrashed at my feet. I didn't have to see her to know she was seizing. My dad couldn't get to her. I bent my knees slowly, still holding my hand up as if that would stop Jack from sending a bullet toward me. Even though the police were coming down the hall, we were out of time.

"Jack, *please*? It's Lacey!"

Still crying, he looked at his daughter and unwrapped his fingers from the handle. The gun dangled briefly from his finger before he dropped it to the ground. I followed its path and hit it across the room, where it landed beneath the desk. Then I turned and scooped up Lacey into my arms as she continued to jolt uncontrollably.

The police and EMTs arrived seconds later. I wasn't sure if they had already found Frank, but I didn't care. All that mattered right now was getting my family to a hospital. Lacey was going to travel in one ambulance and my dad in another. Lacey's seizure had stopped, but she still wasn't awake. And my dad's pain was being controlled with morphine. I was a panicking mess, looking between the two ambulances and trying to decide which one to ride in.

"Lucas, no," my dad said as I reached for the handle to take a step into the back of his ambulance. "Family comes first. Go with Lacey."

My lip trembled. "She's not my family. I don't think they'll let me."

"She's pregnant." Behind the grimaces from his pain, he smiled. And in turn, I did the same. "A baby, huh?"

My head bobbed *yes*. It didn't hide the panic I was feeling. I didn't know if Lacey was okay, let alone our baby. I had never been so scared.

"That's your family, Luke. Go be with Lacey. I'll see you there."

It was probably the first time he didn't have to tell me twice.

Waiting was the worst. The ambulances had arrived at the same time, but again, Lacey was sent one direction and my dad was sent in the opposite. As for me, I was stuck in a room with a TV playing some old cowboy TV show on repeat without sound; shitty, stale coffee; and uncomfortable chairs. Those didn't matter, though. I was too nervous to sit. I paced the room, sharing my nerves with everyone else who was stuck here too. It probably didn't help that I was covered in blood. When another person asked for the TV to be changed to the news, I wasn't surprised to see the first headline scrolling across the bottom reading: *Weekend shooting at Drake-Mason Pharmaceuticals: One arrest, one at large, two hospitalized.*

I stopped and read it repeatedly as it looped.

"Luke!"

I turned, hearing a voice I needed right now. I had texted Justin as soon as I got here, knowing he would get in touch with Rachel. If their expressions even remotely resembled mine, I knew I was a walking disaster. The two of them immediately engulfed me in a three-person hug. I needed this. I needed our friends here. I needed someone because my entire world was collapsing around me.

"Have you heard anything?" Rachel sniffled against my wreck of a shirt.

"No." My voice cracked. "Lacey is in a trauma room, and they took Dad into surgery immediately."

"Are you okay?" Justin asked. "Do you need anything?"

I squeezed them tighter, clenching my teeth to stop myself from absolutely losing it. I needed them to keep me standing. Without me telling them, they knew. They both tightened their hold on me, and together we waited for any news.

People came and went in the waiting area. Justin and Rachel took turns fetching food or drinks. I couldn't eat. I bit the corner off a strawberry Pop-Tart from a vending machine and immediately threw it in the garbage. I kept checking my phone—stupid, because no one else was going to get in touch with me other than the four people already here. I needed some sort of update. But when a surgeon entered the room, covered in just as much blood as me, if not more, I knew wishing for news was a gamble. Bad news was imminent.

"Lucas Drake?"

I stood. "That's me."

"There's a consultation room just down the hall." He motioned to a door. "I think it would be better to talk there regarding your father."

"I can't." My head shook as I crossed my arms over myself. "I'm waiting on two sets of news. It has to be here."

The surgeon looked around the room. Currently, there was only one other person waiting, and they were fast asleep beneath the television. I didn't care if there were people around; I wasn't moving from this spot until I had news regarding Lacey and the baby.

"Please?" I asked again, not willing to wait any longer. "How bad is it?"

His frown wasn't reassuring. "The bullet that struck your father hit the pulmonary artery. There was too much damage. He experienced blood loss faster than we could repair. There was nothing more we could do. I'm very sorry for your family's loss."

I went numb. I was bobbing my head to acknowledge that my dad—the man who had promised he'd see me here at the hospital—was gone. The surgeon kept talking, apologizing, and discussing more of the outcome of the surgery, as if it mattered that I knew. It didn't. My dad was dead, and it wasn't sinking in. I didn't even notice Justin squeezing my shoulder until the surgeon had left the room.

Gone.

My dad was gone.

I barely had time to acknowledge Justin and Rachel when another doctor entered the room. While the last one was in scrubs, blood soaked, obscenely tall, and bald, this doctor was a petite woman of Asian descent. Her white coat was free of stains, and as she called my name, it wasn't as dreary as the entrance of the surgeon.

"Lucas," she offered her hand, "I'm Dr. Larkin. I've been assigned to Lacey Mason, and I'm told you're the one to speak with. Is that correct?"

"That's right. She's my girlfriend."

That was all I could say. I had to bite my cheek, and when I did, I instantly bit so hard I could taste the blood. My nerves were threatening to toss up the contents of my stomach if she didn't give me some good news soon.

"Okay," she said in a calming tone. Her hand landed on the side of my arm as if to keep me steady. "Lacey's blood pressure spiked tonight. This caused her to suffer a stroke and seizures. She's currently comatose."

I dropped my face into my hands, fearful about what she was going to say next. I didn't know if I could take it. I should have never left my keys out. I should have run after her faster. I should have stolen one of my dad's cars instead of calling an Uber. She should have never entered the building tonight. It should have been me and only me. This was my fault.

"Usually, with stroke patients, we have three hours to administer alteplase, which is a . . ."

"A thrombolytic," I finished her sentence with a nod. I knew enough about pharmacy from school to understand their treatment. "To break up the clot."

"Yes," she sighed, "but because of the pregnancy, we could only administer heparin. It's not as invasive, but we're hopeful. We're doing everything we can right now to save them both. I just wanted to keep you updated."

She patted my arm reassuringly before turning and pushing her way back through a pair of double doors that held a yellow STAFF ONLY sign. I was still registering what she said, and she didn't even stick around for my questions. I turned to Justin to gauge his reaction to what Dr. Larkin had just said. Finding him holding his hand over his mouth confirmed what I thought.

"Explain it to me," I said, demanding an answer from the only other person in this room who would understand. "What does she mean by 'save them both'? 'Hopeful'?"

"Luke, I, I don't know . . ." He swallowed hard. "I'm still in school and . . ."

"Justin, please!" I yelled loud enough that I awoke the stranger sleeping in the corner. "Please," I repeated. "Man, I was just blindsided by my dad. He was talking in the ambulance, and now he's gone. I can't lose Lacey too. I need to be prepared for what could happen."

I would not stop asking him until he answered. We both knew it.

"She could wake up and be perfectly fine," he began. "Or she could wake up and not have speech, or have a facial droop, loss of motor functions . . ."

I nodded for him to continue, even though I didn't want to hear any more. My entire body was shaking. I couldn't even look him straight in the eye.

"She might not make it, Luke. She's comatose. If this happens, she could miscarry, or they might keep her on life support until they feel the baby is safe enough to extract . . ."

"So, I could lose my entire family tonight? My father, my unborn child, and the love of my life . . . gone. Just like that?"

Justin didn't answer that question. He didn't have to. It was a yes. That was a major possibility right now. This morning everything had fallen into place, and now it was gone. There was a chance I would leave this hospital with no one.

I could feel myself breaking. I was tuning out both Justin and Rachel, turning away from them so they didn't see me fall apart. That's when I saw someone I never expected to be here. Someone I never expected to see again.

My mom.

She looked exactly the same as the day she left—maybe a little older around her eyes. She stood in the waiting room's entrance, clutching her purse in both hands. She looked hesitant to take another step forward.

"I," she said, then paused, frowning, "I didn't know if I should come. But I saw it all over the news, and . . . was this my fault?" she asked, with a tear running down her cheek. "Was this because of the inheritance? Was it Drake? Is Lacey okay?"

As I walked her way, my head shook *no*. I swore after she left that I would never cry again, but my dad was gone, and I didn't know if my girlfriend and child would make it through the night. I wrapped my arms around my mom, holding on for dear life, and sobbed until I felt like I couldn't breathe anymore.

Little had changed by the following morning. Lacey had been moved to a room in the intensive care unit. I could sit with her now. Still, she remained asleep. At least she was breathing on her own. I was advised that could change. All night I watched every single breath she took while begging her to open her eyes. As hard as it was, eventually I closed mine. I slept for an hour, hunched over her bed and holding her hand. I awoke to beeping machines and nurses changing her IVs. They didn't have updates for me. Just sympathetic smiles as they went about their work.

Around noon, my mom returned with fast food and a coffee the size of my head. By now she knew Dad was dead. I thought it wouldn't faze her—hell, maybe I thought it wouldn't faze me, either—but I saw the heartache that came with the news. Once upon a time, they had loved each other. And even though I was mentally exhausted from the last day, I could finally explain what had happened with Jack Mason and the account Lacey had stumbled into. It felt unreal.

"Have they found this Frank Leonard yet?" she asked, sipping from her own coffee.

My eyes didn't leave Lacey as I shook my head. "The police were here earlier to take my statement. They said it wouldn't take long to find him. He has health issues that can't be ignored. As long as they got Jack, that's good enough for me. They'll catch Frank."

"How did Jack know this man?"

"They started the initial lab together. He had just as much of a beef with Dad as Jack did, I suppose."

Mom frowned in Lacey's direction. "This poor girl has already been through so much. Her beautiful momma was taken much too soon. I never hated Mary for what she did. I was thankful to her for giving me a way out. Lucas, I know I apologized a lot last night, but I don't think I'd be here if I had stayed. I wasn't okay."

It felt like the millionth time I had allowed myself to cry since unleashing my tears last night, but more of them spilled from my eyes. "I know," I said, admitting something I really had known since I was a kid. "I could have tried to find you too."

"It wasn't your job to find me." She dabbed her eyes with the sleeve of her shirt. "I just hate that this is what it took for us to reconnect."

"This wasn't. I think I would have reached out to you about signing the inheritance for me, even though now that doesn't matter. You have no idea how much that meant."

"Are you two done?" Lacey's raspy voice interrupted. "I'm fucking starving. Do they allow snacks?"

My neck pivoted so fast I risked whiplash. My beautiful girl's big blue eyes were wide open. Her smile unleashed my second round of tears as I stood so quickly the chair I had been using flew backward. I dropped my head against hers and kissed her like I would never get to again. My mother patted my back and promised to return with a nurse.

"Pretty girl, you scared the shit out of me." I kissed her again. "Never ever pull this again."

"Never," she promised, clutching my face with both hands.

"You're staying in bed until that kid comes."

"Absolutely."

"No being stubborn."

"I would never!"

It felt like forever since I had laughed. I loved that she was joking, but even more, I loved that she was here right now. For the last twelve hours, I was convinced I would never see Lacey smile again. I was convinced my heart was broken beyond repair. But according to the monitor, my heart was still beating strong within her, and Lacey was sure to watch that monitor to prove it to herself too. Our baby was just as strong as their momma.

We were all going to be okay.

# epilogue
## LACEY

The fireworks had started early. Luke rushed around the house like a chicken with its head cut off on a mission to find the tiny earmuffs we'd purchased for Mia. His fear was adorable. Mia, who was milk-drunk and passed out on my chest, paid no mind to the festivities outside. Our cat had bunkered down beneath the covers, though. Perhaps Mittens would enjoy the noise cancelers if the baby didn't need them.

I should have hated this bed after spending seven months of my pregnancy in it, but I was too busy enjoying these moments with our daughter. The love I felt simply watching her sleep was intense and beautiful. I was happy if she was happy, and Mia Eloise Drake was the happiest baby there was. She had Luke's smile, and my blue eyes, his curls, and my brunette hair. The perfect mix of Mason and Drake.

And she had Daddy wrapped around her little finger.

"I can't find them." Luke returned to the bedroom. "However, I found this. Care to explain?"

I looked up from Mia to see him holding a tiny hanger with a little red bikini. I grinned. He wasn't finding Mia's new swimwear as cute as I was. In my defense, it was Aunty Rachel who had purchased it.

"What's wrong with it?" I tried to stop myself from smiling too hard.

He shook the hanger. "We have no luck with red lingerie."

"That's a swimsuit."

"Same thing."

"It's not."

"We had no luck with your red swimsuit either!"

"Well then, I guess I shouldn't wear the red lingerie I bought for tonight."

His brows lifted before letting his eyes wander around the room—a hopeful chance of seeing this new lingerie. It was tucked away for later. It had been a year since Luke had finally broken his way out of the friendzone, and it was getting used properly tonight.

"I mean," he said, hanging the tiny hanger from the bedroom doorknob, "we should probably try it out. To make sure it's safe. You could try it on for me."

"I could, eh?"

He was tiptoeing his way into the room. With only his pinky, he pulled open the top drawer of our dresser—the panty drawer. His effort was futile. It wasn't in there. He pushed the drawer closed again and muttered, "mm-hmm."

"When are you going to wear something for me?" I giggled, risking waking the baby. "Maybe I want to see some red swim shorts or something."

"Nah, I know what does it for you."

"Oh yeah?" I asked, loving his cockiness.

As if his smirk wasn't sexy enough, Luke began teasing me by lifting his shirt's hemline. His chest and abs rolled as he lifted it—showing off some stripping moves he no longer had use for. He had my attention. I instantly bit my lip and sat back to watch the show. When the shirt came off, and his beautiful chest was on display, I was melting even with the air-conditioning on.

He was so right. He knew the abs did it for me. Channing Tatum had nothing on my man.

Just as he was going for the zipper of his cargo shorts, a cry rang out. Mia made her squinty face, which always accompanied this sound. She was always fussy when waking up from a nap, and there was only one thing that stopped it.

Luke ended his striptease and rushed to the bed, lifting Mia from my arms with the biggest, dorky, excited smile he could make. He loved when she woke up like this, because the only way to stop it was a dance with Daddy. With her thumb in her mouth, Mia giggled, and he spun her around the room. It was a sight that would never grow old.

"It's my turn."

"Like hell it is."

"Rach! Give me the baby."

"She loves me more!"

Justin scoffed and reached out for Mia. Unfortunately for Rachel, Mia was a girl in love. She reached her little arms out, too, kicking her feet with excitement to go into the arms of Uncle Justin. Rachel pouted, dropping back into the deck chair with her lip stuck out and her arms crossed. Stood up by her date and denied by an infant—tonight was not her night.

"Told you she loves me more." Justin placed a sloppy kiss on Mia's cheek and walked off with her to assist Luke with the food.

"That baby has been kissed by Justin more times than me." She glared at his back.

"You're dating someone," I countered. "Maybe, if you ditched Chris the ass, Justin would make time for you."

"He's not an ass."

I lifted my palms. "Then, where is he?"

"Busy."

She was frustrating. Both of them were. In the year-plus that I had been back in the Hamptons, Chris had never once made a showing. He always expected Rachel to be around when it was convenient for him, but he refused to make time for her friends. Meanwhile, Justin watched her as if she were forbidden fruit— beautiful to look at and sinful to touch. He was the one who kept their relationship as friendship only, and she was fooling herself if she believed that would change while she was constantly talking about Chris.

Even though the pair had bickered and fought over who got to hold my baby, the day had been perfect. Instead of joining the beach festivities below, we had our own get-together around the pool. We hadn't decided yet if we would keep Luke's dad's house, but we were leaning toward this being the last year we'd spend on the beach. There was a lot of history here, both good and bad. We wanted to raise Mia where the bad wouldn't outshine the rest. While we loved this beach, we were looking for a place farther inland—with fewer hurricanes.

I took in the sight of our friends laughing and playing in the same place we did as kids. This is all I wanted for my birthday this year. No drama. Just a summer being young and wildly in love with the boy who grew up in this house while I lived beside him. This was the best Lacey Day I could have asked for.

After we had cleaned up and put the baby down for the night, and after the fireworks had finally died down, I was exhausted. Mia had not enjoyed the pops and sparks as much as her parents did, even with the earmuffs Luke had purchased for her. She'd cried herself to sleep, but at least that meant she was going to sleep well tonight. I dropped onto the couch and closed my eyes, knowing I was also going to have a good sleep after a day in the sun.

My eyes hadn't been shut for five minutes when a familiar alarm began sounding from my phone. I leaped from the couch, knocking pillows to the floor, to get at the phone before it could wake Mia. I cursed Luke's name, looking around for him and waiting for the damn text that would stop the noise. Eventually, Luke appeared, holding a pack of sparklers in one hand and his phone in the other.

"Lucas!" I said in a hushed voice. "You wake her, you take her! What's the password?"

"Our daughter's first two initials."

Mia Eloise. I quickly entered the *M* and *E*, and the room fell silent. I glared at him, but he smiled in a way that made my knees go weak. He was freshly showered, with his blond curls loose in the way I loved. While it was nearing ten at night, his normal change to pajamas hadn't happened. Instead, he had changed into another pair of shorts and a tee. It was the second time today this man had me breathless.

"What are you up to?" I asked, pointing at the sparklers.

"Date night."

"Date night?" I looked down at my phone to see the same two words reflected there. "I just put Mia down."

"Yep. She's not invited to date night."

"No?"

"Nope."

"And how do you plan to do that exactly?"

"Mom and Becca already picked her up while you were in the shower."

My lips curved upward. We had a baby-free night? We were going to get to sleep in tomorrow, and that alone was enough to get me excited. I was only minimally panicked that this was the first night without Mia. I trusted Elizabeth with her.

"We will get updates, and they are bringing her back at eleven tomorrow," he added.

"It's late . . ."

"It's the perfect time, because that beach is now empty."

"The beach? I'm in my pajamas."

Luke held out his hand. I may have been tired, but I wasn't going to decline an offer for time with him ever again. I took his hand, and we left through the back door to head for our spot. We took the stairs down to the sand. He was right—the night was beautiful, and the beach was now free of most people. A few houses down, where the fourth of July parties had actually occurred tonight, we could see some staff still cleaning up. But mostly we were alone. This didn't seem to be Luke's first trip out here tonight, because there was a basket waiting for us atop a blanket placed beside a bunch of tiny sandcastles.

"When did you find time to do this?" I asked, peeking into the basket at my feet. My favorite wine was hiding inside, along with a few beers—Luke's preference.

"Our friends assisted. We all agreed that after this last year, you deserved Lacey Day to keep going."

I wouldn't argue. This was perfect. Beneath our drinks were a variety of our favorite snacks and my Bluetooth speaker from the bathroom shower. I picked it out of the basket and held it up.

"What's this for?"

Luke was excited as he took the speaker from my hand and placed it on the blanket. He lit two sparklers for us to dance with. "Last time we danced on this beach, we didn't have music. I came prepared."

With a touch of his finger, the speaker came to life. Again, Luke's hand was extended for me to take. I took it and was pulled in close to sway back and forth. The wind gave us a pleasant breeze on a hot night. My cheek rested against Luke's chin as he pressed his lips to my temple.

I loved when we danced. I loved when *Luke* danced. I loved how happy and free he was, and I loved that I was the one he wanted to dance with the most. It didn't matter where, or when. We danced in the kitchen every single morning while eating our breakfast, and that alone made my day. But this, a date for us on my birthday, was perfect.

"I love you," I whispered. "As much as I hate the obnoxious alarm on my phone, these dates are my favorite."

"Yeah?"

"Mm-hmm."

"I had to do the alarm to get you your passwords. Do you remember them?"

"I do," I assured him. "I'd never forget a moment with you, either, Lucas Drake."

I could feel his smile against my skin. "So, you remember the first one? My middle name shortened."

"Will."

We continued to sway, with our toes sinking into the sand. "What about the second one? I ship . . ."

"You."

"And your mom's name?"

I stopped us from moving to look up to Luke. My heart pounded when I saw the way he was looking at me. Tears rolled down my cheeks as I realized what he was doing.

"Mary."

Even though my feet had stopped, Luke lifted our conjoined hands and twirled me to bring me back into his chest. "And our beautiful baby girl's first two initials?"

"M.E." I giggled and finished his question. Will, you, Mary, and M.E. All this time, he was asking me to marry him. The tears were down my cheeks. "Luke?"

He dropped his head and pecked his lips against mine. "Lacey Jo Mason, I have loved you since the very first day we met on this beach. I promised myself I would not mess up again. I will not lose you again."

"Luke, you put this app on my phone the day Rachel and I first went shopping . . ."

His head bobbed *yes* as he reached into his back pocket. "You mean the day I bought this?" Luke dropped his knee into the sand below us and held out an engagement ring. "I told you, this has been my plan since the day we met. Lacey Jo? Will you marry me?"

Not a chance was I turning this man down. My head was nodding so fast he probably thought I was crazy. Luke slid the ring onto my finger, making our engagement official.

"I ship you, Lacey."

"And I ship you, Luke."

# acknowledgments

Thank you to my readers. This Wattpad ride has been wild and it's because of each and every one of you. I'll never forget that or take it for granted. This book was an absolute blast to write, and it was due to all those nights in the comment section. Sixty-three chapters in fifty-eight days and so many laughs with all of you. I have many more exciting stories in my head to share with you. Don't think I have forgotten our boy, Justin. I know I said never, but #dixoutforjustin.

To Deanna, Fiona, Delaney, Austin, and all the others at Wattpad who have aided in bringing my book to life, thank you for helping me on my writing journey. You've all made me a stronger author.

To my husband and family, thank you for always believing in me. Even when I told you I wrote smutty books. :)

And to Wattpad, thank you for giving me a chance and

allowing me to hold my book in my hands. I shared an Ed Sheeran fanfiction one day on a whim (that tanked). Now I'm here. I'm writing the acknowledgments for my first published book, and I'm crying some serious happy tears. You've made my life so much better these last few years, and I cannot thank you enough for it.

# about the author

May Lynn is the author of the Wattpad Paid Stories hit, *Breaking the Friendzone*. Her love of pharmacy, romance, and mystery led to her writing this breakthrough story, which now holds over five million reads on the platform. May grew up in the Dubuque, Iowa, area and now resides with her husband and their dog and cat in a nearby lake town. When not writing on Wattpad, she enjoys reading, concerts, cooking, and time with family.

Turn the page for a sneak peek of

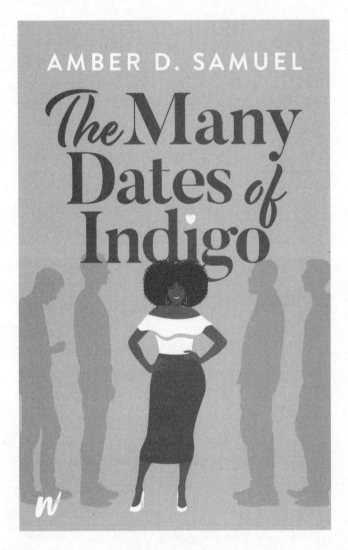

AMBER D. SAMUEL

The Many Dates of Indigo

Available December 2022,
wherever books are sold.

# Chapter 1

*I'm over this shit,* Indigo thought to herself as she watched Saxon rip the pink wrapping paper off the umpteenth gift like the Hulk's sister. Only it wasn't Bruce Banner's sibling; it was hers. It wasn't her older sister's glee as she gushed over another set of pastel booties that had caused Indigo's current irritation. It was the glances and whispers she'd received while being the dutiful daughter.

Months shy of her thirtieth birthday—almost three months, to be exact—concerns for her health and well-being had shifted to interest in her relationship status and womb. No, her family didn't just outright ask her who she was dating or when she was planning to get pregnant. There were subtle hints cast here and there.

"Indigo just loves the single life," Aunt Maureen whispered to her cluster of church friends. There was a big nugget of truth in the statement. Indigo did love being single. Being able to do what she wanted, go where she wanted, eat where she wanted, and not have to let another soul know every detail of her weekly or daily plans was bliss for an independent spirit like her, but it was growing tiresome. She wanted someone to care about her itinerary and yearn to be added to her schedule permanently. She was also growing tired of being ultra-independent. She loved being a boss and taking care of business, but she also craved being pampered, adored, and loved.

"Still no ring," Cousin Tracy harped as she inspected Indigo's left hand after giving her a bear hug. That one hurt because even though Indigo prided herself on being an original, she *had* had an engagement ring picked out before the age of ten. It had happened during a simple stroll down the sidewalk of the River Oaks shopping district. She and her best friend, Tate, had walked behind their mamas, who'd talked about whatever adults talked about in the '90s, when a glimmer from a sizable cushion-cut diamond ring in the window of a jewelry store captivated all of her interest. Her mama calling her name snatched her out of her trance, but she never forgot the gem.

Sure, she had a bank account fat enough to buy herself the ring, but she wanted all the things the ring and the moment stood for. She wanted a man who would be her partner for their lives' journeys, and her past search to find one had left her with scars.

Presently, Indigo was on her third glass of wine and considered drinking straight from the bottle. Instead of risking a hangover, she snuck out of the living room. As she put distance between herself and the overcrowded room of cooing women, she felt the pressure fall off her shoulders. She sought refuge in Saxon's kitchen, the place she'd spent many evenings before buying a house in the same community, needing the sweetness of freshly baked desserts for a sugar high.

In all his six-foot mocha glory, her brother, Harrison, stood by the island, whipping pink food coloring into creamy, pillowy frosting. A platter of vanilla cupcakes sat in front of him, causing Indigo's mouth to water. She wanted to snatch one immediately but knew to wait. He hated when people tried his treats before they were finished. Presentation was everything to him. Ensuring people and things looked beautiful was something they shared.

"I thought you would've left by now." He judged the tint of the pinkness and decided to add some more into the bowl.

"I thought you weren't coming," Indigo groaned, climbing atop the bar stool.

"I wasn't," he declared. Being the only brother had perks, but being the only baker in the family had drawbacks. "But Saxon ambushed me at the bakery and had a meltdown." He stopped stirring to give Indigo a fake smile. "So, I'm here. I had to cancel my date because of your sister."

"Our sister," she corrected before taking another swallow from the almost empty glass. "Wait! You had a date?" she asked, getting a nod from her little brother, the youngest of the trio. "With the Tinder chick?"

Harrison glared at her. "Her name is Tulip."

Indigo's nose turned up. "Like the flower?"

"And your name is what?" He snickered. "A color."

She flashed him her middle finger. "A bold, beautiful color with deep meaning."

The sunlight pouring through the window hit the red garnet in her ring. The lotus-shaped jewel had been a gift for her nineteenth birthday from her best friend, Tate. It wasn't the most expensive piece of jewelry she owned, but its meaning was priceless.

Her hand gesture did nothing to erase Harrison's smirk. "It's a hippie name."

"You mean independent thinkers." Indigo shrugged, raising the glass to her mouth. "Who created their own paths, not giving a damn about what others have to say."

"Maybe that's why you're not married." He smeared frosting on a cupcake. "You're free-spirited at heart."

She didn't see anything wrong with being a free spirit. She'd never wanted to follow the crowd or do things just because everyone else was doing them, but this wasn't a matter of following the norm. She felt the clock ticking, and it wasn't in her favor.

And no one let her forget it.

"You're about to knock the hell out of twenty-five, and I don't see anyone giving you grief about getting married."

"Because I'm putting in an effort." He drizzled pink sprinkles onto the cupcakes. "Going on dates."

"And I'm what?"

"Checked out entirely."

"I'm just busy." She slapped the countertop. "I don't think you people understand how much work goes into being—"

"*A boss*." Harrison cut her off, and she rolled her eyes. "We all know that's an excuse. Mom's a corporate lawyer, and she still had time to hook Dad."

"Well, Baker Bob, Dad was a partner at the firm Mom worked at." She straightened herself on the stool, getting serious. "I own a shoe store, and I don't see too many straight, unmarried guys buying Louboutin and Jimmy Choo."

She had been propositioned by numerous married men, but that was neither here nor there. She didn't fancy being a mistress. Plus, she didn't like to share; having two siblings had given her that trait at an early age.

"For starters," Harrison said, wiping the sugar off his hands, "you can stop saying no when someone asks you out."

"So, you're telling me that I should say yes to the idea of hanging out with a stranger?" She shook her glossy curls. "Seems like fraud."

The last time she'd spent time getting to know a stranger who'd found her attractive and engaging, he'd turned out to be an actual scammer. He still wrote to her from time to time.

"It's not!" Harrison threw up his arms. "'Cause that's how strangers become unstrangers."

"Unstrangers?" She burst out laughing. "That's not a word."

He looked at her blankly. "That's not an antonym for stranger?"

"No. Not at all." She stared at him, making a mental note to buy him a thesaurus for his birthday.

He shrugged. "Well, fuck, I'm not an English teacher. Saxon is."

"All I'm saying is . . ." He pushed her hand away as she reached over the island for a cupcake. He handed her the icing-covered spatula instead. "Say yes to a date once in a while."

She twisted her mouth, savoring the sugar on her tongue.

"And don't overthink it," Harrison insisted while lifting the tray of identically frosted cupcakes. "Just go with the flow."

"That's easy for you to say," she said, hopping off the bar stool and following him back into the madness.

Indigo wished she could date as easily as Harrison. Unlike him, she had wounds that still lingered from bad relationships.

• • •

"Enjoy the rest of your Sunday!" Indigo stood in the doorway, happily waving to the last guest as they headed down the now vacant driveway.

"Mmm, this is good." Harrison slouched in one of the living room's striped armchairs with his legs propped up on the coffee table. "Mama, you put your foot in this gumbo." He shoveled in another spoonful of the swampy chicken and sausage delicacy that was reserved for special occasions.

It was also Indigo's favorite. Unfortunately, Indigo hadn't had any since she'd been too busy to stop and eat. Slurping the spicy juice from the crab legs was the best part, but now she was just too tired to fight with the crustacean exoskeleton.

"Thanks, baby," Stella Clark, the matriarch of the Clark clan, said. She headed for the stairs, arms full of vibrant yellow baby blankets. "You better get you a bowl to take home before Xavier gets back."

Saxon waited for their mama to climb the last step and round the corner before she peeled her lips apart. "Keep your paws away from that pot." She pointed her finger at Harrison while sitting back on the couch, stroking her round belly. "That's Xavier and the kids' dinner. You can go to Mickey D's to fill that bottomless pit of yours."

"Anyway, you need to stop stuffing your face." Indigo pushed the back of Harrison's head, sending it forward and almost into the bowl he was cradling like a newborn. "And help us get this stuff to the nursery." She gestured to the baby paraphernalia that cluttered the usually immaculate living room. "I don't want to be doing this all day."

"What else do you have to do?" Harrison and Saxon chirped simultaneously.

She narrowed her eyes at them with her hands on her waist, blocking the television screen that Harrison had commandeered, switching it from soundscapes to *Atlanta*. "Better things than stockpiling your already packed nursery." Indigo slid her bare foot across the hardwood floor. "This isn't how I wanted to spend my last off day of the week."

"Damn!" Harrison dug his spoon into the bowl. "Tell us how you really feel."

Saxon cradled her round belly with a sneer. "What's the matter with you? This is your niece. You don't want to be here for your sister and your niece?"

6

She wanted to ask how many baby showers she had to attend. Shouldn't being in attendance for the first two have filled her quota? But knowing how hormonal and expressive her sister was, the question would only lead to waterworks and their mom hurrying downstairs, ready to give a tongue-lashing to whoever had made the mother-to-be upset.

"I want to be here," Indigo said in a soft tone to erase the now downturned mouth and big eyes her sister was giving her. "I just don't want to be here all day."

Harrison huffed. "Lies. So many lies your teeth should fall out."

"What?" Saxon cocked her head in his direction. "Lying about what?"

"Stop instigating, you little scoundrel." Indigo tossed a cute plush teddy bear at him, but it sailed past his head by a country mile.

Saxon glanced between the two of them with suspicion, reminding Indigo of the days their big sister had been tasked with watching her siblings while their parents worked late, and they would plot to break the rules. "Are y'all keeping secrets behind my back? What is it? We have a code, remember." A code they'd crafted when she went away to college. Austin was far away, and she hadn't wanted to be left out and miss anything in their tight-knit trio. "Spill it, now."

"There is no secret." Indigo dropped to her knees by the coffee table, busying herself folding a pile of onesies. "Chill out, Sax."

Harrison swallowed his spoonful of gumbo. "She's pissed that she's still single and everyone around her is moving on."

"That's the last time I'm having a private conversation with you, Harriet." Indigo gave him the evil eye.

Harrison shrugged, shoveling another helping of food in his mouth. Her threat didn't faze him. He knew it was empty.

7

"Indigo . . ." Saxon said in a motherly, tender tone that clawed at Indigo's insides because it always had a way of dismantling her defenses, causing her to divulge more than she wished.

"Saxon, don't start." She was smoothing her hand over the polka-dotted onesies, trying to free them of the wrinkles that had set in from being bunched up. "We're not going there, remember?" She peeked at her sister with a pointed look.

"See, that's your problem right there." Saxon sternly jabbed her finger at her. "You don't want anyone's help. I could set you up with a great guy right now." She snapped her fingers as if it was going to be that simple.

"Mm-hmm, she getting more stubborn in her old age," Harrison added with a nod of his head. "I have a few homeboys that have some relationship potential."

"I can find my own dates, thank you," Indigo told them.

Saxon shook her head. "That's how you ended up with Corey."

"Which one was Corey?" Harrison tapped his chin with the licked-clean spoon. "The college boyfriend that had the girl back home?"

Saxon shook her head. "That was Darius. Corey's the one she dated in high school; you know . . ." She snapped her fingers at Harrison as if it was going to help him remember. "The one that got her community service."

"Oh!" Harrison threw his head back. "Corey Hall."

"I'm sitting right here." Indigo frowned at them. "So, can we not do this?"

"Maybe we should." Saxon pushed her back against the soft cushion of the cream couch. "Then maybe you'll see that you need to let someone help you find love because your picker is broken."

"Is not." Indigo drummed her manicured nails on the raw wood coffee table. "There's just an abundance of lames out there."

She thought about the gold-toothed father of six who'd asked her out while she was pumping gas last week.

"I mean, maybe she's right because you did pick Ian." Harrison scooted to the end of his chair. "Or should we say Christian Ross or Michael Earnest? What name is he going by now?"

"His government name is Jason Nelson," Saxon said with a sad quirk on her lips.

"A girl dates one con man and she gets branded." Indigo slapped her hand on the table, feeling a little heated. "I don't keep bringing up y'all's tragic little trysts."

Harrison pointed his spoon at himself. "Because we don't let our failed relationships define us, but you—"

"I what, Harris!" Indigo seethed, jumping to her feet. "I ejected myself out of the dating field because I'm tired of getting hurt. You think it's fun to fall in love with a guy, start planning a wedding, only to find out later that he isn't who he says he is? You think that shit's easy to rebound from?"

It wasn't, but it had forced her to subtract her focus on her social life and add to her business endeavors. Twenty-six had been a wild time for her, but it had been lucrative.

"Then what about Tate?" Saxon interjected. "Are we going to talk about that one or—"

"You know what—" Indigo snatched her purse off the armchair and slipped on her shoes. "I'm out!" She marched toward the door and flung it open. A gust of humid air smacked into her face. Out of all her relationships, that was the only one she couldn't handle reliving. "Let the Hamburglar help you organize your baby shit." And with that, she slammed the door behind her.

# Chapter 2

"They don't know what they're talkin' about," Indigo mumbled to herself as she steered her dark-green 1951 Chevy pickup down the idyllic neighborhood street. The community of Forestwood claimed its name from the robust pine trees scattered throughout the planned preserve of contemporary homes and manicured lawns.

Sure, her dating history was riddled with mistakes, but every one had also taught her a lesson. Showed her what she didn't want in a relationship. And her picker wasn't broken. She'd picked a good one once. Too bad her younger self hadn't known that at the time.

And yeah, she said no to a lot of the guys who asked her out. Scratch that. She said no to *all* the guys who asked her out.

She was exhausted from the dating game, from picking the wrong guy to give her heart, mind, and sometimes body to. From Corey to Darius to Jason, she'd found that her luck with love sucked. However, she didn't want to be single for the rest of her life, even though she had no problems with singledom; the years of spending time with just herself had been rewarding and beneficial. Besides growing her business, building a strong social media presence, paying off her debts, and blossoming her savings account, she'd formulated a self-care routine to recharge her battery and restore her soul after her busy workweek. The past four years had been productive, but it was time for a change.

She could feel it in her gut. Her heart was ready; the pain of heartache had subsided, and she no longer flinched at the thought of investing time in another guy who wasn't her dad, brother, or best friend. Especially her best friend, Tate, who had become more than a friend when they were eighteen. Maybe it was Usher, Lil Jon, and Ludacris that had convinced them that they could be lovers also. But it had been a mistake that had taken years to correct.

Now she was ready to bid the single stage of her life adieu. It was time for her to get back in the ring. The world was full of men, and they weren't all Coreys, Dariuses, or Jasons.

*The loser is probably right*, Indigo thought as she eased her pickup into her driveway and shifted the gear from drive to park.

The stereo was barely loud enough to pick up the quiet storm mix she had created on her iPhone. She blocked out all the ambiance of suburban life swarming around: the kids running down the street playing soccer, riding bikes, or skateboarding; homemakers gossiping on the sidewalk; and couples walking their dogs at a brisk pace.

The clack of nails and soft paws swishing on the car window pulled Indigo out of her thoughts. She killed the ignition and swung open the door.

"My baby!" she squealed, patting an overexcited Cane Corso on the head.

"We have a problem," a familiar voice said.

Tate Larsen stood almost a foot taller than Indigo's five-foot, three-inch frame, even in all the heels she wore. He was in his usual attire of basketball shorts with a white University of Houston T-shirt that stretched across his lean frame and contrasted with his golden olive skin.

He flashed her a smile that didn't match his serious words.

Indigo echoed his expression as she stopped petting her baby and stood up straight. "A new one?" She took the leash he handed her.

"Well . . . a new couple moved in two streets down . . ." He combed an ink-stained hand through his wavy chestnut tresses. "And they have a Pomeranian." He twisted his mouth.

Indigo scratched the black-furred head. "Gambit! You made another enemy?" Her tone turned motherly. The dog looked up with big eyes as if he could comprehend every word. "You got to make a friend." She patted his massive head. "Tate's not going to be around forever."

"Hey!" Tate dropped to his haunches and flung his arm around Gambit's thick neck. "Don't tell my homie that." Tate stood before Gambit could drag his pink tongue up his ruggedly handsome face and slobber in his well-groomed beard. "How was the baby shower?"

Indigo folded her arms and tilted her head. "Do you think I'm going to die a spinster?"

Tate's brown eyes went wide. "Huh?"

"I'll tell you over dinner." She strutted to the porch of her modern farmhouse-style abode.

The cool air chilled her cheeks as she stepped inside. Her home could've been mistaken for a Pottery Barn showroom if it hadn't been for the pops of purple accent pillows, Black art on the walls, and lavender lingering in the air. Once she kicked off her heels, she headed straight to the kitchen, in need of nourishment. Tate and Gambit followed close behind. Tate pulled out a ceramic dish of pasta primavera from the fridge and let the door shut behind him. "So . . . did someone call you a spinster?" He set the dish on the island and started fetching other items from the fridge. "I'm lost." He stared at her with a puzzled gaze.

Indigo's chic kitchen was the meeting ground for most of their conversations. Conversations that happened between six and ten p.m., mostly because Tate loved to eat, and she loved to cook. It was a mutual agreement, and she didn't have to clean out her fridge since he'd feast on most of the leftovers.

"Everyone at that little baby shower was pregnant, married, engaged, or in a committed relationship—except for me." Her face twisted with disdain.

Tate switched the oven on. "Harrison was there. He's not married, engaged, or pregnant." He smiled at his attempt at a joke, but she didn't, so he let his smile fade.

"He's the one who brought it up. Then he enlisted Saxon, so they both let me know . . ." She poured herself a glass of tea from a pitcher, wishing it was something stronger, bourbon perhaps. No, too strong. She did have work tomorrow; sweet tea would have to do the job. "That I'm a loser who doesn't date."

"Wait!" Tate stopped scooping pasta into the pan. "They said that?"

"I know how to use context clues." Her mouth quirked to the side sourly. "This is not how I expected my life to be by twenty-nine."

"I think you have a pretty great life." He leaned on the island countertop pensively. "You're a talented, educated Black woman with the best shoe store in Texas."

Indigo narrowed her eyes at him. "Don't use my words on me."

"All I'm saying is, you shouldn't let a man or the absence of one dictate your success." He tossed a green bean into his mouth, gave it two bites, then swallowed it. "Or anyone else."

"I want to be a mother." She spun the glass in her hands.

He was quiet for a moment as he carefully placed pieces of oven-barbecued chicken into another pan like it was gold. "You could adopt. There are a lot of motherless, family-less children out there."

She gifted him a faint nod, acknowledging he was right about that. "But I want companionship."

"You have a sister, a brother, parents, a niece, a nephew . . . and Gambit." He slid both pans into the oven at the same time.

She propped her chin on top of her fist, looking at her baby lying on the kitchen floor, watching all the food with a string of drool hanging from his mouth.

"True . . ." She moved her gaze back to Tate as he set empty dishes in the sink, wrinkling her nose, and she thought of something that would stump him. "But I need sexual gratification." She smirked at the blood draining from his face. "A mind-numbing, leg-shaking orgasm would be nice." She lifted the glass to her lips with a snicker.

She wasn't the type to go out to the club, strike up a conversation, and bring a guy home, or to swipe left, go out for a coffee date, then burn off all that caffeine with a quickie in the backseat. Long-term commitments were her style, and since she hadn't been in a serious relationship in a while, she'd been in a drought. Her vibrator didn't count.

"You can either read the Bible . . . or . . ." He turned on the faucet and pulled a dishcloth off the counter. "Call me up and put me in the game, coach."

Mischief played on his handsome features, making it hard for her to read. Was he serious or playing around? She assumed the latter and rolled her eyes.

"You're dumb." She let out a sigh then added, "You have an answer for everything, don't you?"

He shrugged. "What can I say . . . I'm a writer. We make shit up on our feet." His mood faltered a little as he folded the cloth.

"You still have writer's block," she intuited.

"Like the freaking Great Wall of China."

She glued the palms of her hands to the cold, pale gray granite of the kitchen island. "It'll come to you. Don't rush it, Tatie Tate."

The nickname she'd been calling him since elementary school brought a smile to his lips. "Now look who has an answer for everything."

"What can I say . . ." She spun off the stool with the vigor of a child. "I'm Indigo Clark!"

"You don't wait for things to happen; you make things happen!" Tate boasted.

"Right!" She slapped her bare feet on the shiny hardwood floor that they'd buffed last week. "So, this is me getting back out there. I'm back on the market." She danced to the music filling the background.

"Uh-huh." Tate's face scrunched up with disgust. "Don't say market."

"I'm back in the game."

Tate nodded slowly. "Better, but don't do anything you don't want to do. If you want to say no, say no."

"Trust and believe." She slid her hands into the pockets of her romper. "If I'm not feeling the dude, he'll get the boot. You don't have to worry about that."

"I'll always worry about you." He leaned back against the farmhouse sink. The golden sunset seeped through the panoramic windows in the breakfast nook, painting them with warmth. "You're my best girl . . . friend."

"Come on, Tate. Let's be real . . ." She grinned with a tilt of her head. "I'm your *only* best friend."

"Oh! No!" He slapped his palms on the sides of his scruffy face, *Home Alone* style. "The horror."

Indigo laughed. "You got jokes." She wagged her finger at him as she backed up out of the kitchen. "But if you eat up all that food while I'm in the shower, I'll give you a *Friday the Thirteenth* massacre."

"A man eats the last oxtail once, and he never lives it down." He tossed the dry towel on the counter. "Can you believe that, Gambit?"

"Believe it," she called over her shoulder as she sauntered out of the kitchen.

For a second, her steps slowed as she remembered the look on his face when she'd brought up the notion of her dating again. She had her assumptions about why he felt that way, but he had to know that she wasn't going to be single forever. Right?